THE SILVERSKIN LEGACY
CURSE OF ARASTOLD

About the Author

Jo Whittemore has been captivated by fantasy since she was a child, dressing up as a fairy for Halloween (which also happens to be her birthday). She currently lives in Austin, Texas with her husband Roger, but longs to return to her California roots.

To Write to the Author

If you wish to contact the author or would like more information about this book, please write to the author in care of Llewellyn Worldwide and we will forward your request. Both the author and publisher appreciate hearing from you and learning of your enjoyment of this book and how it has helped you. Llewellyn Worldwide cannot guarantee that every letter written to the author can be answered, but all will be forwarded. Please write to:

Jo Whittemore
℅ Llewellyn Worldwide
2143 Wooddale Drive, Dept. 0-7387-0917-4
Woodbury, Minnesota 55125-2989, U.S.A.

Please enclose a self-addressed stamped envelope for reply, or $1.00 to cover costs. If outside U.S.A., enclose international postal reply coupon.

Many of Llewellyn's authors have websites with additional information and resources. For more information, please visit our website at http://www.llewellyn.com.

THE SILVERSKIN LEGACY

CURSE OF ARASTOLD
Jo Whittemore

Llewellyn Publications
Woodbury, Minnesota

First Edition
First Printing, 2006

Book format by Steffani Chambers
Cover design by Gavin Dayton Duffy
Cover illustration by Anne Stoke
Editing by Rhiannon Ross
Interior art by Gavin Dayton Duffy
Llewellyn is a registered trademark of Llewellyn Worldwide, Ltd.

Library of Congress Cataloging-in-Publication Data (Pending)
ISBN-13: 978-0-7387-0917-8
ISBN-10: 0-7387-0917-4

Llewellyn Worldwide does not participate in, endorse, or have any authority or responsibility concerning private business transactions between our authors and the public.

All mail addressed to the author is forwarded but the publisher cannot, unless specifically instructed by the author, give out an address or phone number.

Any Internet references contained in this work are current at publication time, but the publisher cannot guarantee that a specific location will continue to be maintained. Please refer to the publisher's website for links to authors' websites and other sources.

Llewellyn Publications
A Division of Llewellyn Worldwide, Ltd.
2143 Wooddale Drive, Dept. 0-7387-0917-4
Woodbury, Minnesota 55125-2989, U.S.A.
www.llewellyn.com

Printed in the United States of America

Peaks and Valleys

"Ainsley."

The young man's eyelids fluttered open, reddish orange dust caking his lashes and making the afternoon sky appear as nightfall. He lay with his back against the fractured ground, uncertain of what he had heard, if he had even heard anything. Rubbing the dirt from his eyes, he squinted against the now full radiance of the sun.

Craggy canyon walls ascended for half a mile on either side of him, and high overhead, a creature beat its wings as it circled the fissure. The young man frowned with the realization that the creature seemed to be wheeling directly above where he lay, as if waiting for something unfortunate to befall him.

"*Ainsley.*"

Now he propped himself up on his elbows, stirring the dust beneath him into little clouds. A warm breeze whirled them about and rustled his flaxen hair before vanishing along the canyon run. The word he kept hearing, Ainsley, had a hint of familiarity to it, and the young man mouthed it as he got to his feet and squinted in the direction from which the voice had come.

"Hello, Ainsley."

He whirled around, raising his right hand before him and willing the power of magic to surge from his fingertips and strike the unwelcome visitor. Multicolored sparks crackled and smoked from his fingernails but fizzled out innocuously against the visitor's own outstretched hand.

Laughter resounded between the canyon walls, its vibrations strong enough to knock the young man off his feet and raise a cloud of ash from his pitiful execution of magic. Sprawled upon his back, he regarded his subduer with trepidation

A cleft-chinned man with wavy brown hair stood over him, head tilted back in mirth. As his laughter subsided, the older man peered down at his junior through eyes the color of red-hot coals. "How quickly you've come to rely on your magic. Not a very wise decision."

Ainsley gasped, scrambling backwards through the dirt to distance himself from the visual abomination.

"Come now, Ainsley," said the older man, crouching and extending a well-manicured hand. "You're not afraid of me, are you? Is it my eyes?" He batted them coyly. "I could have matched my clothes to better suit them, I suppose, but red isn't really my color." He gestured to the brown satin robes that enveloped him like ribbons of whipped chocolate. Around his waist, he had tied a golden sash. "But as you can tell, I'm colorblind."

The young man relaxed a little and allowed himself a smile. "Why do you keep calling me Ainsley?" The older man's hand was still outstretched, but he didn't feel comfortable taking it.

The older man straightened and adjusted his robes, tucking a piece of fluttering parchment farther into his pocket. "Isn't that usually how you address someone when that is his name?" he asked with a good-natured grin. "You told me when you first arrived here."

Ainsley cocked his head to one side, the realization massaging his brain. "That is my name, isn't it?" He frowned and rapped himself on the forehead. "How could I have forgotten?"

"A bump to the skull perhaps?" said the man, shrugging his shoulders.

"Maybe." Ainsley glanced around at the looming canyon walls. "Where are my friends? Where's Megan?"

The man proffered his hand once more. "They're fine. I can take you to them if you'd like."

Ainsley smiled and allowed the man to help him to his feet. "How did I get out here?"

"I'm not too clear on the particulars," the man led the way toward a narrow fissure in the canyon wall, "but while you were unconscious, I heard you muttering something about the Staff of Lexiam."

"Of course!" said Ainsley, his thoughts becoming more lucid. The staff of elemental powers was the reason he and Megan weren't back on Earth enjoying the summer break after their first year of high school.

It belonged to Bornias Niksrevlis, the seemingly tame old man in their neighborhood, and it served as a legacy for his family, the Silverskins, who were the only people with enough willpower to resist the staff's overwhelming allure.

Bornias used it to travel between Earth and his home world of Sunil where he ruled a kingdom in the country of Arylon. On Bornias's last trip to Arylon, Ainsley and Megan had accidentally become tagalongs, and the Staff of Lexiam itself, their one means of escaping back to Earth, had been stolen. After a great deal of difficulty, they had finally retrieved it, only to discover that the Quatrys, the gems of elemental magic residing within the staff, had also been stolen.

Their situation had not improved when Bornias had been kidnapped and forced to choose between relinquishing the staff or letting Ainsley and Megan perish at the hand of a sadistic necromancer. With luck, ingenuity, and the magical abilities he'd developed in Arylon, Ainsley had bested his enemy, but he couldn't remember much beyond that.

Ainsley bit his lip. "The last thing I remember is feeling kind of sick after . . ." His voice trailed off when he caught the man studying him with his intense red eyes. "Well, before I ended up here."

The man nodded as if he understood. "Too much magic can be a dangerous thing." He slapped Ainsley on the side of the shoulder. "Let's press on."

Trudging across the arid canyon floor, Ainsley recanted every complaint he had ever voiced about riding a scrambler or being carried through the trees by a bird-woman. He stopped at least a dozen times to shake rocks out of his boots, having at some earlier point acquired large holes in the toes. His companion never complained, however, offering a shoulder for Ainsley to lean on while he readjusted his boots. Just as Ainsley was certain the strange man had taken enough of the stop-and-go travel, they reached the canyon wall.

"Do you want to enter first, or shall I?" asked the man.

Ainsley eyed the fissure warily. When he had viewed it from a distance, he had assumed it would enlarge as he drew nearer. Standing before it, however, he felt like a circus clown trying to squeeze into a full car. He wasn't claustrophobic, but he couldn't entirely trust something that defied basic logic.

"After you," he said.

"It isn't as bad as it looks from the outside," said the man. "You'd be surprised at how deceiving appearances can sometimes be." So saying, he slipped through the crevice with ease and disappeared.

Ainsley sucked in his stomach and followed through sideways, but he soon discovered he could walk facing forward with his belly as far out as he pleased. He reached out to touch the tunnel on either side of him, but his fingertips couldn't make contact. The rock walls seemed to give him the breathing room he wanted.

"Thank you for helping me, by the way," he said. He came upon a low-hanging chunk of rock and ducked lower than necessary, remembering the smack to the skull he'd received the last time he had strutted into a cave unawares. "I'm sorry, but I didn't catch your name."

The man turned to face Ainsley. In the shadows, his eyes gleamed like rubies. "Everyone calls me Penitent." He extended his hand once more, and Ainsley found it in the half-darkness.

"Everyone *calls* you that?" Ainsley stopped him mid-shake. "It's not your real name then?"

Penitent released him. "I buried my real name with my—" Penitent cut himself off with a forced smile. "Your friends will be waiting for you."

He turned and led Ainsley deeper within the stone monolith, the daylight waning behind them. The wind that had been stirring through the canyon faded until Ainsley could hear nothing but his own breathing and foot shuffling.

"How much farther do we have to go, Penitent?" He stretched his arm out before him, groping for his rescuer's shoulder or a slip of fabric, but his hand grasped nothing but darkness. Ainsley paused in his footfalls, a nervous sweat beading on his upper lip. "Penitent?"

At first, Ainsley thought his legs were giving out on him, for his entire body quivered where he stood. Then, he heard chips of rock falling on the stone floor and felt several of them settle into his hair. Dust clouded the passageway, making him gag and cough, but above his own sounds, he could hear a distinct rumble, like thunder, that reverberated through his stomach.

Ainsley covered his mouth and nose with his shirt and crept toward the epicenter of the wall-shaking sound. As he ventured deeper, the path widened until he was standing at the entrance of a cavern whose dimensions rivaled an airplane hangar. An orange glow emanated from a hidden source, lighting the cavern's innards so Ainsley could see well enough that he was now alone.

"Penitent?" he called, voice muffled by fabric.

Something roared in response, and every hair on Ainsley's body stood at attention. He hadn't thought it possible for anything to sound more frightening than a grimalkin's howl, yet somewhere beyond his range of vision was a creature that contradicted that idea. It soon became clear what had happened to Penitent and what would happen to *him* if he lingered at the mouth of the cavern.

Squinting down the tunnel from which he had come, Ainsley checked for any obstacles that might prevent a hasty retreat. Seeing none, he briskly retraced his steps, beating a path toward the exit. He fought to remain upright as the ground beneath his feet trembled once more with rocks tumbling into his path. A baseball-sized chunk of ceiling struck him in the shoulder, and Ainsley stumbled to the ground. From behind him came another guttural roar that shook the very walls of the tunnel until they began to crack and crumble.

Sprawled upon his hands and knees, Ainsley noticed his shadow elongating before him at a rapid rate. He looked down at one of his hands, now bathed in orange light, and cursed under his breath. Scrambling in the dirt, he cut his palms and the knees of his breeches as he struggled to his feet and lurched down the tunnel. The orange glow illuminated his path but also served as a spotlight, making him an obvious target.

"Come on! Come on! Where is it?" Ainsley glanced around in a panic as he reached the point where the tunnel entrance began and where the canyon should have been. Instead, he had reached a t-intersection. "Please let this be it!" he murmured, ducking to the right.

"Ainsley?"

He yelped as a hand grabbed his shoulder, too small to be Penitent's and too gentle to be malicious.

"Ainsley, are you all right?"

His heart leapt at the familiar female voice, and he turned to look at her.

"Megan!" he whispered, covering her hand with his. "Don't panic, okay? We have to get out of here quickly! It isn't safe!"

"Ainsley?" she raised her voice. "Can you hear me?" She snapped the fingers of her free hand inches from his face.

"Stop that!" Ainsley frowned and swatted her arm away. "Yes, I can hear you. Keep your voice d—"

A soft white radiance blossomed behind Megan Haney, framing her silhouette like an aura. She regarded Ainsley with a sympathetic tilt of the head.

Ainsley drew a shaky breath. "What's going on? Are we . . . dead?"

Megan smiled at him, but instead of answering, she called over her shoulder, "Bornias! I think he's coming to."

Ainsley blinked once in surprise, and then the luminescence around Megan became so brilliant that he couldn't stop blinking. Before his eyes, the cavern shimmered and faded until it resembled the interior of a familiar cabin. He found himself sitting on the floor of Kaelin Warnik's home in the retired wizard community of Amdor.

A paunchy old man with a bush of gray facial hair knelt beside Megan. "Do you know who I am, Ainsley?"

Ainsley regarded him with some perplexity. "Of course I do, Bornias."

Megan placed a hand to her mouth and squealed, and a furrow that had split Bornias's forehead smoothed itself. "This is a good sign," he said, patting Ainsley on the side of the face. Then, he smiled. "This is a very good sign." Ainsley glanced at Megan, who was fighting back tears, and the relief he had felt at seeing her dissipated.

"What's going on?"

Megan wiped at her eyes and took several deep breaths. She knew he was addressing this question to her, but for the first time in a long time, she couldn't think of what to say to him.

"It's probably nothing," Bornias spoke up, giving Ainsley's shoulder a reassuring squeeze, "but you may be sick."

"Sick how?" Ainsley wasn't a fool. "Sick as in the Illness?"

Megan made a strangled sound, and Bornias shot her a silencing look. He turned back to Ainsley. "We're not certain, but it's leaning toward that, yes."

Ainsley stared at him for a moment, then rolled to his knees and vomited into his blankets.

Megan turned her head away, her own stomach twisting. "Is that part of the Illness?" she asked.

"No." Bornias patted Ainsley on the back. "It's part of being scared."

The Origin of the Illness

"I don't understand how this could have happened," said Megan, wrinkling her nose as she watched Bornias mop up Ainsley's puke. "I thought the Illness disappeared, like, fifteen years ago."

"It did." Bornias dunked the head of his mop in water and slapped it onto the wooden floor. "But that's not to say it couldn't still occur. Leprosy once ran rampant through Europe and Asia, but you still see cases of it today."

From the far corner of the living room, Ainsley groaned. "Please don't compare what I have to leprosy. I don't even want to think about parts of my body falling off."

"The Illness isn't just a physical deterioration," said Bornias, wringing out his mop and placing it and the bucket by the front door. "It's also a mental deterioration."

"Perfect." Ainsley flashed him a sarcastic thumbs-up. "Who needs sanity?"

Megan waggled her index finger at him. "Don't joke about that! I don't want that to happen, and neither should you." Clearing her throat, she looked at Bornias. "Erm . . . by the way, what *is* going to happen to him?"

Bornias pulled a chair near Ainsley. "Come sit with us. It's only fair that you, both of you, know."

Megan drew near but lingered between sitting and standing.

Ainsley rolled his eyes. "Oh, come on, Megan! I'm not going to throw up again."

"I wasn't thinking about that," said Megan with a huff, but she blushed and plopped down on a balled-up blanket. After tucking her legs beneath her, she stared up at Bornias. "Well?"

Bornias folded his hands in his lap. "It will probably be easier to understand if I explain to you how the Illness came about. Few people know its true origins, and fewer still are able to accept it."

"Well, that's stupid," said Ainsley. "I'd think they'd want to have a source . . . something to blame."

Bornias tapped the side of his nose and pointed at Ainsley. "That would be the logical path to take, wouldn't it? But that would mean admitting something they already knew but didn't want to believe . . . that too much magic can be a dangerous thing."

At these words, Ainsley felt as if ice water was trickling down his spine. "What?"

"He said 'too much magic can be a dangerous thing,'" repeated Megan. She looked at Bornias with doleful eyes and jerked her head toward Ainsley. "Is hearing one of the first things to go?"

Ainsley pushed her. "I heard him the first time! I just . . . it's disturbing, is all."

"It is indeed," said Bornias. "Now imagine if every day of your life was reliant on magic. That would be the last thing you'd want to hear."

"But how can too much be a bad thing?" asked Ainsley. "I thought that was something every wizard wanted."

Bornias brought his hands to his chin and stared into space. "An excellent question." He fished a gold coin out of his pocket and gave it to Ainsley. "I think it deserves a reward."

"Hey, if you're just handing out money!" Megan leaned forward and held out her hand, palm up. "I was the one who got us to start talking about this in the first place."

"So you did." Bornias nodded and extracted another gold coin from his pocket, but he paused before giving it to her. "If you stand on one foot for five minutes, I'll give you *two* pieces of gold."

Megan laughed. "Seriously?" When Bornias showed her the second gold coin, she leapt to her feet, then transferred all her weight to just one.

"This foolishness," Bornias pointed to Megan, "is what too much of a good thing can do to people. Please sit back down." He pressed the money into her palm.

Megan dropped to her knees and fingered the coins, her cheeks reddening to match Ainsley's eyes.

"Greed changes people," said Bornias. "It makes them do things they normally wouldn't do. They'll lie, they'll steal . . . and some will even kill."

"So, what does this have to do with the Illness?" asked Ainsley.

"The Illness was caused by one man's greed and spread by the greed of others." Bornias settled back in his chair. "You're both familiar with Lodir Novator, Raklund's hero who bested a unicorn and a circle of sirens, among other things?"

Ainsley and Megan nodded.

"He defeated those enchanted creatures to gain their magical powers and satiate his jidalya."

"His what-ya?" asked Megan.

"His jidalya . . . his lust for magic," explained Bornias. "His ultimate desire was to vanquish the dragon Arastold, whose legendary powers were known to have rivaled the Staff of Lexiam."

"She could alter the elements and . . . and restore life to the dead?" asked Megan incredulously.

Bornias nodded. "She could also foretell the future of others at a glance."

"Well, we know from the stories that Lodir defeated her," said Ainsley with a shrug, "so then . . . what, he became all-powerful?"

"He might have . . . if he had survived long enough to learn how to use Arastold's magic."

"What do you mean?"

"Before she died, Arastold uttered a curse on Lodir and all creatures like him for having insatiable jidalya. Thinking nothing of it, and eager to return to Raklund to be glorified by his countrymen, Lodir began his long journey home."

"*He* was the one that brought the Illness to Raklund," said Megan.

"That's correct. A few days after Lodir's return, several of his followers were discovered in his study, badly injured, but Lodir was nowhere to be found. These followers, whose jidalya had been almost as strong as Lodir's, contracted the Illness and spread it throughout the kingdom."

"To Lady Maudred's husband and . . ." Ainsley pointed to Bornias but quickly lowered his hand.

"And to my daughter-in-law," Bornias said with a nod. "After that, all humankind with jidalya who came in contact with dragon blood were driven to insanity, their magic metamorphosing them into dragonfolk until they were scorned by humankind and slaughtered as the misunderstood creatures they were."

Ainsley sighed. "Great. So, I get the Illness, and I get to be a social outcast. Could this day not get any better?"

Megan squeezed his shoulder and looked at Bornias. "I don't understand how this could have happened. I mean, yeah, Ainsley's incredibly greedy about magic—"

"Thanks for that." Ainsley patted her leg.

"But he wasn't bitten by a dragon or dragonfolk," she continued.

"You misunderstand," said Bornias, shaking his head. "The transfer of blood doesn't have to be through a bite. Even by simply *touching* it, he could become infected." He leaned forward, studying Ainsley with a scrutinous gaze. "But that's what perplexes me. How and when did you come across dragon's blood?"

"Uh . . ." Ainsley looked down at his hands, rubbing the fingertips together and remembering the gold powder that had burned them. "Do you recall that time Megan and I escaped from your quarters in Raklund to help you find the staff?" He waited for Bornias's nod of affirmation. "Well, before we followed you to the stables, we reached the Illness Room where they housed all the people who had contracted it . . . and there was dragon's blood on the ledge outside the window."

Bornias's face darkened and his head jerked toward Megan. "Did you both touch it?"

"N-no." Megan slid her cushions backwards a few inches. "I didn't."

"But *I* did," said Ainsley. "And now, here I am."

"Indeed." Bornias clasped his hands together and brought them to his lips. "Your fate sealed by a brush of bad luck."

They sat in silence until a knock sounded at Kaelin's front door.

"My arms are full," came a muffled voice from the other side. "Could someone please let me inside?"

Megan was first to her feet, and she crossed the room to peer out the window onto the front porch. A man in his thirties waited patiently, shaking his shoulder-length brown hair to get it out of eyes that looked like chips of creamy jade.

"Hi, Frieden," said Megan, drawing the door wide for the governor of the Protectors of the Staff of Lexiam, Bornias's main counsel. She couldn't help but smile, relieved to see the man that had acted like a surrogate uncle since she and Ainsley had arrived in Arylon. He was thoughtful and patient but protective of his companions and deadly with a sword.

"How is he doing?" Frieden Tybor stepped into the cabin, one of his hands clutching a wooden bowl of hot water and the other a bottle of pebbles.

Megan shook her head. "He's been throwing up. Bornias just finished cleaning, but it might stink a little."

From where he was now sprawled upon the floor, Ainsley hurled a pillow at Megan, connecting with the back of her head. "You can just tell people I'm not feeling well, you know. They don't need the details."

Megan scowled at him as she smoothed her hair down, and Frieden jumped in before a fight could ensue. "I thought the Illness might be taking its toll, so I brought something that should ease Ainsley's stomach for a little while." He shook the bottle of pebbles, making them clink against the glass.

Ainsley craned his neck and squinted at the bottle's contents. "You brought me rocks?"

"Not just any rocks, my young friend," said Frieden. He strode to the kitchen and placed the bowl of water on the table, motioning for Ainsley and Megan to join him. "These are from the bottom of the Riorim River near Hylark." He poured a few of the pebbles into his palm and set the bottle down. "You see how they all have this moss on them?" He pointed to a dry tuft that looked like green saffron threads. "When brewed in hot water, the moss releases a detoxifying mineral that cures numerous ailments."

"I don't suppose the Illness is one of them." Ainsley wrinkled his nose. "Man, I'm so sick of drinking and eating all these strange things. What I wouldn't give for a soda and some French fries." He turned to Bornias, who was rearranging the cushions on the living room floor. "Can you port back to Earth and bring me some junk food?"

Bornias shook his head. "The only person who will be returning there is Megan."

Megan, who had been watching Frieden pour the mossy pebbles into the hot water, glanced up at Bornias with a quizzical expression. "What do you want me to bring back for you?"

"Nothing. You're not coming back."

"What?" Megan yelped inches from Frieden's ear, and he lost his grip on the bottle. It bounced against the table, but before it could hit the floor, Ainsley leaned forward and caught it deftly in one hand.

"Excellent reflexes," said Frieden as Ainsley handed the bottle back. He almost had to yell to be heard over Megan and Bornias, who had launched into a heated discussion.

"Megan, I'm not giving you an option. You are going home, and that is final!"

"No! Ainsley wouldn't leave without me, and I'm not leaving without him."

Bornias tugged at his beard, a warning sign that Megan knew meant he was close to rage. This time, however, he added a sharp twist, which seemed to calm him.

Smoothing his beard with a sigh, he placed his hands on either side of Megan's face. "I admire your loyalty, but I'm concerned about your welfare as well as Ainsley's. If he caught the Illness, there is a strong possibility that you could catch it as well."

Megan placed her hands over his and met his gaze. "No, there isn't. I *know* there isn't. Please, let me stay."

Bornias pulled away and twisted his beard again. "Come with me to Poloi's bookshop. There's something there that I want you to take home to Ainsley's parents. Ainsley, stay and drink that tonic."

"I'll drink it," said Ainsley, eyeing the water in the bowl, which was starting to cloud and smell a bit swampy. "I can't guarantee it'll stay down, though."

"Do your best." Bornias squeezed Ainsley's shoulder, then looked at Frieden. "You'll let me know if there are any changes?"

"Of course." Frieden nodded as Bornias hurried out the door with Megan in tow.

"What kind of changes are you expecting?" she asked Bornias as they crossed the few lawns separating Kaelin's cottage from the one belonging to Poloi, the community's bookseller. She grabbed Bornias's shoulder to halt him. "Is he going to go into a coma or something?"

"Oh, I wish it were a coma." Bornias twisted his beard. "Compared to what he'll be going through, a coma would be merciful." His shoulders sagged as if he was carrying the weight of Ainsley himself, but he trudged on.

Megan's head bowed, and she listened to Bornias's feet shuffling through the grass. For what had to be the hundredth time since her arrival in Arylon, she wished for her parents. For what had to be the first time, however, she didn't want them for herself.

Ainsley's parents weren't nurturers. His father preferred books to people, and his mother, a suave socialite (despite her six-month pregnant belly), chose to love her son from a distance to avoid wrinkling her Chanel blouse. They had hugged Ainsley awkwardly in his childhood and had since devolved to ruffling his hair now that he was a teenager. Megan had a feeling that at a time like this, Ainsley needed more than just a pat on the head.

There's Something About Frieden

If Megan could have seen Ainsley at that moment, she would have applauded her instincts. Waiting for the inevitable bad news, he couldn't remember being more miserable . . . or nauseous. He sat opposite Frieden, holding the bowl of water level to his nostrils, which flared like an enraged bull's.

"Phooo! This smells like raw sewage!" Ainsley made a sour face and held the bowl away from him as if it were a baby in a soiled diaper. A splash of water hit the table, forming a greasy-looking puddle the color of pea soup.

"It probably isn't going to taste any better than it smells," said Frieden. "Just hold your nose and drink."

With a long-suffering sigh, Ainsley pinched his nose and drew the bowl back to him. Eyes closed, he swallowed a mouthful, trying to block any of his senses that might remind him of how putrid the liquid trickling down his throat was.

"That's it. Just one more mouthful," coaxed Frieden.

Ainsley opened one eye to glare at him. "Would you . . . like to try some?" he said with another swallow. He released his nose but immediately grabbed for it again. "Ugh! The aftertaste is worse than the taste!" He grabbed at his shirtsleeve and began wiping his tongue with it.

"Aftertaste?" Frieden frowned at him. "There isn't an aftertaste."

Ainsley paused mid-swipe. "Yeah, right." He smacked his tongue against the roof of his mouth until it was wet again and then emitted a belch that smelled and sounded like a garbage truck. His face twisted into a hideous Halloween mask. "Can I have something else to wash away this flavor?"

Frieden tilted his chair back and grabbed something off the counter behind him. "Nobody has ever complained of an aftertaste. I've had it myself, and I never detected anything . . . and I've got well-honed senses, if I must say so."

He handed Ainsley the object he had grabbed, but Ainsley just stared at it. Other than being purple and covered with a fine layer of fuzz, it reminded him of an orange.

"Is this . . . what is this?" He sniffed it, marveling at the fragrant aroma, a mixture of citrus and cinnamon that seemed to permeate the skin.

"That's a parbar from the tropical island of Obonia. We use them in jams and pies. You just bite into it," said Frieden, miming the action.

Ainsley planted his front teeth into the parbar and bathed his taste buds in the sweetest, most delectable juice he'd ever had. He polished it off in a minute flat and licked his lips. "That was great. I've never had fruit with cinnamon already in it!"

"Amazing." Frieden tilted his head to one side and stared at Ainsley. "The spices in the fruit are so subtle only the most delicate palate can detect them. That's part of the fruit's allure."

"What are you getting at?" Ainsley asked as Frieden picked up the bowl and bottle.

"It's . . . probably nothing." Frieden smiled as he got to his feet and carried the dishes to the counter. "Your perception is just better than—"

Without warning, Frieden snatched the bottle off the counter and flung it at Ainsley. It hurtled toward him with the velocity of a fastball, but Ainsley's right hand shot up and caught it a full arm's length from his face. A split second later, the bottle rocketed from Ainsley's hand back toward Frieden who ducked seconds before the projectile would have connected with his skull. The glass shattered on the wall behind him, but Frieden didn't turn his head or flinch. His eyes remained focused on Ainsley, who was staring at his hand in fascination.

"That was kind of cool," he said, flexing his fingers and grinning at Frieden.

Frieden didn't share his amusement.

Ainsley's smile faded and his cheeks colored. "I mean, I'm sorry about the mess . . . and almost decapitating you," he amended, "but . . . but you have to admit, most people couldn't do that."

"I'm not upset with you," said Frieden, bending to pick up the jagged shards of broken glass; Ainsley stooped to help him. "I'm just concerned at the sudden increase in your perception."

"What does *that* mean?" Ainsley straightened and tossed his pieces into a wicker waste bin where they clinked with a sharpness that mirrored his words. "I'm in the top ten percent of my class. I'm pretty damn smart already."

Frieden shook his head. "I'm not talking about intelligence, Ainsley. I know you're very bright. But you also seem more aware of your surroundings now . . . like a dragon. It's not a good sign."

"Huh." Ainsley brushed his hands on his breeches in a casual fashion, though he was actually wiping away a clammy sweat that now dampened his palms. "Well, maybe I'm just . . . more in tune with nature in this world." This answer sounded feeble even to him, but he couldn't bear the thought of yet another connection to the Illness or to hear that his condition was worsening.

"It's probably nothing." Frieden gave Ainsley one of his paternal smiles and glanced out the kitchen window. "It's a nice day outside. Why don't we sit on the back porch and forget about the Illness for a while?"

It was such a simple suggestion for an activity that most people, including Ainsley, took for granted, knowing there was always tomorrow. Now, however, he had to face the reality that this visit to the lake might be his last, the start of a list of experiences he had never hoped to end. A lump built in Ainsley's throat, and he blinked rapidly to keep his eyes from welling over.

"Ainsley?" Frieden peered into his face, but his image soon blurred.

"Frieden . . . I don't want to die," whispered Ainsley. "I'm not ready." Tears slipped from his eyes and raced each other down his cheeks to splatter on his tunic. He wiped them away with a hasty glance at the front door, but only Frieden saw.

"I understand your fear, and I would be lying if I told you not to worry." Frieden placed a hand on Ainsley's shoulder. "But you must know that I will do everything in my power to keep you and Megan from harm."

Ainsley nodded and tried to fight back another wave of tears until the realization struck him that soon he would be incapable of any such emotion. The Illness would claim his humanity, and he would know no more of sadness or love or joy. He would know only hate and rage. The notion struck a crippling blow, and he crumpled to the floor like a small child, letting his sorrow claim him.

Frieden sat beside Ainsley, stroking his wild hair. "The Illness hasn't turned you yet."

"But when it does, I'll die!" Ainsley pounded the wall behind him with his fists.

"No, no." Frieden held Ainsley's arms at his side. "If things get too severe, we'll hide you someplace where no one can find you."

"What? Hide me?" Ainsley looked up at him and sniffled. "What good does that do? When the Illness reaches a certain point, I just die . . . don't I?"

It was Frieden's turn to look surprised. "Is that what you believe?" He shook his head. "Victims of the Illness didn't die from it. They were killed by people who didn't have it."

"So . . . the Illness itself can't kill me?" Ainsley wiped at his eyes, feeling slightly more hopeful. "That makes things a little better. I mean, you could just put me in a cage on some remote island guarded by trolls until you find a cure, right?"

"I suppose we could do that." Frieden kept his face expressionless, though Ainsley could hear slight amusement in his voice. "How many trolls would you like?"

Ainsley smiled. "Enough to look after the sea monsters circling the island."

"I'll have the Kingdom Coalition get started on this straightaway," said Frieden with a chuckle.

Ainsley wiped at his eyes one last time and sniffled. "Could we act like I didn't just . . . like nothing just happened?"

"Of course." Frieden helped Ainsley to his feet. "And now, I think you really should get some fresh air." He guided Ainsley out the back door. "What would you like to talk about?"

The two of them settled onto the grass, and Ainsley felt himself begin to relax. He listened to the twittering of nearby birds and splashes from the lake as fish darted to the surface to nab unsuspecting insects. After a moment of silent appreciation, he said, "Let's . . . let's talk about your personal life." His face split into a mischievous grin. "Surely being governor has its advantages with the ladies?"

Frieden didn't smile at this attempt at humor. Instead, he plucked a blade of grass and scrutinized it with a frown. "I'm afraid I enjoy that topic almost as much as you enjoy talking about your present predicament."

The corners of Ainsley's mouth evened out. "Oh. Sorry."

"Don't be sorry." Frieden turned to Ainsley, and this time, he did smile. "I've kept my past buried from everyone, including myself, for long enough. You expressed one of your deepest fears to me, and I should be willing to return in kind."

He flicked the blade of grass into the air, and they both watched it flutter and flip toward the ground.

"Her name was Anya," said Frieden. "I met her in Hylark five years ago while attending a diplomatic summit. During one of my respites, I visited the local apothecary to purchase some ointments. I'd noticed some of the motley in the area suffering from antler rot."

"This was back when you were still a . . . one of those friends of nature?" interrupted Ainsley.

"A nascifriend? Yes." Frieden tucked his chin into his hand and gazed into the distance. "Anya was enchanting . . . stardust swirled into human form. Her hair smelled like a valley bursting with the first flowers of spring." Frieden inhaled deeply, as if speaking of her had brought back her fragrance. "When she laughed, the stars sparkled all the brighter."

Ainsley smiled. "She sounds nice."

"Nice does her no justice," said Frieden, blowing on the blade of grass until it whistled. "She agreed to meet me for a moonlit picnic when she closed shop, and that evening when she handed me a sprout sandwich, I knew I was smitten."

A laugh unexpectedly bubbled inside Ainsley, and he coughed to cover it. Frieden gave him a concerned look, but Ainsley waved a hand. "I'm fine," he said, his cheeks aching as he fought back a grin. "She gave you a sandwich, and you fell in love. Go on."

Frieden looked at Ainsley a moment more before continuing. "Her intelligence rivaled the most erudite scholar, and her compassion for nature exceeded my own. She was always so fascinated with the goings-on of the Kingdom Coalition, particularly the elven affairs."

Ainsley sat a bit straighter. Bornias had once explained the Kingdom Coalition to him and Megan as the alliance of Sunil's fair lands for the greater good. Each city or kingdom on the coalition council served a specific duty, and Ainsley knew what elven affairs Frieden spoke of. "You mean magic."

Frieden nodded. "When we weren't together, she lingered in the libraries across Arylon, always studying. I assumed it was for new potions and remedies." He sighed and sagged a little against a tree. "But it wasn't. We were together five months when she revealed her true self."

Ainsley's eyes widened. "Was she Kaelin's sister . . . the one who kidnapped Megan and me?"

Frieden shook his head and reached into the drawstring bag he wore around his neck. Indicating that Ainsley should hold out a hand, he shook a figurine carved out of stone into Ainsley's palm.

Ainsley tilted the figurine back and forth in an effort to discern what it was. After a moment, he balked and tossed it in Frieden's lap. "You're not serious. She was a unicorn?" He felt a little sick, wondering how intimate Frieden had been with her.

"Not just any unicorn." Frieden turned the figurine over in his hand. "Her real name was Anala, and she was the daughter of Onaj, leader of the White Order." At Ainsley's look of confusion, he added, "Head stallion of his unicorn herd."

"Oh. So, why did she turn into a human?"

"Well, she never truly became human, you see. She used an enchantment." Frieden held up the figurine and pointed to the horn spiraling from its forehead. "An unfathomable amount of magic resides in a unicorn's horn. One of the many things it can do is manipulate a less powerful mind, the human mind, among many."

"So she tricked you into thinking she was human?" asked Ainsley.

Frieden held up a finger. "She tricked *everyone* within a mile radius into thinking she was human. As I said, unicorns possess more magic than you or I could ever dream."

"Unlimited magic?" Jealousy stirred inside Ainsley at these words, jealousy of Anala who had so much magic but couldn't think of a better use for it than playing dress-up. He stared at the figurine of her nestled in Frieden's hands and wondered if he could glean any magic from it if he destroyed it.

Ainsley's fingertips tingled and then he saw a wisp of smoke curling upward from the cuff of Frieden's tunic. Horrified, he clasped Frieden's sleeve between his hands in an effort to smother the fabric, which now glowed a threatening orange. When Frieden looked down at him in surprise, Ainsley assumed a sympathetic expression.

"I'm . . . so sorry Anala deceived you," he said, giving Frieden's arm a squeeze to make sure it was no longer on fire. He hesitated before drawing back, praying that Frieden wouldn't notice the singed edges of his cuff. "So, why did she suddenly decide to reveal herself to you?"

"She needed me to help her family." Frieden dropped the unicorn back into its pouch.

"With what?" asked Ainsley.

Frieden shook his head. "I didn't care. She had used me to get what she needed. Her love, like her appearance, was just an illusion."

Ainsley noticed Frieden's expression turn sour. "She's why you stopped being a nascifriend."

Frieden bumped the toes of his boots together, looking like a pouting child. "I harbored ill will toward her and began to notice how many other creatures took advantage of my help. When I stooped to mend a fox's hurt paw, its mate would steal food from my pack. If I freed a wolf from a hunter's trap, it would dash off and kill a farmer's doodahs."

"But that's what animals do," said Ainsley with a shrug. "Their instinct in life is to look after themselves and their family . . . not strange men."

"I knew that, but I was so jaded over Anala that I let it affect my work. Soon, my privileges as a nascifriend were rescinded, and I lost my ability to communicate with any animals that didn't speak a true language."

Just then, a butterfly fluttered toward them and alit on Frieden's knee. As the butterfly's wings trembled in a frantic motion, Frieden allowed it to crawl upon his finger and offered a sympathetic smile. "I'm sorry, but I can't help you. If you go two cottages down, there is a man who can." With a gentle wave of his hand, Frieden shooed the butterfly back into the sky and followed it until it disappeared around the cottage corner.

Sighing, Frieden leaned back on his elbows. "Perhaps I'll be a nascifriend again one day. For now, at least, there are plenty of *people* I can help." He lifted his arm and examined his shirtsleeve. "Even if they *do* try and set me on fire."

Steps, Stacks, and Spirals

Bells jingled against the door to Poloi's bookshop as it closed behind Megan and Bornias. A few wizards browsing the nearby shelves glanced up and gave Bornias a polite nod. He responded in kind and bent low to Megan's ear.

"Feel free to look around. I'll be in the borrower's section." He indicated the front half of the room in which they were standing and walked away.

From what Megan could see, Poloi had certainly taken his job as bookstore owner seriously. The entire cabin had been constructed as one massive floorspace. No bedrooms or bathrooms divided it, only a length of velvet rope that ran the distance of the room. More people milled about in the back half of the cabin, and there appeared to be a line forming beside a wooden desk where a young woman handled money and wrapped books in thick sheets of parchment.

In the front half of the cabin, and to Megan's right, stood a machine that resembled a miniaturized printing press. On a pedestal beside the printing press lay a leather-bound book the size of a headstone whose pages seemed to be turning of their own accord.

Megan's eyebrows furrowed in confusion. The retired wizard community of Amdor was situated in a no-magic zone where even the simplest of enchantments were supposed to be ineffectual. She inched near for a better glimpse at the phenomenon and gasped when she discovered the source. "Oh, how cool!"

A fairy with delicate crystalline wings was carrying the page corners from one side of the book to the other. At Megan's outburst, she fluttered in place and smiled before placing a finger to her lips and continuing her laborious efforts. Megan clamped her mouth shut and watched each page crackle past.

The book appeared to be a card catalog of sorts, arranged by subjects, then authors. The fairy skipped over "Onaj's Horn," "Orbing," and "Outbreaks" before settling on a page headed "Panaceas." She studied it, and, with a shake of her wings, flew to the other side of the room.

Megan found a step stool tucked beneath the printing press and dragged it in front of the book, intrigued at what else the archives might hold. She gripped the edge of a page, feeling its linen texture between her fingers, and continued the fairy's earlier perusal. After a few pages, an entry caught her eye.

"Portals." Her index finger jumped down the listings to one that seemed an easy read, *The Master Craft of Porting*, located on stack 5, step 7. Megan repeated the location to herself as she turned and scanned the room.

"What are you looking for?" A young man's voice spoke in front of her, but its owner was nowhere in sight.

Megan turned her head to either side in an effort to locate her addresser, but the only wizard within speaking distance was older than Bornias.

"I'm here." Something pawed at Megan's boot, and she looked down.

"Woah!" Her feet left the floor before she could stop them, and she found herself perched atop the step stool.

"You don't have to act like some damsel in distress. I won't hurt you." A snowlight-colored ferret blinked up at her through brown marble eyes.

"I'm not," huffed Megan, stepping down from the stool. "I'm just not fond of rodents . . . particularly large ones."

The ferret's fur bristled, and it bared its teeth. "I'm no rodent! Do you know any rodents that can speak human tongue?"

Megan gasped, taking in the way the ferret crossed its paws over its chest. "You're a human?"

"No, I'm a watermelon," sneered the ferret. "While you're here, you should read up on curse etiquette before you offend anyone else."

"Of course! The Curse of Sargon," said Megan, clapping a hand to the side of her face.

With all her thoughts being on the Curse of Arastold, Megan had forgotten wizards were capable of cursing people as well, in this case, turning them into any living form. She also knew from Bornias that curses caused the caster to lose part of their soul, but she couldn't imagine what heinous crime this young man could have committed to be turned into a ferret.

She stooped before him. "I'm sorry. That was rude of me. I'm not used to . . . this."

The ferret lowered itself down to all fours and sniffed piteously. "I accept your apology. Even *I* can't believe I look like this. Steal one lousy horse, and its Ferretboy until I turn eighteen."

"That's all you did?" Megan fought the urge to stroke the fur on his head. "But that's terrible. How old are you now?"

The ferret clawed at the floor in frustration. "Sixteen."

"Well, you only have two more years." Megan did her best to sound cheerful. "That's not too bad."

"Tell that to my former sweetheart." The ferret regarded her with doleful eyes. "If you want to know where to find her, she's betrothed to my former best friend."

"Oh!" Megan didn't know if she was more surprised that the ferret had a girlfriend or that people in Sunil married so young. "I'm sorry. If it makes you feel better, I've never had a boyf . . . sweetheart at all."

"It doesn't," was the blunt reply. "At least you're a biped . . . and you get to wear clothes. Nobody makes trousers for the modest ferret." He sighed. "Well, can I help you find something?"

"Yes, actually. I'm looking for . . ." Megan glanced back at the catalog, "stack five, step seven."

The ferret nodded. "Travel and leisure. Follow me." He padded across the floor, toenails clicking on the wood, and led Megan to a spiral wrought iron bookcase with a large wooden five planted on top.

"How could I have missed that?" Megan wondered aloud.

"I don't know. How could you have missed the fact that I was human?"

Megan looked down at the ferret whose lips were curled in his best attempt at a smile. Megan smiled back, but it was bittersweet. The cursed young man reminded her of Ainsley, whose sarcastic comments had at one time filled every other sentence of his speech and fueled the rivalry between himself and Megan. It had taken a harrowing search for the Staff of Lexiam to mend the rift between them.

Now, just as they had renewed their friendship, Ainsley's obsession with magic was literally going to drive them worlds apart . . . unless Megan could find a way to stop Bornias from porting her home.

"Okay," Megan gripped the railing with determination, "so step seven." She counted the shelves aloud.

"No, no." The ferret placed a forepaw on the wrought iron. "Step seven isn't up here. These are the spirals. Step seven's down here."

Settling himself on his haunches, the ferret grabbed at a silver handle affixed to the floor. He struggled with it for a moment, then turned to look up at Megan, clearing his throat awkwardly. "Say—"

Megan crouched beside him.

"If I were still human, I could sweep you up in one arm," said the ferret.

Megan blushed and tucked a curl behind her ear. "Well, I'm flattered that you—"

"But now I'm a rodent a fraction of your size," he continued as if he hadn't heard her, "so could you please get off the cover?"

"What?" It was then that Megan looked down and realized a square had been cut around the handle. "Oh. Sorry." She scooted backward and pulled her hair around her face, hoping he wouldn't notice her rosy cheeks. He pulled the handle toward himself, and the wooden square slid into the surrounding floor.

"Voila!"

Megan peered down the semilit hollow. The spiral bookshelf continued downward, supported by a staircase that followed its path. Descending seven steps, Megan turned to face the books at her shoulder. With a grunt of satisfaction, she slid *The Master Craft of Porting* off its shelf and carried it to ground level.

"You found it then," said the ferret. "I should get back to work."

"Thanks for the help," said Megan. "It was nice to meet you . . ."

"Brighton." The ferret extended a forepaw. "My name's Brighton."

Megan shook it. "Nice to meet you, Brighton. I'm Megan, and I'm sorry again about the rodent . . . thing."

"No worries." Brighton shrugged his slinky shoulders. Then, Megan couldn't be certain, but she thought his fur turned a little pink. "Maybe in a few years, you can look me up. It'd be nice to have a friend when I'm human again."

Megan gave him a lopsided grin. "Well, we could be friends now, couldn't we?"

Brighton's eyes shone a bit, but all he said was, "That would be fine."

"You should probably go help those men." Megan pointed at two wizards moving their arms in short, brisk waves. "They don't look as if they can wait for you much longer."

"Sounds like my former sweetheart."

Megan laughed. "You'd better hurry then. I'll see you around."

Brighton waved his tail and skittered across the wood floor and out of sight.

Megan stared after him for a moment, grinning, then settled herself on the floor by stack five with her feet dangling into its open passage. Knowing she didn't have much time before Bornias returned, she skimmed the table of contents, not altogether certain what she hoped to find.

One of the chapters near the beginning, "Group Teleportation," seemed promising. She rifled through the pages and thumped the paper with satisfaction when she read the first passages of the chapter:

For the advanced wizard in need of expendable income, group teleportation can be a lucrative operation. By creating one strong portal, the wizard can send numerous travelers to multiple destinations. These are especially popular in large towns or leisure areas.

It is important to note that neophytes to group teleportation may raise numerous concerns prior to their first journey.

One common concern is that the traveler will land in an undesirable location, which another traveler has selected either in jest or malice. Reassure them that, as in singular teleportation, each traveler can only dictate his or her personal destination and cannot alter another's travel path. The exception to this rule, of course, is individuals lacking normal mental function (i.e., the unconscious, the dead, or the severely intoxicated) and those who enter the portal with no destination in mind.

Another common concern is—

"Megan?"

At the sound of Bornias's voice, she snapped the book shut, and it expelled a dusty puff of air. Stifling a cough, she searched for Bornias's booted feet and located them a few stacks over, now and then lifting him to the tips of his toes.

"Uhh . . . coming." Megan clambered down the steps and jammed the book back in its place among the other tomes of travel and leisure. Spinning on the balls of one foot, she placed her left hand on the shelf two steps above and pulled herself up, knocking free the bookend as she did so. Unfettered, the books at the open end of the row tipped and toppled off the shelf like dominos.

"No!" Megan held out a hand to keep any more from sliding down the stairs and out of sight. Only a few volumes remained on the shelf, however, all from a series called The Traveler's Tales. Megan secured them and prepared to flee in guilt, but something tugged at her and made her stay.

The cover of one of The Traveler's Tales held something familiar among its illustration of a rearing unicorn, dancing nymphs, and a hodgepodge of other magical creatures. On the shoulder of a flute-playing satyr sat a fairy who bore an uncanny resemblance to the one who had given Megan her Pearl of Truth.

Fairy pearls, as Bornias had once explained, were rare gifts bestowed by the fey upon those whose need for them was great. Megan had received the Pearl of Truth at a time when she had given up on herself and lost all confidence. The pearl had allowed her to see her true worth. It had saved her from despair and later saved her life when she had risked her own to block a ball of fire from hitting Ainsley.

Megan's fingers found the lump in the skin directly over her heart where the pearl had been lodged. With the recent commotion, she had forgotten about her enchanted gift until she'd seen the fairy on the book cover. Bornias had warned of an increasing sensitivity to deception since the Pearl of Truth had become a part of her, and she wondered now what would happen once she left the no-magic zone.

"Megan?" Bornias called down to her from the top of the staircase. "What are you doing down there?"

"Just . . . browsing." Megan held the book aloft. "Can I take this book home with me?"

"I don't see why not," said Bornias, extending a hand to help her to ground level. "I must say, I'm pleased that you're finally willing to return there."

Megan smiled but said nothing, clutching the book to her chest.

"Let's check out," said Bornias, leading the way to the printing press with two books tucked under his arm.

Megan spotted Kaelin and Rayne at a nearby table and waved to them. "Are they still researching the Tomdex?" she asked Bornias as he placed his first book on the edge of the printing press and fished around underneath his cloak.

"Yes. Unfortunately, all of our efforts cannot center on Ainsley. Ah!" He produced a stencil of the Silverskin crest cut into a steel plate that was roughly the size of a credit card. Opening the book to the inside back cover, he placed his stencil beside a black stamp resembling a crescent moon with a star dangling from the lower point.

"This was a popular book," commented Bornias, pointing to at least a hundred different crests emblazoned on the page. "But then, any information on the Illness was in high demand at one time."

He fed the book into the machine, which Megan now realized must be a stamping device. It rolled out the other side without the steel plate but now stamped with a glistening ink reproduction of the Silverskin crest.

"Bornias, it ate your stencil," she informed him as he placed the next book on the stamping tray and pulled another stencil from his robes.

"I know. I'll get my borrower's mark back when I return the book," he said.

"How many of those do you have?" she asked after all three books had been stamped and they were walking back to Kaelin's.

"I personally have fifteen because I'm a high-ranking official. Retired mages get ten, and actives get five."

"Aren't some of the books in there kind of valuable?" asked Megan, thinking of the Tomdex. "I mean, how do you know some evil person isn't checking them out to learn all sorts of dangerous curses and potions?"

"We don't just let any mage off the path borrow the books," said Bornias, gesturing for Megan to open Kaelin's front door. "There is a rigorous screening process to endure before you're even allowed to enter the bookstore without a member, and only highly accredited members have access to dangerous literature."

Megan thought for a moment as Bornias deposited his armload on the kitchen table. "Does Evren have access to those books?" she asked.

"Yes, he does," a voice answered from the hallway. Frieden and Ainsley appeared, Ainsley looking a bit worse for the wear. He met Megan's eye, and they smiled at each other, Megan accenting hers with a conspiratorial wink that Ainsley couldn't understand.

"Speaking of the Tomdex," said Frieden, "have Kaelin and Rayne figured out what Evren was so interested in?"

Bornias shook his head. "They're going to attempt a trace spell to see if they can pinpoint the last pages he touched."

"But Evren looked at it over two weeks ago." Frieden frowned. "Even the most powerful wizard wouldn't leave a magical imprint after that long."

Not for the first time, Ainsley and Megan felt as outsiders, listening to the converstion. "I'm guessing you guys are talking about some sort of magical way to dust for fingerprints?" asked Ainsley.

Frieden appeared confused, but Bornias nodded. "Something like that. Trace spells have their advantages and disadvantages compared to your forensic science. For instance, trace spells can tell you the actual identity of the user at once, rather than just giving an identifying clue that requires further research. Magical imprints, unlike fingerprints, cannot be wiped or washed or even wished away, but they can fade over time, which is why I say Kaelin and Rayne will *attempt* the trace spell. But enough about that." He beckoned for Ainsley and focused his dark eyes on Ainsley's red ones. "How are you feeling? Do you need to lie down and take a nap?"

"No." Ainsley stared out the window and ignored the concerned looks directed at him. "I'm fine. I'm not a baby."

"Ainsley," said Megan, "we're just concerned—"

"I'm fine!" he snapped. "Quit worrying, *Mom*."

Megan blinked at him, stunned, but her silence didn't last long. "You don't have to be such an asshole!"

It was Ainsley's turn to be stupefied. "Excuse me? This is my life, so why don't you let *me* decide what to do with it?"

"Because you're my best *human* friend, but by tonight, you could be flying around Raklund breathing fire and turning people into flambé!"

"Megan . . ." Frieden squeezed her shoulder, but she shook him off and closed the distance between herself and Ainsley in two giant steps.

"You are so selfish, you know that? You're selfish and greedy, and if you'd listened to me when I warned you about the magic, none of this would have happened. Now you've wrecked all our lives!" she shrieked.

For once, Ainsley didn't meet the confrontation. He tried to back away to give Megan her space, but she grabbed him by the shirtfront. "Don't you run away from this! You can't just die and leave us to fix this mess!"

"Megan," he croaked, "I'm not—"

"You shut up!" She shoved him against the wall, and something crashed to the floor in the adjoining room. Megan tasted a damp saltiness on her lips but didn't bother to wipe the tears away. "All you can say is 'I'm fine, I'm fine,' but what about the people you're leaving be-hind? What if they're . . ." she swallowed hard and her lip quivered so that she could barely get the words out, "what if they're not fine?"

Yelling at Ainsley seemed to drain all her energy, and she slumped to the floor, sobbing until her entire body shook, her breaths coming in short, strained gasps.

Ainsley reached out to place a hand on her head, then thought better of it and slid down beside her. He leaned his weight against hers and tilted his chin so it was resting atop her lowered head.

"Listen. Frieden told me I can't die from the Illness . . . not unless someone kills me, and if we find a cure soon enough, that won't be a problem."

"We will find it." Megan drew back and took Ainsley's hands in her tear-splashed ones. "And," she sniffled, "I swear I won't let anyone else hurt you."

"I know," said Ainsley with a small smile. "Because you want to do it yourself."

Megan couldn't help but sputter out a laugh as she threw her arms around his neck, staring up at Bornias's moist eyes.

"I'm not leaving without Ainsley," she told him. "And I know how teleportation works," she added when she saw the wizard king open his mouth to protest. "You can't send me wherever you want. It's my decision."

Bornias nodded, his eyes becoming lakes, and he fell to his knees, locking both Megan and Ainsley in a bear hug. "I knew you would have to grow up sometime. I just didn't think it would be so soon."

"Come on, Bornias. Enough with the emotion," said Ainsley, struggling out of his grasp. "You wouldn't want to anger Dragonboy, would you? That beard looks pretty flammable."

They all laughed, including Frieden who stood alone to the side. Megan gave him an apologetic smile, and he winked back.

"We should probably be traveling to Raklund while Ainsley is in fair health," he said.

Bornias wiped at his eyes with a kerchief. "Of course you're right, Frieden. Everyone, gather your things, and I'll call for Rayne."

Frieden helped Ainsley and Megan jam their clothes and other belongings into their sacks, Megan wrapping the book from The Traveler's Tales carefully in a pair of pants. An hour later, they stepped out to a dusky sky of crimson and orange, joined by Bornias and Raklund's soon-to-be-crowned king.

A wizard wearing a tunic and suspendered robe skirts held a torch aloft, lighting lamps bolstered to the fence-posts surrounding Amdor. He nodded to the party as they stepped outside the entrance, and they each gave a visible shiver as their magic that had been latent in Amdor was revived.

"Gather 'round," instructed Bornias, drawing his hand from his robes. In it, he now clutched the Staff of Lexiam, a transparent crystal wand topped with a jeweled golden orb. The others formed a semicircle around him, and he began to chant. "Krida doshin pres siosfra." A ring of amber light emitted from the staff, bathing Ainsley, Megan, Bornias,

Frieden, and Rayne in its glow like a miniature setting sun. While the colors changed to account for each element, red for fire; green for land; blue for water; purple for wind, Ainsley nudged Megan.

"Check out that weasel on Poloi's porch."

Megan glanced toward the cabins and almost dropped her bag. A gruff-looking teenaged boy with spiky snow-white hair waved to her. Now that she was outside the no-magic zone, she could definitely tell her Pearl of Truth was working.

"He's not a weasel, he's a ferret," she told Ainsley, waving back and smiling when she saw Brighton blush. "And he's a friend of mine."

"You have some strange friends," said Ainsley, watching the ferret scamper up Poloi's steps and disappear into the cabin.

"Quiet now," said Bornias. "Let our thoughts be of Lady Maudred."

"Lady Maudred?" Ainsley and Megan exchanged a look of dread but settled their minds on the snobbish old woman who had taken care of them in Raklund.

"Stuffytown, here we come," muttered Ainsley.

Raklund Revisited

"Oh, good heavens!" The china cup in Lady Maudred's hand flew skyward as first Ainsley, then Megan, then the remainder of the party materialized in her sitting room.

Ainsley reached out and caught the cup on its return trip toward the floor, holding it upright, hand darting to and fro to catch the droplets that had sloshed out of their vessel.

"Oops, sorry!" he said as one fat drop exceeded his immediate reach and soaked into Lady Maudred's sleeve. He placed the cup back on the empty saucer still clutched in her left hand.

She goggled at Ainsley, and the cup began to clink violently against the china plate, threatening to topple off its perch. "Wh-what is the meaning of this, King Bornias?"

"Uh . . . maybe I should take that." Megan grabbed the tea serving and set it on a nearby end table.

Lady Maudred seemed not to have noticed, reaching for a cup no longer in her lap while she studied Ainsley's eyes. She looked to the guards on either side of her front entry and said, "Leave us, please." As soon as they abided, she fixed Bornias with a grave expression. "Is this . . . is this what I think it is?"

Bornias slid onto the couch beside her. "I'm afraid so, Cordelia. I need your help."

Lady Maudred stared at him in disbelief. "You need my help . . . with *this*?" She shook her head and reached for her teacup on the end table but cradled it in her hands instead of drinking from it. "I'm sorry, Your Highness, but I cannot relive the nightmare. I know too much of the Illness."

"That's precisely why I need you, Cordelia," said Bornias. "I need someone familiar with the Illness to watch over Ainsley, someone I can trust not to cause a panic in the kingdom."

Lady Maudred pursed her lips and swirled the cooling tea in her cup. "I can't. I'm sorry." In one swift movement, she returned the cup to its saucer and bustled her Rubenesque form around the couch.

"Cordelia, this boy isn't beyond hope," Bornias entreated, grabbing her arm. "*He* is someone you might be able to save."

The folds of Lady Maudred's swaying dress settled around her. She turned to face them, hand clutching her chest. It appeared for a moment as if she might collapse, but then her arm fell to her side, revealing a pendant she had been clutching.

She smiled wanly. "Of course I'll help."

Bornias kissed her hand. "I am in your debt, old friend." He turned his gaze on Megan. "Why don't you take some time to get out and explore Raklund?" To Ainsley he said, "You should relax while Lady Maudred and I brew the stage-one antidote. I'm fairly confident we've caught this early enough, but I don't want you to risk exacerbating the condition by running amok."

Ainsley nodded and feigned an amused smile. He didn't want to alarm anyone, but he certainly wasn't in the mood to run anywhere. A few minutes after they had arrived in Lady Maudred's quarters, he had started feeling lightheaded but attributed it to his quick, jerky movements to catch the falling china. Now, however, his skin itched like a thousand mosquito bites, and he was doing his best to scratch his chest surreptitiously. He didn't dare to look, but he felt fairly certain he was breaking out in a rash.

"Rayne and I should be departing now as well," said Frieden. "We need to meet with the Silvan Council before tomorrow's coronation ceremony." He held an elbow out to

Megan. "Would you like to accompany us to the ground floor?"

With a sidelong smile of assurance at Ainsley, Megan reached for Frieden's arm.

"Wait a moment, will you, Megan?" spoke up Lady Maudred. "I have something for you." She disappeared into her bedroom and emerged with her fists clenched before her. "This, I believe, is yours." She opened one hand and the object within launched itself at Megan, clinging to her shirtfront with its clawed paws.

The screams that followed could have shattered Lady Maudred's china. "Get it off! Get it off!" squealed Megan, flapping the front of her tunic in an effort to dislodge her tagalong.

"It's all right, Megan," said Frieden, chuckling with the others. He plucked the creature from Megan's clothing and held it out to her in the palm of his hand. "Just a narshorn."

"It's a rodent!" she corrected, refusing to look at it. "I don't do rodents."

"Well, you shouldn't have incubated it in your pocket then," scolded Lady Maudred. "After having been snug in there, it recognizes your scent and thinks you're its mother."

Megan shook her head. "What are you talking about? I didn't . . ." But then she remembered the narshorn egg she'd slipped into her jeans pocket when she'd first arrived in Arylon. "Ohhh. Crap."

"I assume that is a vulgar term," said Lady Maudred with a disdainful sniff, "which you will please refrain from using in my presence." She grabbed the narshorn from Frieden and forced its wiggling body into Megan's palm. "You'll also take responsibility for your pet."

Megan groaned and looked down at her "pet." The narshorn rested on its haunches and stared up at her through beady black eyes that blended with its slick coat. Megan noticed that while its body was delicate and mousy, its legs were muscular, like those of a squirrel. With a lash of its spiked tail, the narshorn curled into a ball in Megan's hand.

She smiled despite herself. "It's . . . *kind* of cute," she said. She extended a tentative finger and stroked the narshorn's back. "Oh!" she cried, feeling its ribs just beneath its fur. "It's not getting enough to eat." She shot an accusatory glare at Lady Maudred who crossed her arms.

"I'm a noblewoman with many duties. I feed the narshorn when I can, but keeping it alive isn't my main concern."

Megan frowned at her and held the narshorn up to Frieden. "What do they eat?"

"Insects, berries, and nuts," said Frieden. "You could probably take her to the valley behind the mountains if you think she's hungry."

"She?" Megan brought her pet to eye level. "How can you tell?"

"The female's tail spike blends with its fur," said Frieden. "If it had been a male, the spike would be white to attract a mate."

"Well, that's cool. I'm glad to finally have a female companion," she said to the narshorn, who squeaked in response. "I'll call you . . . Bit." Megan lowered Bit into her breast pocket.

Lady Maudred opened her other fist. "I also thought you might like this," she said, holding out a golden pin shaped like a butterfly.

"Uh . . . thank you." Megan reached out for the pin, but it fluttered its wings and alit on her breast pocket where it returned to its dormant state. Bit peered over the top of the pocket and tried to tear off one of the butterfly's unfolded wings.

"Stop. You'll break your teeth." Megan nudged Bit back into her nesting place and tried to extricate the butterfly's legs from the tunic. It clung to her as Bit had. Megan glanced up at Lady Maudred. "What is this?"

"It's a present," said Lady Maudred with a smile.

Megan felt as if a sewing needle were jabbing at her heart. "No, it's not." She narrowed her eyes. "This is some sort of tracking device."

Lady Maudred's eyes widened. "No, no, my dear. I simply—"

From his seat on the couch, Bornias cleared his throat. "Cordelia, you should know that Megan is wearing a Pearl of Truth."

"Oh!" Lady Maudred blushed. "Well, then . . . yes, it's a tracking device."

Megan gave Lady Maudred a dark look that would have made anyone believe *she* was the one in danger of becoming a dragon.

"I only want what's best for you," said Lady Maudred, patting her upswept hair in a poor effort to appear nonchalant. "I want to ensure your safety while you're here." She smoothed her skirts while Megan continued to glare at her. "If you'd like to do some shopping, you're more than welcome to have the vendors bill me."

Megan considered ripping the butterfly off her shirt and throwing it at Lady Maudred, but the older woman was smiling so hopefully.

Megan sighed. "I appreciate your concern. This whole situation's been a bit overwhelming."

Lady Maudred brought her hand to her heart, and her eyes softened. "Someone you care for has been afflicted with the Illness. I can't deny you the right to be angry. When it took my first husband, goodness knows what a horror I was."

Ainsley cleared his throat. "Lady Maudred?"

"Listen to me, talking that way in front of you." She grabbed Ainsley and hugged him to her massive bosom. "I'm condemning you to the Other Side before you've even sprouted wings."

"It's not that," said Ainsley's muffled voice. He extricated himself from Lady Maudred, hair in disarray. "I just . . . when you told us during our last visit that you'd lost a loved one to the Illness, I kind of assumed you meant your son."

"Oh! No, my son died in the service of the Protectors of the Staff of Lexiam." Licking her fingertips, she reached for Ainsley. "Let me fix your hair, dear."

"I've got it," said Ainsley, dancing out of her reach. With a feeling of disgust, he licked his own hand and ran it through his hair.

"Your son was a Protector?" asked Megan.

"Mmm. He was governor," said Lady Maudred, still inspecting Ainsley's head.

"He was one of the men who attempted to destroy the Staff of Lexiam," said Bornias. "A brave fellow who became one of the unnecessary casualties."

"Oh!" Megan cried out in pain and stumbled forward. Frieden attempted to catch her, but Ainsley was faster.

"Are you okay?" He noticed her hand clutching at her chest, but she quickly pulled it down to her side.

"I'm fine," she said, wincing.

"All this talk of death and dying must be getting to her," said Bornias, at which Megan winced again.

Megan pulled at Ainsley's sleeve, and he helped her stand upright. "That must be it," she said with another wince. "I should probably go for a walk."

"Are you sure that's a good idea?" Ainsley asked under his breath. "You're bound to run into a lot more liars wandering around in the kingdom."

"I think it's an excellent idea," said Frieden, taking her hand. "As long as she minds her own business," he raised an eyebrow at Megan, "she should be fine."

She nodded, knowing that it would be up to her to ignore the conversations she heard in the main hall, despite her desire to learn more about this alternate world. With a reassuring smile at Ainsley, she followed Frieden and Rayne to the door. As it closed behind her, she heard Lady Maudred ask Ainsley, "How long have you been scratching like that?"

Ainsley, who had stepped back to scrape his shoulder against one of the support pillars, stopped short. "Not very long. Why?"

Lady Maudred lifted his arm and rolled up one of his sleeves, inspecting the skin on the underside, which he had almost rubbed raw. "It could be nothing, but it might be something." She wrinkled her nose as he brought his arm down, and Ainsley, too, found himself snorting at the pungent body odor that wafted from his armpit.

"I guess I could use a bath."

"Even dragons don't smell this bad, my boy," said Lady Maudred, pulling a perfumed sachet from between her bosoms and inhaling its scent. Tucking it back in its snug hiding place, she rested a hand on Ainsley's shoulder. "I'll return momentarily, Your Highness," she told Bornias before guiding Ainsley through a dining area to the right and halting him in front of a door.

"Other than the entrance to your quarters, I think this is the only door I've seen here," said Ainsley. "Everything else is hidden by curtains."

"Civilized people don't leave their commode on display for all to view, Ainsley." With those words, she pushed open the door to reveal the most pristine bathroom fixtures Ainsley had ever seen. The tub, chamber pot, and washbasin were shimmering steel; lipothis, he guessed. One of the bathroom walls was mirrored glass meant to augment the snowlights hooked to the ceiling. Beside the door stood a linen cabinet made of diamond cubes that distorted a stack of fluffy towels folded neatly inside.

"You're ashamed of *this*? You should see my bathroom back home," said Ainsley. "My mom swears there's something growing in the piles of dirty laundry."

To her credit, Lady Maudred refrained from looking disgusted. "All soiled clothing should be placed in the laundry passage where the chitwisps can access them." She pulled on a handle by the linen cabinet, which revealed a chute similar to one Ainsley had seen Bornias use to deliver firepine pods to the kitchen. "I'll have a clean set of clothing placed outside the door."

Ainsley nodded. "Where are your soap and shampoo?" He peered at the tub to see what else he might be missing. "And where are your faucets in case the water's too cold?"

"Faucets?" Lady Maudred shook her head. "Your Carnival speak confuses me. When the servants bring up the hot water, they'll have already mixed in the soap. If you want to wash your hair with something different, I can provide something from my private bath. As for faucets?"

"Never mind that," said Ainsley. "You answered my question."

Lady Maudred left, closing the door behind her, and Ainsley latched it shut in case she decided he might need help scrubbing up.

He climbed into the steaming, soapy water and immersed himself in its depths. The liquid heat that ensconced him provided a womblike comfort, and Ainsley wondered if it would be possible to hold his breath and stay underwater until a cure for the Illness could be found. Although, he mused, he would need a bigger bathtub once he started to change. Exhaling a bubbly sigh, he sank to the floor of the tub until his lungs reminded him that he was becoming a dragon, not a fish.

Ainsley broke the surface and wiped the water from his face, reaching for a bar of soap. Lathering it to a thick white foam, he scrubbed one arm, reveling in both the relief for his itching skin and the idea of smelling better than a donkey barn.

He moved on to his chest, which had irritated him the most, and was dismayed to find that the soap had left behind a charcoal black residue where he had rubbed it in. Ainsley splashed water onto his chest and tried to rinse away the black spot, but the harder he scrubbed, the larger it became until the span of his chest was darker than tar.

"What the hell?" Ainsley dipped his hands to gather more water, and that was when he noticed the layers of dead skin floating on the surface. Horrified, he glanced at his chest again. He hadn't been adding the black stain; he had been revealing it.

Beneath his human skin lay the scales of a dragon.

"Argh! Damn it!" Ainsley hurled the bar of soap at the wall where it bounced innocuously to the floor. He roared in frustration and pounded the water with his fists, kicking his legs until he'd managed to rid the tub of half its contents.

Someone knocked on the other side of the door. "Ainsley? Is everything all right?" came Lady Maudred's voice.

He glared at the closed door. "Oh, just freaking fantastic!" he shouted back in a syrupy sweet voice.

Lady Maudred grew quiet for a moment before saying, "There's nothing wrong with being upset about this. My poor husband went through a myriad of emotions."

Ainsley heard the door shift and dared Lady Maudred to break into the bathroom. He knew the tub still had enough water to drown someone, and he imagined shoving the old woman's head underwater until the bubbles stopped. "If you miss him so much," he growled, "I can reunite you with your poor dead husband."

Ainsley gasped at his own words, at the inexplicable rage they'd evoked. Despite all the threats he and Megan had exchanged in the past, this was the first time he had ever relished the thought of doing someone harm. His eyes bulged as he shrank down in the tub, and he shivered though the water was still far from cold.

"Did you say something else, my dear?" asked Lady Maudred.

Ainsley drew his legs to his scaly black chest and took a deep steadying breath. "I was just . . . I'm sorry for yelling like that." In his mind, he added, "and sorry for wanting to kill you."

"Oh, my boy." The door shifted again, and Ainsley could picture Lady Maudred leaning her ample weight against it. "If I were in your boots, I can assure you I would be wanting to do more than yell."

Ainsley's skin exploded in goosebumps, and he wondered if she had heard his threat.

"I'm off to gather a few things for King Bornias. He would like you to meet him in my study when you've finished bathing. Your clothes are right beside the door."

"Thank you!" shouted Ainsley. He sat in silence for a moment, listening to the fading of Lady Maudred's footsteps before splashing out of the tub. His feet met more water, and he glanced down guiltily at the lake he'd created in his earlier tantrum.

Tossing a few towels on the floor, he cracked the door open and grabbed the pile of folded clothes from outside the bathroom. He pulled them on and wandered Lady Maudred's quarters until he found Bornias in the study, peering into a black cauldron.

"Isn't that a bit of a stereotype for you?" he asked, indicating a large wooden spoon with which Bornias stirred the cauldron's contents.

"Lady Maudred doesn't make many potions, so she stocks the basics. You work with what you can get," said Bornias with a shrug. "You cleaned up pretty quickly. How was your bath?"

"Just fine." Ainsley flopped onto a hard, high-backed chair and scratched his chest. "It's fine, I'm fine. Everything's fine."

Bornias raised an eyebrow but didn't question Ainsley. Lifting a square bottle to the snowlights, he measured out the contents into the wooden spoon. "Your potion is ready," he said, adding the liquid to the cauldron. It produced a tiny mushroom cloud the color of Ainsley's eyes.

Ainsley laughed but scooted farther from the table. "Um . . . maybe you'd like to test that on someone else first. I'd be more than happy to bite Evren or something."

"Test what? Test this?" Bornias pointed to the cauldron. "This isn't for drinking."

Ainsley didn't bother masking his relief. "Oh good. Is it something less . . . radioactive, I hope?"

Bornias picked up a goblet that had been placed beside the cauldron. "Drink up."

Ainsley regarded the wine-colored potion before tilting the goblet back and draining it in one swallow. "Wow." He belched as he placed the vessel back on the table. "I think that's the first thing I've had to drink since I got here that actually tasted good."

"I enhanced the flavor with berry juice," said Bornias, "but overall, the ingredients should have made it palatable."

Ainsley sat back down and began jiggling his legs while he watched Bornias finish his concoction. "So, how long before I know whether the antidote worked?"

Bornias gave the cauldron ingredients one last stir. "If you're improving, we won't know it for days, unfortunately. But if the antidote *didn't* work and your condition is worsening, we should know by morning."

"Ah," said Ainsley, thankful that the collar of his tunic ended at his neck and no lower. "So, if I wake up covered with black scales or something, we'll know it didn't work."

Bornias gave him a sympathetic smile. "More or less, yes. Now, come stand by me. I sent Lady Maudred to fetch you some things and buy us time, but she won't be gone forever."

"Buy us time for what?" Ainsley joined Bornias and peered into the cauldron, which was filled with inky liquid. "Is this a summoning pool?"

"Not exactly," said Bornias. "Consider this an . . . inter-dimensional videophone." Muttering an incantation, he passed a hand over the brew. The liquid within rippled from one side to the other, and when it cleared, a picture of a stove lamp and fan came into focus.

"What's this?" asked Ainsley. He leaned closer and heard something bubbling, but the liquid in the cauldron remained glassy smooth. From within the cauldron, he heard voices.

"I'll be right there, honey! Just let me give this a stir so it doesn't stick to the pot."

The image in the cauldron flickered as Ainsley steadied himself against the table, mouth hanging slack. He heard feet shuffling closer, and then to his horror, Bornias said, "Hello, Tib."

Ainsley buried his face in his hands when he heard his father yelp in surprise. He thought Bornias of all wizards would have known better than to use magic in front of unsuspecting people.

"Bornias, you devil!" said his father. "You almost sent me to the Other Side. You couldn't think of a more subtle way to reach me than appearing in a pot of chili?"

Ainsley raised his head at the casual tone with which his father spoke. He would have bet the Quatrys that his father would faint upon seeing an old man's face floating in his stockpot. Yet, he continued his conversation with Bornias as if they were chatting on the front porch about the weather.

Bornias looked into the cauldron and gave an exaggerated shrug. "It was the only liquid vessel I could access in your house. All your toilets are blocked for some reason."

"We had to lower the lids. The dog won't stop drinking out of them. Say, why didn't you try his water bowl?"

Bornias crossed his arms. "Would you rather have your wife find you on all fours talking to a dog dish or in front of the stove?"

"I see your point." Ainsley's father laughed. It was a sound Ainsley wasn't privileged to hear often, and he found it enjoyable. "How's my young hero doing, by the way? I haven't heard any updates since he and Megan took down the necromancer."

"Actually, that's why I needed to speak with you." Bornias stepped sideways and grabbed Ainsley by the arm, pulling him in front of the cauldron. "We have a bit of a problem."

"H-hey, Dad." Ainsley leaned over the cauldron and gave a weak smile.

His father's eyes enlarged until the whites around both irises were entirely visible. "Ainsley!" He reached out a hand, and then seemed to remember that more than a layer of chili separated him from his son. "What happened?"

"I'm a little sick," said Ainsley, attempting his best casual shrug. A lump rose in his throat, and he grabbed Bornias's arm. "He can fill you in."

"Stay right there," his father commanded. "Bornias, what the hell happened?"

Bornias rested his hands on both sides of the cauldron and sighed. "It's all my fault. I should have watched him more closely. He's brilliant with magic, but he's never been around it, so it overwhelmed him."

"Yes, but that alone wouldn't have caused this."

Bornias twisted his beard in one hand. "It's a long story, but he and Megan found some dragon's blood. Add fuel to fire and?" He clapped his hands together.

Ainsley's father was silent for a moment. Then, "Bornias, I want you to come get Claire."

"No!" Ainsley and Bornias exclaimed as one.

Ainsley stepped in front of Bornias. "Dad, we can't bring Mom here. She's six months pregnant. If I get any worse, she won't be safe."

"Besides that, you'll be opening a very large can of worms," said Bornias. "I don't think this is the best time to tell your wife, 'Surprise! I'm from another world!'"

"Yeah, and . . . *what*?" Ainsley spun around and faced Bornias, the argument he had been about to make dislodged by this new information. "Say that again? The part about my father being from another world."

"Your father is from Arylon," said Bornias with a frown. "I thought you would have gleaned that from our conversation."

"I figured out that he knows about this place," Ainsley gestured wildly with his arms, "but I thought he was going off stuff you told him."

"Oh." Bornias reddened and scratched his cheek. "That would have been a better story, wouldn't it?"

At that moment, Lady Maudred chose to make her entrance, waving a piece of parchment. "Your Highness, I found most of what you were looking for, but there are a few things we'll have to order from Pontsford." She walked toward Bornias, who intercepted her before she could reach the table.

"That's fine, Cordelia. Thank you."

"How is that potion working?" She brushed past Bornias and stopped in front of Ainsley, pulling back his shirtsleeve and inspecting his skin.

"Hmmm." She reached for the goblet. "A little more potion probably wouldn't hurt. Is it in this pot?" She peered into the cauldron and let out an ear-piercing shriek, sending the goblet flying into the air.

Ainsley caught it easily, but he wasn't quick enough to catch Lady Maudred, who collapsed on the floor in a dead faint.

"Ainsley," his father said with a sigh, "fetch my mother some smelling salts."

To Market, To Market

Despite her own protests, Megan had been grateful to leave Lady Maudred's quarters. The lie Bornias told had almost been too overwhelming to handle, and she hoped that when she returned later, Ainsley would have learned the truth about his father. She didn't feel right being the one to tell him.

Skimming her fingers across the stone wall, she descended the steps one at a time, wondering how the Pearl of Truth would react when immersed in a throng of people, dozens of whom were likely to be untruthful at some given point in their shopping.

On the second-floor landing, Megan paused and studied the activity on the ground floor. To her dismay, it seemed to be more crowded than usual with merchants posting boards outside their shops that boasted sensational sale prices within. Most were scrawled with reminders that Carnival in Pontsford was at hand. Megan listened to the buzz of casual chatter but couldn't isolate the din into separate conversations. With a grateful sigh, she skipped down the steps and joined the early evening shoppers.

Unlike many of them, however, she knew exactly where she wanted to go.

She strode to a wooden door engraved with a picture of a needle and thread and the name "Sari," the tailor who had outfitted Ainsley and Megan when they first arrived in Arylon in their out-of-place Earth clothes. When she knocked on the shop door, she expected to have to reintroduce herself, but Sari smiled at Megan and hugged her.

"Cordelia's young friend, welcome, welcome!" She grabbed Megan's hands and pulled her into the room. "You and your brother are my inspiration."

Megan almost corrected Sari, but then remembered that she and Ainsley had been posing as Frieden's niece and nephew. "How so?"

"That fabulous Carnival fabric you were wearing," Sari said, referring to Megan's blue jeans. She fluttered away and returned with a bolt of black cloth, thrusting it at Megan. "I've improved it! Feel!"

Megan grabbed the loose end of the bolt and rubbed the cloth between her fingers, marveling at its satiny softness. She tugged at it with both hands and found it to be as durable as denim. "It's amazing."

"And half the price of your foreign fabric, I'd wager." Sari winked and returned the bolt to an empty spindle. "I'm taking it with me to Carnival next week when all the dignitaries arrive in Pontsford, and," she blushed, "I'd like to name it after you and your brother."

"Really?" Megan racked her brain, trying to think of all possible combinations of her and Ainsley's names. "How about . . . aingan? Or megley?"

Sari rubbed her finger across her lip in thought. "I don't like megley . . . too close to motley. But aingan has an exotic sound to it." She gestured to her fabric and spoke to an invisible crowd. "Lords and ladies, the most regal thread this season isn't spider's silk, it's aingan."

Megan played along and cheered. "We love aingan! Five thousand bolts, please!"

Sari beamed at her. "I have a gift for you and your brother. I was only able to get one, however, so you'll have to share." She scurried away again and ducked under one of the cutting tables. When she reappeared, she clutched a brown satchel in one hand. "A peddler was selling these enchanted bags, and I traded him a bolt of aingan for this one."

"Oh . . . thanks," said Megan, turning the plain-looking bag over in her hands. "How exactly is this enchanted?"

"It's weightless. You can stick any of your traveling items in it, and all you'll ever feel is the weight of the bag itself."

"Really?" Megan regarded the bag now with a less critical eye. "That's awesome. Thank you."

Sari bowed. "Anything I can do for my inspiration. Was there something else you needed?"

Megan tucked the bag under her arm. "A new cloak actually. Can it be made with a pull-away clasp?" she added, thinking of the grimalkin that had chased her up a tree and ripped the cloak off her back.

"Of course!" Sari called the request to an idle table, and in five minute's time, she was draping the cloak around Megan's shoulders. "No charge," said Sari. "Just thank your brother for me."

Megan hugged Sari. "I will. Hopefully, we'll see you in Pontsford."

Stepping into the hallway, Megan was surprised at the number of people gathered about the shoe shop a few doors down. She didn't remember finding it that interesting on her last visit, but as she joined the crowd, she realized the attraction was not at that shop but the one beside it. A man in striped robes beckoned to a group of giggling girls, some of whom Megan recognized as Ainsley's admirers when they had first arrived in Raklund.

"Which of all you beauties would like a new look for Carnival?"

"I would." One of the girls, a redhead, stepped forward, flipping her waist-length hair over her shoulder so that it smacked several passersby across the face. The merchant helped her onto a tall stool where spectators could view the demonstration. The girl allowed herself to be lowered onto the seat as if she were a princess assuming the throne.

"Now, good lords and ladies," the merchant turned back to the audience, hands cupped around his mouth. "We all want to look our finest for that special someone we're meeting . . . or hope to meet at Carnival, correct?"

A young man in the crowd catcalled and was rewarded with laughter from the audience. The merchant winked at him. "The one thing most of us don't have, however, is a lot of time for primping and preening once we get there." The audience murmured in agreement. "And we can't beautify ourselves at home because by the time we reach Pontsford, any style will have been replaced by a windswept look." The audience laughed again. "That's where I come in."

The merchant grabbed the front of his robes and whisked them to either side, revealing a multipocketed belt slung holster-style that was stocked with a comb, scissors, and several bottles. "Watch my hands if your eyes can keep up," he said. In a matter of seconds, the girl's hair had been parted and twirled into a dozen tiny buns, each adorned with a thimble-sized flower.

"A blossoming beauty if ever I saw one," said the merchant with a flamboyant wave of his arms.

The women in the audience cooed, and the hallway resounded with applause.

"That hairstyle will stay intact for a fortnight," the merchant raised his voice to be heard over the din he'd created. "A few splashes of my special tonic will keep it clean and smelling like a hylark." He pulled a fuchsia-colored vial from his belt and handed it to the redhead, whom he then escorted offstage.

"Now, I know some of you may think that this was easy because the girl has gorgeous hair, but I can work with even the unruliest of masses." He scanned the crowd and his eyes settled on Megan. "You!"

Megan balked as everyone shuffled about to look. She glanced behind her, hoping to see someone wearing a clown wig, but the merchant called, "I'm talking to you, dear. The pretty brunette trapped under the shrubbery of hair."

"Oh, no, thank you." Megan held up her hands and backed down the hall. "I'm fine the way I am."

"Of course you are!" the merchant called to her. "But Carnival is a special occasion, and I'll bet you have a young man or two you'd like to spend time with while you're there. Maybe a rugged lad with a soft spot for animals or perhaps a tragic fellow who's cursed—"

"I said no thank you!" Heat blossomed in Megan's cheeks and she wrapped her arms around her chest, feeling as if the merchant had peered into her soul. "I'm not some vain little twit!"

He held her eye for a second, then nodded. "Very well. Perhaps another volunteer?"

Megan turned and hurried down the hall, distinctly aware that half the crowd was watching the merchant and the other half was watching her. She was so busy looking for a safe place to hide until the crowd dispersed, she overlooked a gray-haired dwarf headed her direction and barreled into him.

"I'm so sorry!" She stooped to collect the pipe she had knocked from his hand, and realized it was familiar to her.

"In trouble again, are we?" asked a gruff voice.

Megan straightened, her grin matching that of the old blind dwarf who had once helped her and Ainsley escape from Lady Maudred.

"Sir Inish!" She grabbed for his leathery hand, placing the pipe into it. "How are you?"

"Good evening . . . Megan, was it? How are you?" He tilted his head in the direction from which Megan had come. "Unless my ears deceive me, you seem to be running from something."

"There's a merchant who's styling people's hair, and he makes me feel a little uneasy," she explained.

"Ah, the new fellow across from my office," said Sir Inish with a nod. "Telepaths like him trouble me a bit as well. I always feel naked around them."

"Telepath?" Megan turned to look back at the merchant. "You mean, like, he can read minds?"

Sir Inish nodded again. "Normally, his kind aren't allowed to live in areas with a high population, but he swore a blood oath that he would avoid the political officials and wouldn't use his powers for ill gain. Plus, he was willing to pay handsomely for his shop."

"Huh." Megan watched the merchant hand out samples of his secret potion. "I wonder why he wanted to stay here so badly."

"Past troubles?" Sir Inish shrugged. "Nobody knows, but I'd be careful around him."

Megan snorted. "Now that I know what he is, I'll stay as far away as possible." The merchant happened to glance in her direction, and Megan turned around, eager to change the topic to something else, less the telepath pick up her thoughts.

"So, what have you been up to? Have you been training the Silvan Sentry?" she asked, recalling his former position as captain of Raklund's military forces.

He nodded and sighed. "Nonstop. They have a great deal to learn, though I have to admit," he held up a finger for emphasis, "they have been improving."

"Well, that's good," said Megan. "Are you taking a break right now?"

"Actually, I just finished speaking with Governor Frieden . . . er . . . your uncle," he corrected himself with a grin. "He tells me you're fond of the blade."

"That's true," said Megan, recalling with some remorse the sword Frieden had given her, which had been reduced to molten steel by Losen's evil mother, Sasha. She hadn't come across another one since.

Sir Inish tapped his pipe against the wall to empty it and tucked it into his vest pocket. "He also tells me you have difficulty maneuvering with anything heavier than a rapier."

Megan was thankful Sir Inish couldn't see her blush. "That's also true."

"Have you at least been practicing with a real sword?"

Megan bit her lip and thought. "I can carry one, and Frieden and I have sparred once or twice."

"But he cares about you." Sir Inish shoved a pudgy finger in Megan's face at an alarming angle that allowed access to the inside of her nose. "He's being cautious when he duels you, not attempting to bring you to your knees for a swift beheading."

Megan's hand strayed to her throat. "I would hope not."

"You should hope *so*! Meet me on the second-floor landing at dawn tomorrow. I'll show you what facing a *true* opponent is like."

The thought of holding a sword again quickened the beating of her heart, and Megan hugged the old dwarf. "I'll be there!"

Tib and His Amazing Disappearing Act

After Ainsley had used the smelling salts to rouse her, Lady Maudred had spent the better half of five minutes shrieking at Tib and Bornias for giving her wrinkles that "no amount of elven magic could reverse." She looked livid enough, at one point, to dive into the cauldron and drag her son home.

And then she remembered Ainsley. She smothered him with fifteen years worth of grandmotherly love, mixed with a bit of her stiff personality, fussing over how thin and tired he looked.

"I have the Illness. I can't really help it," Ainsley pointed out.

"Yes, let's speak more on that," said Ainsley's father. "What plans have you to combat this?"

"Ainsley has already taken the antidote," said Bornias, peering into the cauldron. "We'll know shortly if it was effective."

"In the meantime," Ainsley cleared his throat and blushed, "can you come here, Dad?"

For a moment, the only sound was the bubbling of chili from the other side of the cauldron.

"There's nothing I want more than to be with you, son," Ainsley's father said at last. "But, I physically can't."

"And why is that?" Lady Maudred looked ready to kick the cauldron across the room.

Then they heard voices from the other side of the cauldron. Ainsley's father dropped his voice to a loud whisper.

"Listen, I have to go or I'll have family members angry at me in *two* worlds. I'll speak with all of you later. Bornias, tell them what's going on. Mother, Ainsley, be strong. I love you."

Ainsley hesitated, then hurried forward. "Hey, Dad!" But the liquid in the cauldron had already returned to its murky state. He and Lady Maudred turned to Bornias who was fiddling with the laces on the front of his jerkin. When he realized neither one of them intended to leave, he sighed.

"Please don't give me those ill-treated looks. It was Tib's request that neither of you know about the other's world."

"But, how did he end up on Earth in the first place?" asked Ainsley. "And how come he can't come back now? You do it all the time!"

"I'd like to know myself," said Lady Maudred. She placed a hand on Ainsley's shoulder, and he winced. "For now, I think Ainsley should lay down in Tib's room while you clean up this mad-wizard mess." She indicated several decanters stacked precariously on a chair now dripping their contents onto the stone floor and forming a yellowish pool.

Ainsley knew someone who would be as interested in Bornias's explanation as he. "Grandmother?"

She raised a hand to quiet him. "Please call me Gran, not Grandmother, dear. Grandmother makes me seem cold and fussy."

Ainsley bit his tongue. "All right then, Gran. Does your tracking device know where Megan is? She should probably know what's happening."

"The goldenwing? Of course!" Lady Maudred cleared her throat. "Megan," she spoke in a raised voice as she fussed with her sleeves, "could you please return to us as soon as possible?" She cocked her head as if listening for something, then nodded in satisfaction. "She just finished speaking with Barsley Inish and is on her way."

"I hope he spoke with her about her swordsmanship." The bottles in Bornias's arms clanked together as he fought to keep them from slipping. "I don't feel comfortable with her holding one until she's been better trained."

"We can ask when she arrives," said Lady Maudred. She pointed to the cauldron. "Will you be using this again?"

Bornias leaned over to inspect the potion, and a half-full bottle rolled from his arms into the cauldron with a splash. He sighed. "I don't think I will now. This is ridiculous. I'm no scullery maid." With an incantation, he released the bottles in his arms, where they levitated in anticipation of his instructions. "Into the kitchen." He waved his hand, and the vessels whizzed through the air and out of the room, the wind whistling across their open mouths.

"Why don't I show you to your father's old bedroom." Lady Maudred guided Ainsley from the study and down the hall to a thick navy curtain, which she pulled back with a flourish.

Ainsley felt as if he were looking into his father's office back home. Books and papers covered every flat surface with the exception of the bed, which itself had runes and writing scratched into the wooden posts. His father seemed to have been preoccupied even when he was asleep.

"I don't know anyone who was as dedicated to his work as your father," said Lady Maudred. "He would have been a complete recluse if it hadn't been for the Protectors." She pointed to a framed picture that had been mounted at the head of the bed.

Ainsley's father stood with arms crossed over his chest and an olive cloak draped over his shoulders, flapping in a nonexistent breeze. Ainsley guessed he must have been about twenty years younger when this portrait was painted. No gray tarnished the beautiful blonde hair Ainsley had inherited, no wrinkles creviced the bronze skin.

"We had that painted when your father was just a few years older than you. He *hated* everything about it. He hated posing for it . . . the painter had to guess how your father's eyes naturally looked because he kept crossing them . . . and he wouldn't even let us display it in any of the common rooms!"

Ainsley smiled, his fingers tracing over ridges the brushstrokes had made. "That sounds like my dad. He's not much on keeping up appearances."

"He learned that from your grandfather, I'm afraid." She pointed to the pin on her chest, and Ainsley leaned in to inspect the miniature portrait of a wild-haired man with a thick mustache and eyebrows. "I'm surprised you didn't grow up some feral child wearing nothing but a loincloth."

Bornias appeared, wiping damp hands across his chest. "I should make this quick. The rehearsal for Rayne's coronation is near at hand, and I need to be present."

Lady Maudred clicked her tongue at the wet streaks on his shirtfront, and they shrank until they were pinprick-sized dots. "I do own towels, your Highness," she told him. "They're much more absorbent than clothing."

"I'll be wearing my royal robes anyway," said Bornias with a shrug. "Nobody will see them."

Lady Maudred raised an eyebrow and turned to Ainsley. "I'm *really* surprised you didn't grow up some feral child."

Bornias settled himself on a bench at the foot of the bed. "Ainsley turned out fine. He's a bit on the obsessive side about magic, like his father, but otherwise an admirable youth."

"My father's into magic, too?" asked Ainsley with an excited jump onto Tib's old bed. "That was kind of a conflict of interest, being governor of the Protectors, wasn't it?"

"Your father's obsession with magic is quite different than yours." Bornias turned sideways on the bench to face Ainsley. "You wish for immeasurable magic you can control without a thought. Your father wishes to understand magic and limit its use. It was that drive that took him from this world."

"Wait! Wait!" Megan burst through Lady Maudred's front door and skidded to a stop in the archway to Tib's room. "Don't start without me!" She threw an armful of parcels on the floor and looked at Ainsley. "How are you feeling?"

"Itchy and confused," Ainsley admitted. "My father's from this world."

Megan nodded. "I knew that." At Ainsley's confused look, she pointed to her chest. "The pearl told me."

"He was governor of the Protectors before Frieden, and he was Lady Maudred's son," Ainsley added. "Did you know that?"

"That I did *not* know." She bounded onto the bed beside him, despite a disapproving look from Lady Maudred. "So how did he end up in our world then?" she asked Bornias.

"Do you remember when I told you that many of my followers had tried to destroy the Staff of Lexiam?"

Ainsley and Megan nodded as they recalled the first day they had arrived in Arylon and learned of the staff's disappearance.

"You told us all the people who attempted to destroy the staff were destroyed by it," said Megan, "or something like that."

Bornias shook his head. "I didn't say they were destroyed by it. I said they were vaporized."

"Same difference." Megan shrugged.

"Ah, but it isn't." Bornias glanced around and picked up a bottle from the bureau. "In here is liquid." He shook the bottle, and they could hear sloshing. "If I put it into a spray form, or *vaporize* it, it isn't destroyed, is it? I have merely altered its state of being." He passed a hand over the top of the bottle and a spray nozzle appeared. Bornias gave it a squeeze, and a heady aroma filled the room. "Now, these particles are airborne, rather than confined to a liquid form."

"So, you're saying my father tried to destroy the Staff of Lexiam and became like a . . . a cheap-smelling cologne?" Ainsley fanned the air in front of him. "How did his particles make it from here to Earth?"

"Your father and I have spent many an afternoon researching this, and the only theory we have is that when the staff attempts to destroy a living being, it also creates a tiny tear in the fabric of space. When the living being is vaporized, it passes through the tear and emerges wherever that particular tear happens to lead."

Ainsley considered this for a moment, and all he could think to say was, "Wow."

"Wow, indeed," said Bornias, passing his hand back over the bottle and removing the spray nozzle. "You can imagine how disconcerting it was for your father to re-solidify in a foreign world. He was very lucky that Megan's father happened upon him and believed his story."

"*My* father?" Megan's eyes widened. "My father knows about Arylon and everything and he never told me?" She snapped her fingers with a triumphant smile. "That's why our parents have always lived next door to one another, isn't it?"

Bornias nodded. "Your father has always been like a brother to Tib, taking care of him and teaching him about Earth."

Lady Maudred leaned over and gave Megan an unexpected squeeze. "I knew there was something I liked about you."

Megan blushed but grinned. "Your son does an excellent job fitting in. Your grandson on the other hand . . ."

"Hey!" Ainsley kicked at Megan from beneath his blanket.

"You mustn't overexert yourself, dear." Lady Maudred grabbed Ainsley's legs to still him, and then turned to Bornias. "Now, why is it that I cannot see my son again, your Highness?"

"Oh, you could go see *him*, but he can't come to see you. For some reason we haven't yet discovered, the staff blocks his return to Sunil. He spends every free moment researching and trying to find a way home."

Megan nudged Ainsley in silence, and he nodded, his heart feeling a little lighter now that he knew his father's obsession with books.

Lady Maudred's eyes welled up with tears. "If only he had let me know he was still alive. I could have come to visit. I could have acted like I belonged on Earth." She reached into her sleeve and removed a tissue, dabbing at her eyes. "I've missed so much of his life."

Bornias stood and placed an arm around her shoulders, though with their height difference his arm made it around just one shoulder. "He truly wanted to let you know he was okay, but he knew you would demand to see him and then the questions from his wife and Ainsley would begin. 'Where does your mother live?' 'Why can't I ever go spend the night at Gran's?' It was a very difficult spot for him to be in, and he thought it would be quicker and easier for him to just discover a way to come home. Now that Ainsley and Megan are here, however," Bornias shrugged, "it's only a matter of time before Tib has to tell his wife the truth."

"But she's pregnant!" Ainsley struggled to get out from beneath his sheets. "She can't handle news like that! I have to let her see that I'm okay."

"Lay back down." Lady Maudred grabbed his shoulders and sat him firmly on his bed. "You'll only make things worse showing up at her doorstep looking like you do now."

"Besides, your father and Megan's father have both your mothers convinced that nothing is amiss. If we can defeat the Illness, there may be no need for anyone to panic."

That being said, Bornias yelped and doubled over, clutching his stomach.

"Bornias!" cried Ainsley and Megan. Lady Maudred rose to fetch one the guards, but Bornias waved his hand in refusal. "I'm fine." He straightened up, and Ainsley and Megan could see that the face of his belt buckle was now sprinkled with spectacularly colored fireworks. "I really must ask Frieden to make his messages a bit more subtle, though. Perhaps I will after the coronation rehearsal." He turned to Megan and held out a hand. "Would you like to come?"

"I would," she admitted, "but I'd also like to stay here with Ainsley . . . just until he gets better."

"Very well." Bornias turned to Lady Maudred. "I'll return in the morning. Make sure he remains as still as possible."

Lady Maudred nodded as Bornias sat on the edge of Ainsley's bed. He spoke to Ainsley in a whisper only the two of them could hear. "Whatever you do, try and fight the Illness. The jidalya will tempt you in sleep and in waking, but no amount of magic is as precious as your life."

Bornias got to his feet, and they watched him disappear down the hall.

When they heard the front door slam, Megan turned to Ainsley. "Well, what do you want to do now?"

Ainsley's stomach gurgled. "I think I want to eat."

"That sounds like an excellent idea," said Lady Maudred. She stood in the bedroom doorway and whistled low and long.

From afar, Ainsley and Megan could hear the clatter of dinnerware, and then Lady Maudred stepped to one side of the archway as an entire table laden with food floated into the bedroom. It eased to a halt beside the bed and shuddered to the floor, its contents shaking slightly but remaining upright.

"I thought it might be wiser if we eat in here," said Lady Maudred, shifting the navy curtain so it blocked the archway from outside view. "Help yourselves."

Neither teen bothered to feign patience as they both reached for the same plate. Ainsley released his grip first and started removing lids from the covered dishes. Megan followed behind him, spearing and scooping a little of almost everything she saw.

"I recognize the roast," said Ainsley as he forked a few slices onto his own plate. "We had it the last time we were here, but what's this?" He pointed with his utensil to the other entrée, a mixture of steaming spiced vegetables and shreds of what looked like tree bark. Megan had noticed it, too, and completely avoided adding it to her dinner options.

"Mmm. It appears the cooks prepared a specialty," Lady Maudred wafted the scent of the dish to her nostrils and sighed with contentment. "It's Mariner's Mash. Potatoes and various sea greens mixed with crisp-fried Mammoth crab."

"Mammoth crab? As in, incredibly huge or incredibly hairy?"

"Mammoth as in incredibly huge." Lady Maudred smiled. "They're a delicacy because they're so difficult to catch, but their meat is plentiful and tender."

Ainsley plucked a piece from the entrée and chewed it. "This is really good!" He served himself, and Megan, a large spoonful, and they settled on the bed and started to eat.

"We've seen so little of this world. What's your favorite place, Lady Maudred?" Megan asked after the older woman had situated herself at the desk with her own meal.

"My favorite place?" Lady Maudred swallowed a forkful of Mariner's Mash. "Probably where this Mammoth crab came from, the Port of Scribnitch."

"Really?" Megan frowned, not being able to visualize the genteel Lady Maudred traipsing about on a boat dock. "Why?"

"The Port of Scribnitch heads the Kingdom Coalition's commerce division, and it is *the* culture center of Arylon.

Exotic imports arrive every day, which provide excellent shopping opportunities, and even more exotic people come to visit from all over the world. The food is exquisite, and the buildings reflect the various cultures that have graced Arylonian soil."

"That place sounds awesome." Megan polished off her last bite of dinner. "Maybe we can go there before we have to head home."

"I hope so," said Lady Maudred. She shifted in her chair and accidentally kicked Megan's shopping parcels. "Oh! I had forgotten you went shopping. How was it?"

Ainsley groaned at the thought of more girl talk, but while Megan related the tales of Sari's new material, the telepath, and her meeting with Sir Inish, he found himself listening with rapt attention.

"I also found a basic pet store," Megan pulled a glass jar of brown pellets from her enchanted sack and unfastened the lid, "so now Bit won't starve." She plucked out a few pellets and held one over the breast pocket where the narshorn was resting. Bit emerged a moment later, nose twitching, and grabbed the food between her paws, gnawing on it with her tiny teeth. "Here's some more in case you get hungry." Megan dropped the remaining pellets from her hand into the pocket, and Bit disappeared from sight.

Lady Maudred yawned. "Oh, excuse me! It's been a long day. I hope the two of you don't mind if I leave you for a soak in the bath."

"It's fine," said Ainsley, putting his plate on the table. "We'll keep ourselves entertained."

Lady Maudred whistled to the table, and it followed her out the door. She turned at the entrance, the table nearly bumping her backside, and waggled a finger at her grandson. "Entertain yourselves *without* magic."

"Of course!" Ainsley grinned at her innocently. When the curtain had swished closed behind her, he turned to Megan. "So, feel like climbing out on any ledges to pass the time?"

"I think we're still living with the consequences of that." Megan smiled. "But it does seem a little dull without Frieden or Bornias around, doesn't it?"

"Well, they always had stories to tell us about Arylon."

"So do I!" Megan found her original knapsack on the floor and transferred its contents to the new, enchanted one in her search for the book from The Traveler's Tales. "A-ha!" She held it up for Ainsley's inspection. "What do you think? I can read you some of these."

Ainsley rolled his eyes. "I'm not six years old, Megan, and you're not my babysitter. No thank you."

"Okay." Megan shrugged and tucked the book under one arm. "I'm going to go read by myself, then. Have a good night."

Ainsley watched for a moment to see if she was bluffing. The last thing he wanted was to be alone in the dark with the Illness. When Megan pulled back the curtain, he grunted in protest. "Wait! You can tell me your stories."

Megan turned and saw a rueful smile on his face. "I don't want to fall asleep with terrifying thoughts running through my mind."

Without a word, she climbed onto the bed beside him and propped herself up. Ainsley lay back against his pillows and stared at the ceiling where his father had stenciled constellations in white ink. Comforted by Megan's presence and so many reminders of his father, he smiled to himself and listened as Megan read about the origin of fairy pearls.

Trip the Sword Fantastic

Megan awoke to a gentle shaking of her shoulder and a sweet cinnamon smell. She opened her eyes and looked up at Lady Maudred.

"It's time to get up if you're to meet Sir Inish at dawn."

Megan yawned and looked around. She was no longer in Tib's bedroom but a smaller one with a mauve curtain. A tray of food had been set on the nightstand and a change of clothing lay draped over a folding privacy screen.

"How's Ainsley doing?" she asked, grabbing for a slice of toast covered with a thick jelly of oranges and cinnamon.

Lady Maudred shooed her out of the bed and made it behind her. "He seems a bit troubled in his sleep, but it doesn't appear his condition has worsened."

"Does Bornias know?"

Lady Maudred shook her head. "He came by last night after the rehearsal but won't return until the afternoon. I think he feels he might postpone any deterioration of Ainsley's health if he stays away."

"You'll let me know if something happens?" Megan swallowed a piece of bacon and stepped behind the privacy screen, sliding out of one tunic and into the other.

"Of course," said Lady Maudred. "By the same method I used yesterday."

At those words, the golden butterfly that had affixed itself to Megan's earlier outfit finally released its grip on the fabric, leaving six tiny pinholes. To her dismay, it alighted on her new shirt in the exact same spot. Bit, not to be outdone, scrambled out of the discarded shirt's pocket and leapt to Megan's shoulder.

"I wouldn't forget about you." Megan stroked the narshorn's head. She changed her pants and stepped out from behind the screen to see Lady Maudred now holding a glass of milk out to her. "That's not beetle's milk, is it?" asked Megan, eyeing the frothy white. "If it is, I'm not drinking it."

"Well, of course it's n——"

"I'm wearing a Pearl of Truth," Megan reminded her.

Lady Maudred sighed and placed the milk back on the nightstand. "Go meet Sir Inish. By the time he's finished with you, you'll wish you'd drunk five glasses of this, I'll wager."

"I doubt it. See you later!" Megan hurried out the door and down to the second floor landing where Sir Inish waited with his back against the wall.

"Good morning, Sir Inish!"

The old dwarf smiled. "You're prompt. I appreciate people who respect my time." He bent his arm at the elbow and offered it to Megan. "Shall we?"

Megan linked her arm through the old dwarf's. "Show me what I'm missing."

When she and Ainsley had last come to Raklund, they had been hurried up to the third floor by Lady Maudred and denied the privilege of exploring the second. From the brief tour they had received then, Megan knew at least that the second floor housed the Raklund library, but Sir Inish led her past its iron doors with handles soldered to look like the Silverskin crest. He paused at the end of the hall before another set of iron doors directly above the infirmary. This set, however, provided no handles with which to open them. Sir Inish withdrew something from his pocket, and, after feeling around, pressed it against a coin-sized reproduction of the Silverskin insignia inlaid in one of the doors.

Both doors clicked and opened inward, and Megan could hear the energizing sound of steel clinking against steel, accompanied by sporadic grunts and shouts.

She stepped into a room whose ceilings were supported with pillars that bordered five sunken pits, each roughly the size of a lap pool. In three of the pits, pairs of men clashed swords and maneuvered around and over stones that a bored-looking woman kept turning into trees or flaming buildings or small children.

A man in a maroon cloak circled the pits, barking instructions. "Use the flames to your advantage! Heat your blade and double the damage."

"Ew." Megan wrinkled her nose as they walked past the pit. "That's a bit mean, don't you think?"

"*That* is why you're here," said Sir Inish. "To understand that all battle isn't chivalry and honor. Are you ready to begin?"

Megan sputtered. "What . . . now? You want me to go in there and fight those guys?"

"No, you'll be fighting me," spoke a female voice.

Megan turned to find the redheaded girl from the hairdresser's show smirking at her. "Can you handle a vain little twit?"

"Megan, this is Rella Forgeway," Sir Inish beckoned to the redhead, and she placed a hand on his arm, "one of my best students."

"You flatter me, Sir Inish," said Rella with a laugh. It sounded like china shattering to Megan, but Sir Inish smiled. "I don't flatter. I praise."

Rella circled Megan. "I'm actually a little surprised, Sir Inish. She doesn't have the look of a swordswoman, does she?" She indicated her own clothing, which she had changed from yesterday's modest dress and vestal cloak to tight, curve-hugging breeches and a cleavage-baring bodice.

Megan glowered at her, but Sir Inish just smiled. "As you know, I'm not one to judge on looks."

Rella laughed, but she also blushed. "Of course, Sir Inish. I apologize." She turned to Megan. "Pit four is free. Are you ready?" Even with her hair up in its multitude of buns, she still managed to give it an arrogant flip as she walked away.

"But . . ." Megan faltered, knowing her next words would validate Rella's swordswoman insult, "but I don't have a sword."

Rella stopped and looked over her shoulder at Megan with a smug grin. "You don't have a sword? Did you lose it in your last battle?"

Megan crossed her arms. "As a matter of fact, I did."

Rella crossed her arms as well, pushing the backs of her hands against the sides of her breasts to enhance her cleavage and make Megan appear woefully underdeveloped. "I love exchanging battle stories. For what cause were you fighting?"

"I was retrieving something very valuable that you might have heard of . . ." But Megan trailed off when she remembered that nobody other than the members of the Silvan Council had ever known the Staff of Lexiam was stolen.

"I'm sorry. What was that?" asked Rella.

"It was a . . ." Megan's eyes darted around the room for ideas but none came to her. "A horse," she said with a wince. "It belonged to Governor Frieden." She winced again.

"Impressive," said Rella, though she looked as if Megan had proclaimed victory over a tangle of yarn. "You should have no trouble besting me then." She sauntered to a weapon rack against the wall and withdrew a pathetic travesty of a sword. The dented and warped blade wobbled in its pommel, flaking rust onto the ground as she handed it to Megan hilt-first.

"There aren't any better swords there?" asked Megan, giving the weapon a practice swing and feeling as if the blade might fly loose at any second.

"All of the spares are roughly the same quality," said Rella, descending into the pit.

"Well, this should be interesting," Megan murmured, turning the blade over in her hands. She almost dropped it when she heard a humming from her left breast.

The golden butterfly fluttered its wings, and Megan watched the metal connecting the hilt and blade of the decrepit sword glow red-hot, then turn black and emit a puff of steam. Megan held her hand close to the soldered metal, and when she felt no heat from it, she wiggled the juncture experimentally. Though the sword still looked dull and shabby, the blade no longer wobbled.

"Thanks, Lady Maudred," whispered Megan.

"You can't charge into battle on a horse with broken legs," came the tinny response.

Megan smiled and jumped down into the pit.

"If you don't mind messing up that hairdo," she told Rella, "I'm ready to go."

The words had scarcely left her lips when Rella charged at her, sword set to plunge into Megan's heart. Megan screamed in surprise, and then Rella screamed in pain.

Bit launched herself from Megan's breast pocket and sank her teeth into Rella's sword hand. Rella's sword clattered to the ground, and she fought to shake Bit loose.

"I am so sorry!" Megan closed her hand over Bit, who fidgeted to get back to Rella and steal a few more nibbles.

To Megan's surprise, Rella waved a dismissive hand and sucked the bloody puncture mark. "I underestimated you. Here I thought you were unprepared, but you had a sneak attack. Very well played." Rella examined her hand and picked up her sword. "One word of caution, however. Your opponent will now be on guard for your pet, and it may become mincemeat."

"Got it." Megan held Bit at eye level. "Thanks for that." She stroked the narshorn's furry head, and its eyes closed, "but right now I need you to protect yourself."

The narshorn opened its eyes and squeaked, brandishing its barbed tail at Rella before diving into Megan's pocket.

This time, Megan waited until she was actually ready before announcing it. Rella was an aggressive opponent, forcing Megan to retreat and parry several blows in succession.

"You . . . can't be timid with your weapon," grunted Rella. "You're not at Carnival waiting for someone to ask you for a dance."

She feinted a strike, but Megan saw through it and struck Rella's blade in a backsweep, knocking the sword from her grip.

"A daring move." Rella stooped and retrieved her sword. "Either you predicted my feint, or you're incredibly lucky."

Megan gave a half-smile and waited for Rella's next attack. Rella, however, seemed to have reconsidered her strategy and had switched to defense. The two girls stood on the opposite sides of the pit, regarding one another.

"I don't hear any movement!" Sir Inish commented from above. "Can it be that you are both so well practiced that you are prepared to face *any* adversary?"

Ducking her chin, Megan swooped forward and raised the sword to her left shoulder, slashing at a downward slant when she reached Rella. To her horror, Rella did nothing to stop the steel blade headed straight for her jugular. Megan yelped and altered her swing so that it arced to the left, and at that moment, Rella raised her left arm and pounded her fist against the back of Megan's right hand, smacking her sword loose.

"Ow!" Megan massaged her hand and scowled at Rella. "What the hell is your problem? I save your life and you try to break my hand?"

Rella looked unconcerned. "Will you be this lenient with your enemy on the field of battle?"

"We're not on the field of battle." A blush crept up Megan's neck as she snatched her sword off the ground.

"Nevertheless, you cannot show a moment's hesitation if it comes down to your life or the life of your adversary."

Megan regarded Rella dubiously. "Do you really expect to spend a great deal of time killing people?"

Rella backed to the edge of the pit and stood en garde. "I avoid confrontation when possible, but in defense of my people, I would stop short of nothing. Let's go again."

———

Rella worked Megan for two more hours until her muscles began to ache and she was spending more time picking up her sword than actually fighting. At last, Sir Inish called an end to the practice, and Rella sheathed her sword and extended a hand to Megan.

"I judged you unfairly. You're a decent opponent," she said as Megan took her sweaty hand and shook it. Rella held Megan in her grip for a moment and regarded her with a solemn expression. "But you lack the understanding of the power you wield. With that sword, you can bring down your enemies and protect the ones you love. You mustn't be afraid of it or what it can do. Otherwise, your enemies gain the advantage."

Megan nodded, and Rella finally released her grip. "I'm sorry I misjudged you, too," said Megan. "I thought you were one of those pretty girls with nothing else on her mind but finding the next mirror." Megan winced, realizing her apology hadn't sounded any better than her original insult, but Rella smiled.

"My sword is my companion, but it certainly can't bring me flowers and chocolate. Besides, every girl loves a little flattery."

Megan returned her smile, and the two climbed out of the pit to let a pair of teenaged boys use the sparring spot. One of them ogled Rella's outfit openly, but to Megan's pleasure, she caught the other staring at her.

"See what I mean?" Rella winked and, calling a good-bye to Sir Inish, sauntered away.

"How did the practice go?" Sir Inish asked Megan after she'd returned the sword to its place on the rack.

"Pretty well. Rella's a good teacher," said Megan. She linked her arm through his, and they strolled toward the entrance.

"She's one of the few people I can still trust in these times," said Sir Inish in a low voice. "That's why I wanted you to train with *her*."

Megan looked at the blind dwarf. "What do you mean 'in these times'? The Staff of Lexiam is secure, and Losen is in a no-magic cell somewhere downstairs."

"I'm not speaking of the staff," said Sir Inish, "although, I believe it is still in danger."

"Then what *do* you mean?" Megan guided Sir Inish around a group of Silvan Sentry who were engaged in a deep conversation. The moment they saw Sir Inish, their heels clicked together, and they chorused a salutation to their former captain.

"*That* is what I'm referring to." He jerked his head back after he and Megan had passed the soldiers. "They're part of a conspiracy . . . a coup to overthrow the government of Raklund and upset the Kingdom Coalition."

Megan's brow furrowed, and she looked over her shoulder at the Silvan Sentry who were now scattered about in various activities. "It looks to me like they're finally giving you the respect you deserve."

Sir Inish grunted and shook his head. "Trouble is brewing. I can smell it in the air and feel it in my joints."

"Well, I hope you're wrong," said Megan as a soldier rushed forward to open the door for them. "But let me know if there's something I can do."

"I will," said Sir Inish. "If I find out before it's not too late."

Family Feud

"Ainsley?"

Ainsley heard his name echoing off the cavern walls, and he grinned as a figure ran toward him.

"Penitent! I'm so glad to see you!" Ainsley sprinted to meet him halfway. "Where did you go?"

Penitent squeezed his shoulders. "Somehow we got separated." One of his hands clutched the side of Ainsley's face, and he studied him with blood-colored eyes. "Are you okay?"

"I'm fine. Something was chasing me earlier, but I escaped and found my friends." Ainsley frowned. "I don't know how I ended up back here, though. I guess the Illness must have transported me."

"How far has it progressed?" Penitent's hand squeezed Ainsley's shoulder.

"I took some antidote, so hopefully I'll be fine." Ainsley placed a reassuring hand atop Penitent's.

"You won't be." Penitent's fingers dug into Ainsley's shoulders. "Ainsley, you must listen to me." Frightened, Ainsley tried to back away, but Penitent followed him step for step in an eerie sort of dance. "You cannot fight it with magic. That is what it wants."

Ainsley's brow furrowed. "But . . . but you need magic to beat magic."

"No, Ainsley. It doesn't—"

A deafening roar drowned out his words. Ainsley spun around and saw a familiar orange glow brightening the cavern. His heart pounding a hole through his chest, Ainsley willed magic, any magic, to come to him.

Give me just enough power to defeat my enemy, he thought. Seconds later, a refreshing burst of vitality surged through his body, and his fingers glowed with a white light.

Penitent jerked on his arm. "Didn't you hear me?" His frantic eyes searched Ainsley's. "You cannot use magic to defeat this."

Ainsley laughed and pulled away, the power that flowed through his body granting him a new confidence. "Watch me."

Then, the mysterious creature that had stalked him through the dark tunnels appeared. A pair of dark ruby eyes floated among a sea of smooth ebony scales that covered its massive head and flowed to the base of its clawed feet. Its torso filled half the cavern, and had the creature rested on its haunches, the crown of spikes encircling its skull would have pulverized the stalactites above.

"It's a dragon," whispered Ainsley. A lump filled his throat, and it seemed to block the earlier waves of confidence from reaching his brain. His knees now shook and his bladder threatened to give way.

Head tilted back, the dragon roared once more, a crackle of fire accompanying its herald as it blackened the ceiling with six-foot flames. Ainsley swallowed hard and tried to imagine the dragon spewing something less horrific, like chocolate syrup or gold coins, but the intense heat pushed away all thoughts that didn't involve charred flesh.

With the rise and fall of its enormous clawed feet, the dragon lumbered toward Ainsley and Penitent, its pace eerily casual as if it knew it could end either man in a single move. The dragon's midsection came into view, and with it, a pair of leathery wings that were folded against its body. The additional space of the cavern allowed the dragon an opportunity to stretch them, and it did so, the tips of each wing brushing against the cavern walls.

Ainsley steeled his resolve and willed the magic to course through his veins once more. Again, the tips of his fingers glowed with the promise of power. The dragon, sensing the growing threat, snarled and quickened its pace. Through its nostrils, it drew a deep breath, the suction pulling Ainsley's feet from beneath him, dragging him across the cavern floor and over various debris.

Its breathing stopped, and Ainsley lay sprawled on his back a few yards from the dragon's mouth. He could hear the sound of rocks settling back into place and his own labored breathing. Then, the dragon's mouth opened, and a stream of fire spewed forth. All thoughts of magic left him, and Ainsley threw his hands up to protect himself, squeezing his eyes shut.

The flames enveloped him, but he felt nothing more than mild warmth, as if he were wrapped in a blanket. Opening one eye, he saw a thin outline of what he could only describe as *energy* separating him from the flames. He raised a fiery arm, and the energy layer stayed with him. Grinning, Ainsley jumped to his feet and shook his body from head to toe. The fire fell away, forming a small circle around him, and Ainsley snuffed it out with the bottom of his boot.

Crossing his arms, he looked up at the dragon and smirked. "You'll have to try harder than that."

At those words, the dragon leapt forward, its jaws bearing down on Ainsley. He stood his ground and raised his arms directly above his head, calling upon the moisture that dripped from the stalactites and pooled in the caves. As he brought his arms down in a wide arc, a protective dome of ice formed above and around him. The dragon bumped its snout against the curved shelter and gnashed its teeth, which slipped against the slick ice.

With a forward thrust of his fists, Ainsley's protective dome shattered into tiny ice shards that pierced the dragon's sensitive underbelly like a thousand spears. The dragon roared with rage and belched fire once more, but Ainsley gathered it in his hand and, feeling giddy with power, extinguished it with the clench of a fist.

He darted beneath the dragon and placed his hands on its stomach, willing all its magical energy to come to him. An amber glow pulsed under his fingers, and he laughed as the dragon howled in protest, its life force draining into Ainsley's body. Then, with a shudder, the dragon disintegrated into a pile of ashes.

Ainsley wiped dust on his pants and grinned at Penitent who crouched in a corner of the cavern, his face more ashen than the dragon's remains.

"See?" said Ainsley. "It wasn't difficult at all with magic." He pursed his lips and whistled a tune, accented with bursts of fire.

Penitent shook his head. "Don't you realize what you've done? You cannot destroy magic."

Ainsley concentrated on several globes of fire and ice he was now juggling. "What do you mean? I didn't destroy it. It's mine now."

"No, it isn't." Penitent pointed behind Ainsley. "Look."

Ainsley gave a sidelong glance at the pile of ashes, and his fiery juggling balls smashed on the ground, doused by the frozen water that followed.

"I'll be damned," he said, dropping to his knees.

Within the pile of ashes, something had moved. Ainsley scrabbled at the cinders until a baby dragon popped its head out and gave a muddled cry.

"Penitent, look!" He pulled the whelp free of the mess with a great effort, its size already that of a full-grown Great Dane. "If I raise him to be friendly, think how much magic I can get out of him!"

The baby dragon blinked up at Ainsley and then, without warning, it tackled him to the ground, snarling and clawing. Ainsley encased himself in a layer of ice, but the dragon's claws pierced the surface like ice picks and smashed his defense to pieces.

"Help me, Penitent!" cried Ainsley as the dragon launched a stream of fire at him. He caught it in his hand, but this time, he felt the uncomfortable heat along with a stinging sensation. "I'm losing my magic!"

"No, you're not." Penitent's voice sounded distant, but Ainsley couldn't take his eyes off the dragon to search for him. "The dragon's magic is more powerful now, and it will continue to amplify every time it is destroyed."

Ainsley succeeded in kicking the dragon away and scrambled to his feet at a run. Seconds later, he was face-down in the dirt with the beast snarling in his ear. Ainsley rolled onto his back and made one more attempt at magic, but the dragon had his arms pinned, and its jaws, already armed with fangs, were closing in on his jugular.

"Ainsley?"

He gasped and shot bolt upright in his father's bed, smacking foreheads with Megan who had bent over to check on him.

"Owww!" She lay back on the foot of the bed, cradling her skull. "A little warning next time might be good."

"Sorry." Ainsley licked his lips and swallowed, wishing for a glass of water. "Bad dream."

Megan winced as she pulled herself back up. "You don't look so great. Do you want me to get Lady Maudred?"

"No," he said, fighting to keep his breathing even. "Just something to drink."

Megan reached for a pitcher and mug that Lady Maudred had brought and filled it halfway "Try just a little bit first. You look ready to puke."

Ainsley rolled his eyes, but accepted the drink and leaned back against the headboard. Something jabbed him between both shoulder blades, and he sat back up, sloshing water across the bedcovers.

"What's wrong?" asked Megan, turning pale and stepping back a few paces.

Ainsley thrust the mug at her. "For crying out loud, I'm not going to be sick!" Then he turned and studied the wooden frame behind him. "That's weird. I felt something poking me, but there's nothing here." He twisted his arm behind his back and felt the skin by his closest shoulder. "Oh, damn," he whispered.

"What? What is it?" Megan pushed his hand aside and replaced it with her own. A welt about the size of a baseball throbbed in her palm. "Ugh, gross!" She wiped her hand on the bedcovers.

Ainsley reached by his other shoulder blade. "There's one here, too." He whipped his shirt over his head. "How bad does it look?"

"Woah!" Megan jumped back and collided with the dresser behind her, knocking the pitcher and mug to the floor with a crash.

"What?" Ainsley twisted his head to peer over his shoulder. "Am I growing Siamese twins or something? Tell me! I can't see anything but the welts."

Megan steeled herself and reached forward to touch the lower half of Ainsley's back, which was now covered in black scales. "Let's just say those welts aren't your biggest problem anymore."

Ainsley kicked off the blankets and scuttled across the room to a standing mirror. With his back to it, he looked over one shoulder at his reflection, and his heart slipped into his stomach.

Hurried footsteps sounded outside the door and abruptly came to a halt. Ainsley and Megan looked up at Lady Maudred, who had braced herself in the doorway and was panting like a marathon runner.

"Oh, thank the Other Side you're both still alive," she gasped, one hand now lowering to clutch at a stitch in her side. "I heard a crash and assumed the worst."

Ainsley's eyes blazed. "What, you thought maybe I'd turned Megan into flambé? I wouldn't hurt her. You, I might, however."

"Ainsley!" Megan gaped at him, but he didn't need to be reprimanded. Already, his wave of anger was receding, replaced by one of guilt.

"I'm sorry. I didn't mean it." Eyes lowered to the floor, he pulled his head as close to his shoulders as possible, wishing he could withdraw into himself like a turtle.

"It's quite all right," said Lady Maudred, though she still looked taken aback by Ainsley's sudden flare-up. "These flashes of anger will come and go."

"Will these come and go, too?" Megan whirled Ainsley around so his back faced his grandmother. Lady Maudred gasped and fell against the dresser, burying her head in her hands. Ainsley turned away to face his reflection.

Already, the dark scales on his chest had spread to his abdomen, where the skin had developed a calloused texture. He wrapped an arm about his stomach and noticed that it, too, had taken on an ebony cast. Head raised, he stared at the blood-colored pupils and wild hair of the creature that had claimed him.

"Ainsley?" Megan reached forward with a tentative hand and touched his shoulder.

He turned away from his reflection and smiled at her. "I'm okay. I've been through worse things than this, right?"

Tears welled in Megan's eyes, and she bowed her head. "Of course."

Ainsley's smiled faded. He wrapped his hands around the nearest bedpost and pulled with all his might until the splintering of wood drowned out Megan's sobs. With a roar of anger, he swung the bedpost at the mirror. Megan screamed, shielding herself with her hands as slivers of glass rocketed across the room.

An angry buzzing filled the air, and the reflective shards lost their velocity, falling to the ground with the tinkle of a thousand wind chimes. Ainsley's feet left the ground, and he was flipped upside down so that his hair brushed the floor.

"Hey!" he cried. "Put me down!"

From where she stood by the dresser, Lady Maudred's bosom heaved, and she drew herself to her full height. "Are you quite finished destroying your father's things?"

Ainsley scowled and righted himself, gesturing at a bookshelf. An armful of books flew toward Lady Maudred, but she cleared her throat, and the books stacked themselves by the bed in a neat pile.

"Need I remind you that I have been practicing magic for a good fifty years longer than you?" she asked, crossing her arms over her chest. "You're but a novice."

"I'm far more powerful than you'll ever be!" snarled Ainsley. He balled his hand into a fist and opened it, palm toward Lady Maudred. Spurts of fire swerved around Megan and made a beeline for his grandmother, who didn't flinch. Puckering her lips, she whistled, and the fires fizzled out with a puff of smoke.

"What other magic have you for me?" she asked.

"Stop this!" Megan waved her arms in front of Ainsley just as he turned a quill into a dagger and hurled it toward his grandmother. It slid from his grasp before he could halt it and sliced across Megan's left forearm. "Ah!"

"Megan!" Ainsley ran to her, feeling young and stupid, not at all like a powerful sorcerer. "I'm sorry. I'm so sorry. That wasn't meant for you."

"It's okay," said Megan through clenched teeth. She gripped the laceration with her right hand and raised her left arm above her head, blood dribbling through her fingers.

"Here. Use this." Ainsley grabbed an ornamental sash off one of his father's robes and held it out to her.

"Wait, wait," said Lady Maudred, postponing her magical quarrel with her grandson. "You need to put healing salve on it first."

Megan wrinkled her nose. "Ugh. Not that stuff that smells like wet dog."

"I still have some in my other pair of pants!" Ainsley dumped the contents of his travel bag on the bed and unearthed his pair of jeans. Digging in the pocket, he retrieved a half-empty jar of mossfur. He uncapped it and gagged. Even at several feet away, Megan coughed and covered her mouth and nose with the sash.

"Oh, man! I don't know if it's possible, but I think that stuff went rotten."

"It is, and it probably has," said Lady Maudred, dipping a finger into the jar and spreading the contents on Megan's wound. "But, the longer it ferments, the more potent it becomes."

"Thanks," she said as Lady Maudred secured the makeshift bandage around her arm.

"No thank you is necessary," said Lady Maudred. "I shouldn't have let the situation get out of hand. I apologize that you were the innocent victim in a stubborn showdown."

"She's right," said Ainsley. "I just wish there was a way to prevent this from happening again."

"Perhaps there is." Lady Maudred rummaged among her son's cloaks and extracted a pair of steel manacles. "Magic binders."

"Handcuffs? You can't be serious. I'm not Losen." Ainsley looked to Megan for support, but she smiled ruefully and nodded.

"It's probably a good idea. If this is what happens now, imagine what you'll be like when . . . you know."

"But those aren't going to work on me. Magic restrictions don't work on curses."

"No," said Lady Maudred, "magic restrictions don't *reverse* curses. Besides, your magic isn't derived from the curse, so it can be restricted."

"Fine." Ainsley blushed a shade lighter than his eyes and held his hands out to his grandmother. As the locks clicked and his magic drained away, he stumbled forward, holding a hand to his head.

Megan gripped his shoulders to steady him and looked at Lady Maudred. "Why didn't you guys use these on people that had the Illness in the past? Things might not have turned out so badly then."

"When Ainsley's condition reaches a certain point, his magic will be more powerful than a pair of binders," said Lady Maudred. "That's what happened to the others, and that's why they were locked in the Illness Room."

"Until they became dragons and flew away," Ainsley pointed out. He skulked to the bed and flopped down, chains clanking. "You might as well put me there now and start preparing for the great Ainsley hunt."

"Stop it!" Megan kicked the bottom of his boot. "We'll find a way to cure you, won't we, Lady Maudred? There has to be a way to get the antidote. I mean, you guys figured out a way to cure the first stage of this. It shouldn't be too hard to come up with the second and the third."

Lady Maudred shook her head. "It was luck that we stumbled across *any* sort of relief. Governor Frieden happened to know a woman who specialized in herbal remedies, and she gave it to him. She disappeared before he could get anything further from her, however."

"I'll go ask Frieden where she went and get her to help us." Megan headed for the curtained archway.

"It won't do you any good," said Ainsley with a glum expression. "If the woman is who I think she is . . . she's not really a woman, and she and Frieden aren't on speaking terms anymore."

Megan halted and did her best to not appear disappointed. "Oh, well, then. We'll just find someone else who knows."

Ainsley grunted in exasperation. "Megan, nobody else knows how to cure this. Otherwise, they would have come forward before Bornias's daughter-in-law got affected." He lifted one hand to run his fingers through his hair, but the chain between his cuffs stopped him several inches short. With a sigh, he lifted both hands and repeated his effort. "Going to the bathroom's going to be an adventure. I wonder if Losen wears a pair like these in the prison."

Then, in one of the rare moments that Ainsley and Megan shared, the exact same thought struck them simultaneously. He looked at her, and she grinned back at him.

"How dumb are we?" asked Megan, smacking herself on the forehead. "We've wasted all this time!"

"If we hurry, we could have this whole mess taken care of by tonight!" He grabbed a cloak off the rack and wrapped it around his shoulders, pulling the hood low over his eyes.

Lady Maudred watched their excited movements with a frown. "I seem to be missing some major epiphany."

Megan helped Ainsley drape the excess fabric of the cloak over his hands so they were well hidden. "When we were in the Swamp of Sheiran, Losen told us how his father had died of the Illness while Losen was searching for a cure."

Lady Maudred looked unimpressed. "That's how it usually happens."

"But, after his father died, Losen *found* the cure," said Ainsley with a smug grin. "And he just happens to be sitting in a jail cell downstairs with a lot of time on his hands."

Dungeons and Darkness

Raklund prison seemed to Ainsley and Megan the perfect place for Arylon's filth to be housed. Water leaked from the ceiling and ran down the walls, coating them with a slimy film. Steps cut into the stone spiraled downwards at a steep angle with a slick handrail acting as the only guidance.

"Man, this place is creepy," whispered Megan.

"It's a prison, Megan," said Ainsley, speaking to her over his shoulder. "It's not the Taj Mahal." He turned and almost collided with his grandmother's backside.

A gate with jagged metal bars separated them from the rest of the prison, including a prune-faced man holding a lantern.

"Good evening, Scovy," said Lady Maudred with a curt nod.

The man doffed the scrap of fabric covering his com-bover and bowed at the waist, the light from the lantern splashing on the wall as he shook its flame. "Lady Mau-dred, always a pleasure. What brings you to my part of the kingdom?"

"My grandchildren and I are here to see the prisoner brought in last week, Scovy. He's a friend of the family."

"Excuse me, my lady." Scovy squinted one eye and looked past Lady Maudred. "You all right back there?" He pointed to Megan, who had her hand pressed against her heart.

"Fine. I'm fine." She wrapped her arms about herself and tried to look casual.

Scovy studied her for a moment and turned back to Lady Maudred. "I apologize, my lady." He bowed again. "So, you're here for the jewel thief, Losen?"

"Jewel thief?" Ainsley snorted, and Megan prodded him in the back.

"You don't think he did it either, eh?" Scovy shook his head. "A nice lad like that couldn't be capable of anything worse than killing a fly."

"Listen . . ." Ainsley started forward, forgetting his need to be inconspicuous. Megan, who *hadn't*, grabbed him by the back of the robes and pulled him into the shadows. His hood slipped and he turned to hide his face from Scovy, revealing his angry red eyes to Megan instead. "You almost got me noticed!" he accused in a harsh whisper.

"No, *you* almost got you noticed." She lifted the cowl of his robes back over his head and tugged it down over his eyes a little rougher than necessary. "Keep quiet!"

"Are the two of you done fighting over who gets to go through the gate first?" asked Lady Maudred with a pointed stare.

"Uh, yeah. I'm going first," said Megan, stepping to the front. She waited for him to unlock the gate, but instead he extended a hand through the bars palm up. "Uh," she looked at him, stupefied. "I . . . don't . . . have the key. You do. Or, do you need money?"

"Take his hand so he can pull you through," said Lady Maudred under her breath.

"Oh." Megan blushed. "This is like the entrance into the Hall of Staves, then." She grabbed his hand, which was surprisingly warm considering the cool, damp environment. With a gentle tug, her torso slipped through the steel and through to the other side.

"I don't know if I'd compare this to the Hall of Staves. These aren't the most lavish accommodations, are they?" he said with a grin, reaching back through for Ainsley. "Come on, lad!" He waved his hand at Ainsley who just stared at it, feeling the weight of the manacles on his wrists.

"I . . . don't think I can." He looked up at Lady Maudred, who stared back blankly. "I'm *bound* to get hurt in there." Recognition flashed in Lady Maudred's eyes and she gave a small nod.

"You'll be perfectly safe, I assure you," said Scovy. "This is a no-magic zone, and all the prisoners wear magic binders for added protection."

"Well . . ." Lady Maudred hummed to herself in the background, and Ainsley felt a weight lifted from his wrists, along with the rejuvenation of restored magic. "Okay." He accepted Scovy's hand, and as he passed through the bars, he felt the magic drained from him once more. "Damn."

"Whoops!" Scovy caught him as he stumbled. "You *are* a bit delicate, aren't you? No wonder you're afraid of getting hurt in here."

Ainsley wasn't sure if he wanted to throttle the prune-faced warden or Megan, who was doing her best not to laugh aloud at the thought of "delicate" Ainsley. Lady Maudred joined them a moment later, and the trio followed Scovy down a corridor partitioned off into cells on either side.

At first, Megan averted her eyes and stuck close to her companions, remembering the surly behavior of all the criminals she had seen in the movies. Ainsley, however, stared down the occupants of each cell, and when he couldn't see a particular inmate well enough, he ventured up to the bars and peered inside.

"This is kind of disappointing," he said.

Megan chanced a peek at the inmate in a cell to her right and soon found herself staring openly. The man sat primly on the edge of a blanket-covered bale of hay, holding a mirror in one hand and combing his goatee with the other. No scars or tattoos marred his bare arms, which stuck out from beneath powder blue robes, and his hands appeared to have all their fingers. When he saw Megan, watching him, he looked up and waved his comb.

"I have to agree with Ainsley," said Megan, returning the greeting. "These don't exactly look like hardened criminals." She pointed to the man in the cell to her left who cradled a ball of yarn in his lap while his knitting needles clicked a woven pattern into shape.

"Well, they're not your standard street thugs," agreed Scovy, "but *these* men commit crimes that involve magical prowess, something far more deadly than any dagger-wielding highway robber."

"What'd *he* do?" Megan gestured to the inmate who had returned to his grooming.

"Sir Durnstock? He's close to the gates, which means he's one of our lesser offenders. Let me think." Scovy scratched his head and stared up at the ceiling. "Ah, yes." He snapped his fingers. "He cursed a minor and refuses to reverse it."

"The little bastard deserved it!" Sir Durnstock waved his comb at Scovy. "I would have done the same thing even if the penalty had been a *year* in this cesspool."

Scovy rolled his eyes. "You're being released next month, you martyr. Keep complaining if you want to make it two."

Sir Durnstock retracted his comb and shifted on his hay bed so that his back was to the cell bars. Mirror held aloft, he began plucking his eyebrows, muttering obscenities about Scovy's mother under his breath.

"So, uh, where's Losen?" asked Megan, doing her best to tune out Sir Durnstock's expletives. "Jewel theft isn't that big an offense, is it?"

Scovy gestured for them to follow. "You know, I didn't think so either, but Governor Frieden insisted that he be housed with the permanent offenders."

They traveled the length of several more cells until they reached a solid steel door, which Scovy had to pull them through. "The greater the offender, the stronger the security," he said, gripping Ainsley's hand.

The minute Ainsley reached the other side, he crumbled to the ground. Megan hurriedly helped him to his feet as Scovy reappeared gripping Lady Maudred's fingers in a delicate manner.

"Are we ready to press on?" asked Lady Maudred with a careful eye on Ainsley, whose knees were shaking enough to shift the fabric of his robes.

Ainsley leaned against Megan. "I think so. It's just my ankle acting up again," he lied.

"Let us stick together, then," said Scovy, "and stay out of their reach. These wizards aren't as pleasant as the short-timers."

Lady Maudred fell into stride beside him while Ainsley and Megan took up the rear. It quickly became obvious the precautions Scovy had taken to ensure his charges remained under his control. The corridor expanded before them, keeping the offenders at more than an arm's distance, and snow lights dangled before the entrance of each cell, lighting every crevice of the criminals' homes.

In most cases, however, it wasn't necessary. Half the prisoners were rattling their bars and spitting or cursing at Scovy. The other half were lost in their own ministrations, creating poppets from old doodah bones and scraps or writing on the stone walls with chunks of lighter-colored stone.

"*This* was more what I expected to find in a prison," Megan whispered to Ainsley, wishing she'd had even her shoddy practice sword with her. She pulled at her pocket, and Bit popped her head out, blinking against the brightness of the snow lights. "Be on your guard, okay?"

The narshorn squeaked and crawled up to Megan's shoulder, ears and whiskers twitching.

Ainsley leaned close to Megan to be heard over one prisoner catcalling to Lady Maudred. "No offense, but if we're in real danger, I don't think that little guy is going to do a heck of a lot more than poop on your shoulder."

"This *girl* you mean," said Megan, releasing Ainsley to stumble along on his own, "and she's already come to my rescue once. I know she would again."

Ainsley shrugged but said nothing more. Walking on his own was a daunting enough task that required his full concentration. Just as he considered dropping to the ground and letting Megan drag him the remaining distance, they reached a t-intersection at the end of the hall. One of the corner cells was empty.

The other was occupied by a young sallow-skinned man who lay on his back with his eyes closed, jaw slackened by slumber. Bruises painted the arm draped across his stomach in blues and greens, souvenirs from his confrontation with Ainsley and Megan. His face also showed signs of battle, but it was now fuller, as if he had eaten a few good meals since arriving in Raklund. His dark hair, at one time dingy and long, had been washed and shorn to a stubble. The overall effect revealed the handsome charmer the necromancer could have been.

"Good evening, Losen," said Scovy. "Some friends are here to see you."

Losen stirred and blinked a few times before turning his head toward his visitors. He studied them for a moment before recognition flashed in his eyes. "Well, hello." He sat up, running his hands over his non-existent long hair. "What brings you here?"

Lady Maudred turned to Scovy. "Do you mind terribly if we have a moment alone with Losen?"

"Not at all, my lady. I'll swing back around with his evening meal in just a little bit." He bowed and sauntered down the hall, ducking on occasion to avoid the projectiles aimed at him.

Ainsley, Megan, Lady Maudred, and Losen all watched until he had disappeared through the solid metal door. Then, Losen approached the bars of his cell and glanced from Ainsley to Megan, finally settling his gaze on her.

"You're still alive, I see. I'm happy for you," he said without a hint of glee. "When I thought I'd killed you, the guilt I felt surprised me."

"Guilt isn't a bad thing," said Megan. "It's a sign of humanity."

"Tell that to your people," said Losen, nodding toward Lady Maudred. "They could use a lesson in compassion." He then turned to Ainsley, sizing him up. "You're also still alive, unfortunately. I had hoped you might die of internal bleeding or something even slower and more painful."

"Funny. I had hoped the same of you." Ainsley lifted his head high, and the cowl of his robe promptly fell away, revealing Ainsley's entire face, including his angry red eyes.

"O-ho!" Losen leaned through the bars and grinned. "I see you *are* dying a slow and painful death. Someone on the Other Side must have heard my prayers."

"You jerk!" Megan clenched her first and reeled it back, but Lady Maudred grabbed her arm.

"Violence will only hurt our cause."

"Oh, come now, what's a little violence among friends?" Losen pressed his face through the bars. "Go ahead and hit me if it will help."

Megan crossed her arms over her chest and clenched her jaw. "As tempting as your offer is, Lady Maudred's right."

"Very well, then." Losen retrieved a wooden bucket that smelled of stale urine from the corner of his room. After ensuring it was empty, he flipped it upside down and sat himself upon it. "Why are you here?" he asked.

"Don't play dumb," spat Ainsley. "You see what I look like. Why do you think we're here?"

Lady Maudred shushed him with a nudge. "We're here because we need the cure for the Illness."

Losen crossed his legs at the ankle and leaned back on his bucket so that it creaked in protest. "And what's in it for me?"

"What is your price?" countered Lady Maudred.

"Full amnesty for my mother and myself." His words came quickly, as if he had been considering an exchange for some time. "Plus societal reinstatement."

Lady Maudred shook her head. "I can't give you those things. You know that. As a threat to the magical world, you must remain here. Please suggest a different exchange."

"Hmmm." Losen scratched his chin and leaned forward, propping his head on his fists, as if deep in thought. "Nope. You have nothing else I want. Good day." He straightened and returned the bucket to its corner.

"Please!" Megan shook the cell bars. "We need the cure!"

"What cure?" Losen lay back down on his makeshift bed and closed his eyes. "There is no cure."

But then the images flashed before Megan's eyes, a montage of light and dark, softened and hardened by the emotions Losen had felt in his discovery. Lightning ripped through Megan's chest, an unspeakable torture that she could only explain with a raw, bloody scream. Her hands slipped from the bars and clutched at her heart, then clutched at air as she fell back toward the stone floor, sinking into darkness.

11

What She Saw

"Megan!" Ainsley spun and grabbed hold of the front of her tunic as she fell, the sudden stop making her head bob about like a rag doll's. His grip was weak and he could hear stitches popping on both sides of the garment, but he managed to slow her momentum as she reached the floor.

"It's okay. You're going to be okay," he told her more as a comfort to himself than anything, for Megan's eyes remained closed.

Lady Maudred dropped to her knees beside Megan and attempted to rouse her.

"Is she . . . is she breathing?"

Ainsley looked up to see Losen with his face pressed against the bars. Losen's panicked expression mirrored the one he had worn in the Swamp of Sheiran when he'd almost killed Megan with a ball of fire meant for Ainsley.

And, as before, Ainsley felt an unspeakable rage. He grabbed the collar of Losen's robes, and when Losen tried to back away, Ainsley yanked hard so that the necromancer's face smashed against the bars.

"What the hell did you do to her this time?" Ainsley ignored the blood from Losen's nose that spattered across Ainsley's cheek, and moved his hand around to Losen's neck. "You'd better start talking, or I start squeezing."

Losen's hands scrabbled at Ainsley's, and he backed away, but Ainsley held fast, matching his every backstep so there was never a change in the distance between them.

"I didn't . . ." Losen gurgled and fought for air as Ainsley's grip tightened. "I didn't do anything to her. I swear. I didn't even mean to hurt her the first time."

From behind him, Ainsley could hear Megan groaning and shifting on the floor. He scowled and gave Losen's jugular one last pinch before shoving him down upon the haybale and turning to help Megan.

It was then that he realized he was on the wrong side of the prison bars.

"What the hell?" He shook the iron cage and smashed into it with one shoulder but felt no give.

"Ainsley?" Megan blinked up at him, her last memory of him having been standing beside her. She staggered to her feet and peered through the bars at him. "How did you do that?"

Lady Maudred, who had been crouched beside her, looked up and clapped a hand to her mouth.

Losen laughed, his voice still raspy from having his windpipes squeezed. "You're getting a little too powerful for your own good, aren't you? It won't be too long before the Illness ravages you and takes your soul."

Ainsley whirled to face Losen but felt something catch on the bars behind him. He turned and saw that the back of his robes were sticking out as if he were hiding something beneath them. Lifting the cloth, he gasped, his reaction echoed by Megan and Lady Maudred.

The lumps that had been forming between his shoulder blades had split open, and a pair of leathery black wings now lay folded against his back.

"It's too late now, Dragonboy. Your fate is sealed." Losen pointed at Ainsley and laughed riotously.

"Oh, no, no. Hell, no." Ainsley covered himself back up, as if he might make the wings disappear if he could no longer see them. A sick feeling rose in his stomach and his heart hammered in his ears. He wished he could rip the hideous disfigurements from his body, but he knew the evil wings would grow back. They wanted him to soar above Arylon so he could decimate villages with bursts of flame and devour innocent people whole.

Ainsley's legs wobbled and the room spun before his eyes, accompanied by the sound of Losen's laughter.

"Not . . . too late," he slurred. "I don't want to be . . ." He felt himself slipping into a sea of insanity and grasped the iron bars tighter in hopes he might be able to hold on.

And then, Megan wrapped her hands around his and smiled, looking into his wild eyes.

"I know the cure."

The spinning room lurched to a halt and the pull of dementia relinquished its grip on Ainsley. Megan struggled to catch him through the bars as his tense muscles relaxed.

"You do?" he gazed up at her, wishing they were on the same side so he might hug her until she popped. "How?"

Megan allowed him to slide to the floor and then crouched beside him. "Losen told me."

They both turned their heads to look at the necromancer, who had stopped laughing and now eyed Megan warily. "I didn't tell you anything."

"Yes . . . you did." Megan met his stare. "I could see through your lies. I have a Pearl of Truth, remember?"

"But, that's not possible." Losen shook his head. "This entire area is magic-proofed." As if to test this theory, he spoke an incantation and pointed at Megan. Nothing happened.

"It *is* possible." Lady Maudred spoke from behind Megan, and both teens turned to face the older woman who had also taken to sitting upon the floor. "If the magic is stronger than that which binds it, nothing can contain it. It explains how Ainsley was able to pass through the bars, and it means your lie," she pointed at Losen, "must have been quite strong to invoke the power of the Pearl of Truth."

"No, no, no." Losen shook his head and ran a trembling hand through the stubble on his scalp "You're just trying to trick me into telling you so you don't have to set me free. Well, I won't tell you anything."

"You don't have to," said Megan with a smug smile. "Let me guess . . . the dragon Arastold has the cure, and she's up in the . . . Icyllian Mountains?"

Losen opened his mouth to protest but thought better of it, strolling toward the bars instead. "You may be right," he sneered at Megan, "but you'll never get out of here in time to save your friend." He reached for a rope that dangled from the ceiling and gave it a hard yank.

Seconds later, the sound of a dozen ringing bells rent the air, echoing up and down the corridor and causing the occupants of other cells to go into a frenzy. Ainsley and Megan exchanged a frightened look. From afar, the thunder of feet and the sound of steel blades carried toward Losen's cell.

"Get back on this side. Quick!" Megan grabbed Ainsley's arms and pulled, but he collided solidly with the iron bars, banging his forehead against them.

"I . . . I can't!" He blinked rapidly in an effort to clear the stars from his vision.

"What do you mean?" Megan couldn't keep the anger and panic out of her voice. Shouts issued from either end of the t-intersection as the guards drew closer. "You did it before. Do it again!"

"Help! Help! I'm over here!" Losen yelled and grinned at Ainsley and Megan. "A boy with the Illness is trying to kill me!"

"Shut up!" Ainsley hissed at him. He grabbed Losen by the back of the neck and smacked his forehead against the stone wall. With a moan, Losen crumpled to the ground. Ainsley grabbed the blanket off the haybale and tossed it over him. "Help me with this," he said, struggling to cover himself from head to foot with the robes.

"Was that really necessary?" asked Megan. She and Lady Maudred yanked the cloth over his hands and adjusted the back of his robes. "I mean, he's evil and all, but you might have killed him."

"It was either him or me . . . now be quiet!" Ainsley hurried to the bale of hay and lay facing the wall just as four guards turned the corner.

"What's going on here?" demanded one of them.

"What do you mean?" asked Megan, blinking up at him with wide eyes. "We're just here visiting my brother, Losen."

"Why is he lying over there, then?"

"He's not feeling well, poor thing," said Megan. "That's why he called for you."

"We heard him mention something about the Illness?"

The volley of questions was starting to annoy Megan. "He has food poisoning and is delirious. He'll be fine after he sleeps."

"What's this?" He pointed to Losen's blanket-covered form.

"Just some . . . clothes for him," spoke up Lady Maudred. "Is he not allowed to have them?"

The guard, a stocky, platinum-haired man with flinty eyes, bowed to Lady Maudred, though it was plain he felt it unnecessary. "Of course, my lady, but they should have been cleared through security first."

"I apologize, Captain Kyviel," said Lady Maudred. "We'll know better next time."

Captain Kyviel nodded back and turned to Megan. "Please tell your brother not to pull the alarm unless it's an absolute emergency. Tummy aches don't count." He directed these last disparaging words to Ainsley.

"Yes, sir," said Megan. "Of course."

Captain Kyviel gestured for the other three in his party to follow, and they turned away. Megan breathed a sigh of relief and exchanged a smile with Lady Maudred. Ainsley, too, closed his eyes and relaxed.

But then one of the guards said something to Captain Kyviel that made all four Silvan Sentry turn back around.

Megan swallowed and tried her best to look unconcerned. "Is there something else?"

Captain Kyviel scratched his head. "Well, now that I think about it, the last thing we need is a prison full of sick patients. I should probably look at him and make sure he doesn't need to be quarantined."

Ainsley's eyelids jumped open. He tried to mentally coerce Captain Kyviel away, but it did no good. He heard booted feet clomping toward the iron bars, and every muscle in his body stiffened.

Megan stepped between Captain Kyviel and the cell. "I . . . um . . . you probably shouldn't touch him. He's really contagious right now. He's been, you know . . ." she mimed throwing up. "It's a whole stomach bug thing."

Captain Kyviel's lip curled in disgust, but he nudged Megan aside. "Prisoner!" he called to Ainsley. "Bring your worthless body over here!"

Ainsley lay still and emitted a snore that fooled no one.

"If I have to step inside that cell, you won't like it!" warned Captain Kyviel.

Ainsley took his time as he rolled to his feet, keeping his head bowed, and shuffled toward the bars.

"Let us see what sickness you're spreading in my kingdom," said Captain Kyviel, grabbing the cowl of Ainsley's robe.

"Please," Lady Maudred rested a hand on Captain Kyviel's arm. "His eyes are very sensitive to the light. Perhaps we could forego—"

Captain Kyviel flipped back the hood as if Lady Maudred had said nothing. Megan gasped and covered her face with her hands. When Captain Kyviel cleared his throat, she knew it was all over.

"Hmmm. He doesn't look too bad," said Captain Kyviel. "Maybe a bit tired and sweaty, but stomach troubles do that to the best of us."

"What?" Megan lowered her hands and stared past Captain Kyviel at Ainsley whose face had morphed into a close approximation of Losen's. The scaly black patches had been replaced by sallow skin, and the red eyes were now sullen and dark. He even wore the same bruises and scratches as his archetype. Megan's jaw dropped open so that Lady Maudred had to nudge her to snap it shut.

The only indicator Ainsley gave that anything might be amiss was the sheen of sweat on his forehead. The amount of strength needed to maintain the glamour of normalcy in a no-magic zone left him light-headed. If the Illness hadn't increased his powers, he doubted he could have even created anything at all. He almost cried with relief when Captain Kyviel pulled the hood back over his eyes.

"Go lie down. We'll have a healer bring you medicine."

Ainsley nodded, letting his glamour drop with a cathartic shudder. He was so caught up in the moment, he didn't notice the pale hand reaching for him from the floor of the cell.

Out of the corner of her eye, Megan saw the real Losen stir under the blanket. "Ainsley!" She lunged forward, but it was too late.

Losen yanked on the rear of Ainsley's robes, which slipped down around his shoulders, revealing a shock of blonde hair and eyes like fiery embers. Before Ainsley had time to react, Losen kicked the backs of his knees so that his legs buckled beneath him and sent him sprawling on his rear end.

For a moment, nobody moved. Captain Kyviel stared from Ainsley to Losen while his brain processed what had just occurred. The other guards watched Captain Kyviel, unsure of their next move. Megan backed away from the group, doing her best to remain unseen.

"Oh, my goodness!" exclaimed Lady Maudred, placing a hand to her bosom. "Who was that young man hiding under that blanket, and what has he done to my dear Losen?"

"*I'm* Losen." Losen jabbed his chest. "*He's* just an imposter . . . and he has the Illness!"

"What?" Lady Maudred backed against the wall with a flabbergasted expression. "This isn't possible!"

"*They're* in on it, too!" Losen pointed at Megan and Lady Maudred.

All eyes were now on the two female figures slowly backing toward the exit.

"I'll bet you didn't see that coming," said Megan with a feeble laugh. "Surprise!"

"I don't like surprises," snarled Captain Kyviel. He snapped his fingers at the other guards. "Lock them away with the other degenerates. Treason will not be tolerated in Raklund."

Two of the guards made a grab for Lady Maudred, while the other went for Megan.

"Unhand me!" exclaimed Lady Maudred. "Do you have any idea who I am?"

"Make this easy on yourself, girl," the guard told Megan. "Just face the wall and put your hands behind your back."

Megan stared past the guard at Ainsley who was now being interrogated by the captain. With a sigh, she turned away and stretched her arms behind her. The guard stepped toward her, head lowered, and reached in his cloak for the bindings while Lady Maudred protested in the background.

"Let the girl go! She's an innocent! I'll get you out of this, Megan! Don't worry!"

Megan tilted her head toward the older woman, who was proving a handful for the guards, and mouthed a single word. Lady Maudred continued to struggle but a sparkle now shone in her eyes, and she nodded.

Just as the guard reached for Megan's wrists, she snapped her head back and caught him in the jaw with the top of her skull. The guard screamed in pain and stumbled backwards, dropping the binders on the ground. Megan whirled and reached for the sword at the guard's waist, sliding it from the scabbard and across his stomach in one fluid movement.

It was a surface laceration but enough to make the guard double over and drop to the floor from the combined pain in his jaw and torso. The other two guards looked up in surprise and loosened their grip on Lady Maudred.

With an unladylike roar, Lady Maudred jerked free and snapped one of the snow lights from the ceiling, swinging the globe from its chain like a flail. She charged at one of the guards, beating him several times in succession so that he backed away. The other guard chased after, clenching and unclenching his hand around his sword, uncertain if violence against the wife of the Silvan Council leader would cost him his job.

"What the devil is going on?" Captain Kyviel turned away from Ainsley and gaped at Megan as she clasped the fallen guard's fasteners around his wrists. He pointed at Losen. "You, ring the bell for backup!"

Losen just stared at him blankly. "Do you really want to watch her and the old lady take down more of your men?"

"Damn you!" Captain Kyviel reached through the bars and rang the bell himself. This time, there wasn't a rapid shuffle of footsteps.

"Where's your backup?" asked Ainsley with a smirk.

Captain Kyviel drew his sword and waved it at Ainsley. "I'll deal with you in a minute, Plaguebearer." He advanced on Megan, who was careful to keep her distance. "Put down the weapon, girl. I'm not opposed to hurting the fairer sex, so don't think I won't."

Megan remained stone-faced. "Let my friend and I go. You don't want a fight from us."

"A fight?" Captain Kyviel laughed and walked a circle around Megan. "How cute. A fight . . . from you. Put the sword down."

Megan smiled back. "You'll have to make me."

Captain Kyviel's expression of mirth faded, and he lunged forward, arcing his blade down upon Megan's sword hand. Megan leapt back, her posterior colliding with the bars of a cell behind her. Bit, who Megan had almost forgotten in her pocket, launched herself at Captain Kyviel's face and began beating him with her barbed tail. Her reflexes were far faster than his and she avoided his many slaps and swipes while inflicting damage of her own.

Megan grinned and leaned back to watch the spectacle for a moment. "Go on, Captain! You can—" A pair of bony hands grabbed Megan from behind and held her against the cell bars.

"I've got her, Captain!" cried the prisoner.

Megan wrenched and clawed at his hands, but the prisoner held fast, not seeming to care about the skin Megan scraped away. Bit leapt from Captain Kyviel to the prisoner and started gnawing at his fingers.

"Not so tough now, are we?" sneered Captain Kyviel, wiping at the bloodied puncture wounds on his face.

Megan spat on his shirtfront. "You're pathetic."

Captain Kyviel slapped Megan hard across her cheek so that her entire head turned parallel with the cell wall.

"Hey!" exclaimed Ainsley. "Leave her alone!"

Ignoring him, Captain Kyviel grabbed Megan by the chin and snapped her head forward. "I told you I don't have a problem hurting the fairer sex," he said, his voice menacing but soft. "You would be wise not to meddle with me."

Megan blinked back tears, wishing she could let them fall to cool her throbbing cheek. Her arms still pinned, she drew both legs in and kicked Captain Kyviel in the stomach. He stumbled, wincing, but managed to grab her legs so that she was suspended between the prisoner and himself.

"Release her," he told the prisoner.

Megan's stomach lurched into her throat as gravity claimed her upper body. The back of her head slammed against the cell bars, and she was too dazed to try and cushion her fall with her hands. With a bone-jarring bump, she landed on her right side, her wrist twisted beneath her.

"Megan!" Ainsley gripped the iron bars of his prison, shaking them with his entire body in an effort to find a weak point. "Damn it!" He looked on helplessly as the captain of the Silvan Sentry continued to torment her.

"Oh, dear," said Captain Kyviel, clucking his tongue at Megan in mock sympathy. "It looks like you've had a bit of an accident. Let me help you up." He crouched and grabbed for her sprained wrist. Megan whimpered in pain but didn't make any move to stop him. "Oooh. Does that hurt?"

Ainsley couldn't stand it anymore. He backed against the wall and charged the bars with his shoulder. This time, however, they posed no barrier and he passed straight through, skidding to a halt inches behind Captain Kyviel.

The captain straightened and turned to face Ainsley. "What have we—"

Ainsley drew back his fist and punched Captain Kyviel squarely in the jaw. Before the older man had time to react, Ainsley struck again, this time at his windpipe. Captain Kyviel stumbled forward, gasping for breath.

"I told you to leave her alone," said Ainsley. He scooped Megan up in his arms, ignoring her pummeling fists, which struck at him in confusion. "Gran, come on!" he called.

There was no response.

Ainsley shuffled across the floor with Megan and peered around the corner. Several figures were sprinting toward them, but none were Lady Maudred and all of them carried swords at the ready.

"Shit!" Ainsley readjusted Megan's weight in his arms and ran as best he could toward the solid steel door. "Please work, please work, please work," he chanted to himself, flinching as he reached the door and passed through to the other side with ease.

"Ainsley!" Lady Maudred grabbed him by the shoulders as he came through. "Thank goodness you both made it." She eyed Megan, who had slipped into unconsciousness, with some sorrow. "Pull your hood down and follow me!" Seeing that his arms were full, she did it herself.

"How did you get in here?" he asked with a frown. "How did you get past the guards?"

"I took care of the two who attacked me, and when the others found me, I told them I was escaping from you two. As the wife of the Silvan Council leader, I have a lot of clout, you know."

Ainsley gave her a look. "Thanks, Gran."

Lady Maudred sighed. "Well, I'm sorry, but I couldn't do you much good if I got caught. Now, come with me . . . quickly."

Ainsley jogged behind her until they reached Sir Durnstock's cell. The neatly groomed wizard was busy knitting what looked like a staff case.

"What ho, Lady Maudred?" He spied Megan slung across Ainsley's arms. "What happened to this one?"

Lady Maudred approached the cell bars. "Sir Durnstock, we're in a bit of trouble. If we can free you, will you cast illusions upon us?"

"Gran," interrupted Ainsley, tapping her shoulder. "I can do that . . . or you can."

"I haven't the energy," Lady Maudred shook her head, "and you'll tax yourself enough before we're out. Besides, Sir Durnstock is set to be released in a month's time." She looked back at Sir Durnstock. "Will you help us and keep our silence?"

"They serve me toast with no butter!" said Sir Durnstock. "I'll do anything to escape these crude accommodations." He peered through the bars, glancing up and down the hall. "But how do you propose we escape? I don't see old Scovy."

"We don't need him," said Lady Maudred. She turned to her grandson. "Can you pull him past the bars?"

"I think so." Ainsley lowered Megan to the ground and held his hands out to Sir Durnstock. "Grab hold."

Sir Durnstock complied, and Ainsley furrowed his brow in concentration, trying to summon the emotions he had felt before that allowed his magic to swell beyond the prison's limits. On the floor beside him, Lady Maudred attempted to rouse Megan.

When she at last opened her eyes, she smiled up at Lady Maudred. "I bet you think I'm weak for fainting twice down here."

Lady Maudred helped her to sit up and began feeling Megan's head for bumps. "On the contrary, you're one of the strongest young people I know. I just happen upon you at inopportune times."

Megan winced as Lady Maudred passed over the spot where her head had hit the iron bars. "My wrist hurts, too."

"Healer Sterela can take care of both of these things," Lady Maudred assured her.

"Not if he finds out we're fugitives."

"Healer Sterela won't even know who we are . . . if we can release Sir Durnstock to help us." She looked back at Ainsley who had managed to pull the wizard through with him. "Excellent! Now, we need you to do that one more time so we can be free of this place entirely." She pointed to the main gate at the bottom of the stairs leading to Raklund.

"I think I can manage that. Are you okay to go through?" he asked Megan.

She nodded. "Thanks for the help earlier. It took you long enough."

Ainsley grinned. "Let's go. Everyone hold hands."

Hello, Goodbye

"Are you sure there isn't anything further with which I can assist you?" Sir Durnstock fingered his wand. "I don't feel as if we've made an even exchange."

Ainsley and Megan looked at one another. She was now a tall blonde in a regal gown with sleeves long enough to cover her scratched and bruised arms. Ainsley had refused to remove his robes, knowing there couldn't be too many red-eyed teenagers running about in the kingdom, so Sir Durnstock had settled on shortening his cloak and changing its color.

"If we need anything further from you, we'll let you know," promised Lady Maudred, who had become a svelte redhead. "For now, I suggest you leave the kingdom and stay in hiding for at least a month. You might want to disguise yourself as well."

Sir Durnstock bowed before tapping himself with a wand and turning his hair a shiny flaxen. "There we are."

"That's all you're going to do?" asked Megan. "That's not much of a disguise."

"It's a sin to alter perfection, don't you know," he said with a wink. "Your faces are still the same, so don't let people get too close to you, and your illusions will fade in a day's time, so do what you need, and do it quickly."

With a final bow, he disappeared among the shoppers, who had become a thick lunchtime mass.

Lady Maudred turned to Ainsley. "You know I would rather not do this, but . . ." she held out the magic binders.

"Do you really think those are going to work on me?" asked Ainsley with a raised eyebrow. "After what you just saw in there?"

"Well, I don't know how much good they'll do, but they should curb your inhibitions somewhat."

Ainsley turned so his back faced the hallway. "Fine. Just do it here where nobody can see."

Lady Maudred snapped the binders into place, and Ainsley settled his robes around himself.

"Now, I suggest we make haste to my quarters," said Lady Maudred. "Before the entire kingdom realizes what we're about."

While they walked, Lady Maudred pulled the golden butterfly off of Megan, whispered to it, and sent it fluttering into the air. "King Bornias will meet us upstairs shortly," she explained to Ainsley and Megan who watched the butterfly flit out of sight. Then, she drew forth another goldenwing and sent it airborne toward the infirmary. "That one was for Healer Sterela."

"Do you think it's a good idea for him to see me like this?" asked Ainsley, pointing to his face. "He's going to know what's wrong and then he'll tell everyone."

"Not if I can help it," said Lady Maudred.

"Please, no more magic," said Megan. She winced as they hurried down the hall, the movement jostling her sprained wrist. "Ainsley and Sir Durnstock already lost parts of their souls today. Nobody else needs to."

Lady Maudred stopped Megan at the base of the stairs that led up to the rest of the palace. "What do you mean? Souls are only lost through dark magic, and none among us performed the like." She removed a satin sash from around Megan's waist and tied the ends together, fashioning a makeshift sling.

"Ainsley turned into Losen and Sir Durnstock changed *our* appearances." Megan lowered her head and allowed Lady Maudred to slide the sling around her neck, cradling her arm in the low-hanging loop it formed.

"I didn't turn into Losen," said Ainsley. "Remember what Bornias told us? You can only assume the appearance of someone else if they've offered you a willing handshake

. . . and Losen and I aren't exactly best friends." He took Megan's free arm and helped her up the stairs. "All I could do was what Sir Durnstock did."

"Which isn't a curse or dark magic because it wasn't performed with evil intentions," said Lady Maudred, following behind them. "In fact, we probably did Sir Durnstock a favor in allowing him to help us."

"How's that?" Megan turned around to look at her.

"Are you familiar with the Sunilian Theory? No, no, of course, you're not," she waved away the question at the quizzical looks she received. "The Sunilian Theory is our basic premise of life: Good cannot exist without evil, love cannot exist without hate, and blessings cannot exist without curses."

Ainsley and Megan stopped walking and stared at Lady Maudred blankly. She sighed. "What I'm saying is that just as the universe doles out punishment for the ill use of magic, it also rewards those who use magic for benevolent purposes."

Megan chewed her lip in thought. "So . . . instead of losing part of his soul, Sir Durnstock will . . . gain part of it back?"

"Exactly!" Lady Maudred ushered both teenagers up the stairs. "If he has ever done something to lose it, then yes. If his soul is pure and unaltered, however, he receives a blessing."

"Excuse me?" Ainsley lurched to a halt and was almost trampled by his grandmother. "*I* helped save this country with my magic, and I wound up getting cursed. That theory sucks. I should have a halo and wings by now."

"You have wings," Megan pointed out.

Ainsley gave her a withering look. "Not Satan-spawn wings. *Angel* wings."

Lady Maudred squeezed his shoulder. "You're not being punished because you performed good magic, Ainsley. You're being punished for your obsession with it. There's a difference."

"Funny, *I* don't see it," said Ainsley. Stomping up the stairs, he called over his shoulder, "A good deed should be a good deed."

"Ainsley, wait for us!" called Megan. She turned to Lady Maudred. "What do we do about your guards? Won't they be after us now, too?"

Lady Maudred frowned. "You raise a good point."

She bustled up the stairs with Megan trailing behind, doing her best not to move her arm. When they reached the third floor landing, however, the corridor was empty, and Ainsley was nowhere in sight.

"Uh . . . do your guards take firepot breaks?" asked Megan.

Lady Maudred's brow furrowed. "No, they don't. Stay behind me."

With a low whistle, the front door of Lady Maudred's quarters creaked open, revealing the sitting room and two figures resting on the couch.

"Nervous for a minute, weren't you?" asked Ainsley from where he sat.

Megan and Lady Maudred let out a combined sigh and hurried into the room, Megan closing the door behind them and drawing the latch.

"What have you done with my guards, your Highness?" Lady Maudred glanced around the room. "Should I be looking for any potted plants that weren't here this morning?"

"No, no." Bornias waved his hand and smiled. "I disguised myself as Captain Kyviel and told them to wait for me in the main hall. Needless to say, we don't have a lot of time."

"I should say not," said Lady Maudred. "Especially once the whole Silvan Sentry develops an interest in us."

Bornias leaned back and stroked his beard. "Yes, Ainsley tells me you just came from there with some exciting news . . . and judging from your makeovers, I'd say it must be something big."

Megan grabbed one of Bornias's beefy hands. "We know how to cure the Illness!" she blurted.

"What?" Bornias jerked back his hand as if Megan had just bitten it. "There is no cure."

"Yes, there is." Megan squeezed onto the couch between Ainsley and Bornias. "I got the truth out of Losen using the pearl. Arastold has the cure, and she's been living in the Icyllian Mountains."

"Arastold?" Bornias looked past her to Ainsley. "Is this some kind of joke?"

Ainsley shook his head. "I don't think so."

Bornias hoisted himself off the couch and started pacing the floor. "I suppose you believe this, too." He paused and looked at Lady Maudred.

"I do, your Highness," she said with a curtsy. "I think it seems logical that the cure for the Illness lies with its creator."

"Does it not also seem logical that Losen could be lying to you and sending you off into the frozen wilderness for his own sheer pleasure?"

Lady Maudred's face colored to match her hair. "Your Majesty, if you had seen Megan down in the prison, you would not question this."

"Bornias," Megan tugged at his sleeve. "I promise what I saw was real. It even overpowered the no-magic zone we were in. It *has* to be the truth."

Bornias shook his head. "Nevertheless, I don't think it's wise to go traipsing off without verifying any of this."

"Fine." Megan flopped down on the couch beside Ainsley. "Let's waste precious time that Ainsley doesn't have."

Bornias reached for his beard and gave it a sharp tug. "Megan, we can't—"

The banging of fists on the front door filled the sitting room. "Bornias!" Frieden's muffled voice carried from the other side. "Let me in. Quickly!"

Bornias hurried to the door and unlatched it, almost knocked down by Frieden who slammed it and relocked it. He turned to Bornias with sweat beading on his forehead, hair swinging into his panic-stricken eyes. "Ward the entrance. More are coming."

"How many?" Lady Maudred bustled to Frieden while Bornias waved his staff at the door, turning it into a snarling grimalkin.

Frieden looked at Lady Maudred and only a slight flash of surprise at her appearance registered on his face. "Captain Kyviel and fifteen or so more. Healer Sterela told them you'd be here."

"That snake!" she growled. "When I get finished with him, *he'll* need a healer."

Frieden grabbed her by the shoulders to maintain her focus. "Do you have any way out of here other than the front door?"

Lady Maudred looked taken aback. "Of course not. Nobody would dare attack me in my home."

"Well, there's a first time for everything, Gran." Ainsley got to his feet and listened at the wall where the door had once been. "They're on the steps between the first and second floor and coming fast."

Frieden began issuing orders. "Ainsley, stay on lookout. You've got the best senses of us all. Megan, Lady Maudred, gather supplies. You two and Ainsley need to leave the city. Bornias, you have to port Lady Maudred, Ainsley, and Megan away and get out of this room yourself."

Bornias shook his head. "If we run, we only look guilty."

"If we stay, they'll kill Ainsley." Megan jerked on his arm like a child in a candy store. "Bornias, please let us port to the Icyllian Mountains. It won't hurt for us to at least look for Arastold."

"They've reached the second floor landing," interrupted Ainsley. "And I hear more footsteps joining them."

"Look for Arastold?" repeated Frieden.

"We went to see Losen," explained Megan, "and the Pearl of Truth told me that Arastold has the cure and is living in the Icyllian Mountains."

"They're almost here!" hissed Ainsley.

Bornias ushered everyone into Tib's bedroom and turned the velvet curtains into a door before slamming it and pressing his back to it. "I'm sorry but leaving Raklund isn't an option right now. No offense to you, Cordelia, but Ainsley and Megan need more protection than you alone can offer."

Lady Maudred drew herself to her full height and gazed down at Bornias imperiously. *"That* is a matter of opinion."

Frieden put a calming hand on her shoulder. "Bornias, I can go with them and communicate to you anything that happens."

Bornias glowered at each hopeful face in turn. Through the door came the muffled sound of fists pounding on the wall and the wail of the grimalkin.

"Bornias, please," entreated Megan. "We're out of options."

The grimalkin yowled again, interspersed with the crumbling sound of rock as Lady Maudred's front wall was slowly being reduced to rubble. Bornias glanced over his shoulder and sighed, then pulled the Staff of Lexiam from his robes. "*Krida doshin pres siosfra*," he said.

Ainsley and Megan grinned at one another as light shot from the Staff of Lexiam, forming a circle around Bornias that changed from red to green to blue to purple before returning to red and repeating the sequence.

"Gather your things," said Bornias. "You don't have much time."

Ainsley and Megan snatched up their knapsacks and threw in the few belongings they'd removed since arriving in Raklund.

"I'll get food and water from the kitchen," said Lady Maudred, nudging Bornias aside.

"I'll come with you," said Frieden, but Bornias grabbed his arm.

"Stay. Nobody knows your involvement in this either."

"*I'll* go with her," volunteered Ainsley, following on the heels of his grandmother.

"Frieden, help me find a weapon of some sort," said Megan, using her one good arm to pull open a wardrobe door. "His dad had to have a sword or something."

They rifled through the drawers and bookshelves but found nothing more dangerous than a letter opener.

"Maybe on *top* of the bookshelf, then," said Megan. She grabbed the bench at the foot of the bed and started to slide it across the floor, but the slat of wood that formed the seat lifted away from the base of the bench, swinging on twin hinges. "Look, there's a secret compartment."

Inside, Megan found a book of runes, an ivory bowl and a dagger with the Silverskin insignia on it. "This'll have to do for now," she mumbled, scooping everything into her enchanted knapsack and slinging it over her shoulder.

"We need to leave," Bornias peeked through the crack in the bedroom door. "What is taking Cordelia and Ainsley so long?"

Megan ducked under his arm and looked, too, though she was more concerned about what hunted them. The front wall of Lady Maudred's quarters now had a gaping hole through which Megan could see several people hammering away at the remaining barrier. The grimalkin lay on its side, slain by numerous arrows and sword slashes. "The guards are almost through!"

Just then, grandmother and grandson appeared at the kitchen entrance, carrying bulging bags. Arrows screamed toward them, but Lady Maudred hummed under her breath, and they clattered harmlessly to the ground. Ainsley, who still wore binders on his wrist, ran with the bags hoisted over one shoulder. The front wall collapsed completely, and the thunderous boom startled him. He skidded on one of the fallen arrows and, unable to throw his hands out for balance, fell hard on the floor. Lady Maudred, who hadn't heard him over the explosion, kept running.

The guards were upon Ainsley in an instant, ripping the bags from his grasp and using them and their fists to subdue him.

"This one has the Illness!" one of them exclaimed, to which there was a flurry of responses.

"He'll infect us all, the plaguebearer!"

"He's not fit to remain among society!"

"Kill him!"

"We must kill the other two as well! They could be carriers of the Illness!"

The voices pounded against Ainsley's brain harder than their fists upon his flesh. He hated the Illness and how insecure and angry it made him feel. He hated that he had put his friends' lives in danger and that his own grand-mother had to run for her life because she was associated with him. He hated everything he had become . . . but he loved the thrill of power.

With a cry of anguish, Ainsley willed the power of the Illness to envelop him, absorbing all the horrible emotions he had been forced to feel and turning them into even more power he could hold over his enemies. The binders fell from his wrists with a clank.

"Ainsley, no!" Megan's knapsack slapped against her shoulders as she threw open the door and ran toward him. She dropped to the floor as a screaming guard hurtled through the air toward her and winced when she heard him strike the wall. Straightening, she ran toward Ainsley just as he dispatched the last guard by turning him into a potted plant. Before he could pull down his trousers and water the newly transformed foliage, Megan grabbed his arm with her good one and yanked him off balance. "We have to *go!*"

Ainsley met her eye, and for one brief moment, Megan was terrified that he might not leave, that he would continue to destroy Raklund little by little.

"Please . . . don't make things worse."

Her words stung Ainsley, and had it not been for the fact that Captain Kyviel was in charge, he might have turned himself in to avoid feeling any more guilt. "Okay," he said instead, and ran with her to join Bornias and the others. "Let's go."

"Draw near to me and let your thoughts be of the Pass of Light at the base of the Icyllian Mountains," said Bornias. They gathered close, and the staff's purple glow shone brighter and brighter until a light as golden as the sun replaced it. "Good luck to you all," said Bornias.

Megan gave Ainsley's hand a squeeze, and he could see a bloody smear across her cheek from the graze of an errant arrow, an injury, like her wrist, that was his fault.

I've done enough damage, thought Ainsley. He closed his eyes, and a single tear spilled down his cheek. *I don't want to go to the Pass of Light. I want to protect everyone from me. I want to go where my kind belong.*

The Darkest Part of Night

The scents and sounds of life abandoned Ainsley as he was swept away from Raklund. When his feet pressed against soft ground, he still felt as if he were in a lifeless void. He opened his eyes to a dismal image of carnage.

He was standing alone in a forest that looked as if it had been the victim of a catastrophic blaze. The ground was coated in ash, which no plant life had made any effort to push through. Massive trees loomed around him, each trunk as wide around as a castle turret and tinged a lifeless gray. A few were severed and charred to jagged stumps, and Ainsley had a sick feeling he knew what had caused such damage. The tallest of the nearby trees had suffered more hardships than the rest, its trunk twisted into a giant question mark shape. Its bare-leafed branches resembled skeletal fingers scratching at the early evening sky, across which menacing clouds now rolled.

A frosty wind dodged through the trees, nearly knocking Ainsley to his back. He wrapped his robes tighter around himself and listened against the whisper of the wind. He knew it would be almost impossible for any creature to thrive here without vegetation or drinkable water. He knew, also, that any creature who had inhabited the area would have been chased away long ago by the dragons who had wrought such destruction.

"So, this is hell. I always thought there'd be more people." With a shaky sigh, Ainsley drooped onto a deadened tree stump. He supposed he deserved to be here, where he could inflict no more harm than had already been done. Nobody would have to watch him get sicker and become more horrific in appearance until he was more beast than man. He wouldn't have to endure the whispering and averted gazes of people who feared the Illness, and when self-control finally abandoned him, everyone would be safe from his draconian rage because he would be here alone.

But he wasn't.

Ten yards behind him, Megan rolled onto her back and coughed clouds of dust. Doing her best to whisk the soot from her eyes, she glared at Ainsley's hunched form perched on a tree stump. She hoisted her bag over her shoulder and stood, gathering her skirts in her free hand.

She had every intention to yell at him until she was hoarse, but as she drew nearer, she saw that his head was buried in his hands, and it sounded as if he were weeping.

Megan's jaw trembled and her own eyes misted over. She hadn't seen Ainsley cry since the second grade, and back then she had felt just as terrible as she did now.

She had been thinking of Ainsley's Illness in terms of how it affected her. She was upset with him for not listening to her, she didn't want him to give up and leave her, and now she was angry with him for wanting to be by himself, without her. She hadn't considered how he might be feeling about his own misfortune.

"I'm a terrible friend," she whispered. Tears started trickling down her cheeks and soon she couldn't control them. "Oh, Ainsley, I'm so sorry!" She ran toward him, crying.

Ainsley jerked his head up. A pale, ghostly figure was coming straight toward him, arms outstretched, wailing and calling his name.

"Shit!" He toppled off the stump and stumbled backwards, making a cross before him with his fingers. "Begone, evil spirit!"

Megan screamed and whirled around. "Where?" Feeling her long blonde hair and skirts twirl with her, she looked down and remembered the glamour that had been cast upon her, now coated with gray ash that gave her a zombie-like pallor. She couldn't help but see the ridiculousness of it all, and she started to laugh. Another cloud of dust issued from her, and she let out a hoarse cough, which amused her even more.

Ainsley's eyes narrowed at the familiar guffawing, and he noticed the spirit's arm sling as she was doubled over in hysterics. "Megan?"

Megan gripped his arm. "Oh, Ainsley, I'm so sorry!" she said, fighting to keep a straight face.

"It's not funny," he said with a scowl. "I really thought you were a ghost."

"A ghost who knows your name and came to this empty forest just to haunt you?"

"Shut up," said Ainsley, but he grinned. "What are you doing here?"

"Isn't it obvious? I followed you here!" Megan waved her uninjured arm, and soot filled the air like a flurry of gray snow. She coughed and waved her hand to get rid of the ash cloud but only succeeded in making more. "I knew you wouldn't go along with everyone else." Bit poked her head out of Megan's bodice and let out a dusty sneeze.

"You can't stay here," said Ainsley, shaking his head. "You're not safe with me."

"Yeah, well, you're not safe with yourself," Megan tried to find a clean spot on her sleeve to wipe her face. "Brilliant hideout, by the way. Nobody will *ever* spot your blonde head and bright red eyes in all this gray."

Ainsley held a length of his cape out to her. "I didn't know I was coming *here* exactly. I just asked to go where my kind went."

"Well, let's see if we can find out where this place is." Megan finished wiping her face and slid her knapsack off her shoulders and onto the ground where it sent up another spray of ash. She sat on Ainsley's roosting stump and pulled a roll of parchment from her bag, unfurling it over her knees.

"How do you even know where to start looking?" Ainsley peered over her shoulder while she studied the map.

"Well, I'm just going to take a wild guess and say we're *here*." She jabbed a finger at a spot on the parchment with several vertical hash marks drawn upon it. In the midst of the scratches, a single question mark rose tallest.

"The Folly," Ainsley read aloud. "That's comforting."

Megan smirked. "Good news, though. We're only about 150 miles from the Pass of Light. We can probably reach it in about a week."

"Except that *we're* not going," said Ainsley. "This is where I belong, and this is where I'm staying." He sauntered away, kicking up piles of soot as he walked. "I'm going to see if I can find some firewood."

"Ainsley!" Megan hurriedly rolled the map and shoved it in her bag before chasing after him. "Please don't be like this."

"Like what? Unwilling to rejoin a society that wants to kill me?" Ainsley paused before a slim tree that appeared to have only slight fire damage and shook its trunk. "Man, I wish I had an axe. Maybe I can get some of the branches." He pointed to several halfway up the tree.

"You can't reach an of those. They're thirty feet off the ground." Megan crossed her arms. "Besides, you're changing the topic."

"Am I that transparent?" He slipped off his cloak and grabbed for the lowest branch on the tree that he could reach, drawing himself up.

"Stop!" Megan tugged on his leg but Ainsley jerked free and continued climbing. "Ainsley, why are you giving up? So many people care about you and want you to get better. *I* care about you."

Ainsley flinched but didn't slow his ascent. "I'm not giving up. I'm accepting my destiny."

"Destiny?" Megan raised her hands in exasperation. "There's no such thing as destiny, Ainsley! Things happen because people make them happen. You weren't *destined* to catch the Illness. You abused magic and this was the consequence."

Ainsley clenched his jaw and reached for a thick branch, yanking on it with all his strength until it snapped free. "Heads up!" he called, dropping it to the ground.

Megan scurried out of the way and waited for the dust to settle. "You had better be careful!" she called as

Ainsley finally reached his desired branches. "You might be *destined* to fall!"

Ainsley clutched the trunk with one hand and looked down at Megan. "If you think——"

His fingers slipped and he lost hold of the tree, hurtling backwards toward the ground.

"Ainsley!" Megan screamed, sprinting toward him.

Ainsley concentrated on creating a wind to cushion his fall, and in a matter of seconds, he was floating upright. "Damn, I love magic," he said with an impish grin.

Megan didn't return his smile. "You . . . um . . . might not want to thank magic for that one, Dragonboy." She pointed behind him.

"What do you mean?" Ainsley glanced over his shoulder and startled himself so much that the wings now working to hold him aloft almost stopped beating. "Woah."

Megan circled around him. "How did you do that?"

"I don't know. I don't even know how they're moving right now." Ainsley relaxed his back muscles experimentally, and the wings became motionless. He dropped a few feet and tensed his muscles. The wings began beating at full force, propelling him upwards. "This is awesome!"

He relaxed slightly and hovered in the air near the branches he had wanted. With both hands free, he was able to rip several from the tree in a few minutes' time and toss them to the ground.

Megan dodged each one and seethed while she waited for Ainsley to slowly drift to the ground. "Are you done goofing around?"

"Goofing around?" Ainsley kicked the various branches into a pile. "Both of us are going to benefit from this fire, you know." Bending down, he placed a hand on one of the branches, and it ignited, the flames quickly spreading to the other pieces of wood.

"That's not what I meant, and you know it. Lady Maudred and Frieden are out there someplace risking their necks to help you. Bornias is probably dodging questions left and right back in Raklund, I end up trapped in the middle of nowhere looking like I rolled around on the carpet at a smoker's convention, and the one person who should care most about this, you, is content with losing himself."

Ainsley opened his mouth to retort, but bowed his head and nodded. "I know, okay?" He lowered himself onto the tree stump.

"Then, let's *go*." Megan dropped to the ground before him, placing her hands on his knees. "We can cure this. I know we can."

"Megan," Ainsley smiled softly at her, "what if I don't want to be cured?"

Her hands slid from his lap into her own. "You can't mean that."

He shrugged and worked a hand through his hair. "I love having magic," he said. "I don't want to go back to living without it."

Megan felt her eyes tearing. "So, you'd rather go insane and kill everyone, including the people you love, until you get hunted down and killed yourself?"

Ainsley shook his head. "Of course I don't want that."

"You can't have it both ways, Ainsley."

"Bornias uses magic, and he's fine. My father used magic, and he's fine, too. My grandmother, Kaelin," Ainsley began counting on his fingers.

"You're not any of those people," Megan gripped his kneecaps. "You weren't raised like any of those people. You see magic differently than they do."

"Yeah, they take it for granted, and I see it as a gift."

"No, they respect it, and you take advantage of it," Megan got to her feet, "kind of like you do with everything in your life."

Ainsley glowered at her. "That was cheap, Megan."

Megan raised her eyebrows at him. "Yeah, well, so are you." Snatching her knapsack from the ground, she carried it to the opposite side of the fire and began removing things from it.

"You're not leaving then?" asked Ainsley, opening his own knapsack without looking at her.

"In the morning." She unrolled her blanket and spread it on the ground. "Don't worry. I'll be gone before you wake up. Ouch!" Megan cradled her wrist and blushed before walking around to Ainsley's side of the fire. "Under normal circumstances I wouldn't ask, but can you please use magic to heal this?"

"Those bones will age quicker than the others," said Ainsley. "Are you sure you want to do that?"

"Well, I won't be able to protect myself as well unless I do." She slid her arm from the sling and held it out to him.

Ainsley gingerly held her wrist between his fingertips. "You shouldn't travel alone, you know."

"If I don't find Lady Maudred and Frieden," said Megan, wincing, "we'll never be able to get the cure back to you."

"You're still going after the cure?" Ainsley jerked her arm in surprise, and Megan yelped. "Sorry, sorry."

"Of course, I am. Even if you've given up on yourself, I haven't. I can track down the cure and bring it back to you. Who knows? Maybe Frieden and Lady Maudred have already found it."

"I seriously doubt that." Using magic to find its source, he concentrated on the injury to distract himself from the guilt Megan's charity made him feel. "The damage isn't too bad," he said, kneading Megan's wrist so hard she had to blink back tears. "I can only feel a small crack in one of the bones."

"Quit squeezing and just mend it," said Megan with a wince.

"Okay, okay." Closing his eyes, Ainsley channeled magic through his fingertips and into Megan's fractured wrist. The magic acted upon the bone like water across dried mud, settling into the damaged area and melding the crack together.

Megan smiled as the pain diminished and the strength returned to her wrist. "Thanks," she said, flexing it experimentally. "I'll be a fair opponent now."

"I don't think you should go out there by yourself," said Ainsley. "You don't know what sort of dangers lay between you and the Pass of Light."

"Well, I'm going," said Megan. "I can take on anything I come across. I've taken pretty good care of myself up until now."

Megan hoped Ainsley wouldn't call her bluff. Granted, she had survived grimalkins, a necromancer, an evil cat-woman and a slew of Silvan Sentry, but she hadn't done any of it alone. Ainsley had always been there. Unfortunately, he was aware of this as well.

"Megan, don't be so stupid. You can't even defend yourself."

"I have this," she produced Tib's dagger from her knapsack, "and the Pearl of Truth."

Ainsley rolled his eyes. "So what, you'll use your pearl to figure out a thief doesn't want to just 'borrow' your money and then slice and dice him with your knife?"

Megan smiled coolly at him. "I'll manage."

"Forget it. I'm going with you to the Pass of Light to make sure you don't get yourself killed. After that, I'll come back here and live out the rest of my days." With that, he fished a piece of fruit from his bag and plopped down on his blanket.

"Fine. I can't stop you, I guess." Megan retreated to her own blanket, reveling in her small victory. Ainsley could use whatever excuse he wanted, she mused, just as long as he came with her. She smiled and gazed at the sky, which had slipped into evening.

White stars blinked against the black of night, and a stiff breeze flickered the campfire flames. The only sound came from Ainsley crushing mouthfuls of fruit between his teeth, and he did this for as long as possible to fill the silence of the dead forest. With his every slobber and smack, Megan winced and waited for it to end.

When Ainsley was finished, he tossed the core aside and rummaged through his bag for another one. The instant he planted his front teeth in its flesh, Megan was upon him.

"Do you not have anything a little quieter that you could possibly eat?" She stormed around the fire, snatched the fruit from him and threw it into the darkness.

"Hey! That was my dinner!" Ainsley got up and scanned the ground.

"Eat some jerky or bread or something soft." Megan lifted his bag and pawed through it. "*Anything* that's less crunchy."

Ainsley, who had stooped to examine an object, gave her a weary look. "We don't have anything else, Megan." He picked up the object, but it crumbled in his hand. "Ugh. Dirt."

Megan paused with a pair of stockings in her hand. "What do you mean? You and Lady Maudred took those two bags of food from her kitchen."

"Correction. We took those two bags of food, and the guards took *my* bag of food from me." Giving up on his search, he walked back to the campfire and snatched his stockings and bag from Megan's hand. "Like I said, *we*," he pointed from Megan to himself, "don't have anything else."

Megan sank onto his blanket. "So we have a week's travel ahead of us and no food?" She clutched at her stomach, which had chosen that moment to begin growling. "How are we going to survive?"

"We'll just have to hunt for it," said Ainsley, sitting beside her. "You have a knife, and I can fly and scan the area for animals."

Megan blinked at him. "So, then we have to chase the animals down and kill them?"

"Well, I don't think they're going to walk into our camp and jump onto the fire, Megan."

Megan got to her feet. "But . . . but I don't even know what creatures live where or what fruits and vegetables are safe to eat." She hurried to her knapsack and dumped its contents onto her blanket. "There has to be something to eat! What about the food we ate at Lady Maudred's? Maybe I tucked some scraps in my bag without thinking about it . . . or maybe I still have food left from when we went to visit Kaelin! Doodah meat should last a while, don't you think? I bet in one of these side pockets . . ."

Ainsley walked away, rubbing his temples. He hummed to himself in an effort to drown out Megan's rambling, but with his heightened sense, he was able to hear her even over his own voice. The situation was exacerbated by the lack of any other sound for miles, and Ainsley felt anger beginning to swell inside him. He silently begged for a herd of scramblers or pack of grimalkins to charge through the camp, for anything to replace Megan's voice.

And then he heard several voices. Some were whispering, others were laughing, a few were even singing. Ainsley spun round, peering through the darkness, but no bodies accompanied the voices.

His heart pounded loudly in his chest, but the voices were louder still. "I'm going insane," he whispered.

Megan popped her head above the campfire, clutching a shirt in one hand. "Who's out there?" she asked.

Ainsley could have kissed her. "You hear them, too?" he asked, his heartbeat slowing to normal.

"Of course, I do. I mean, they're muffled but I can hear them. They're coming from over there, right?" She pointed east of their camp.

Now that his wits were about him, Ainsley, too, realized the voices were isolated to one part of the forest. "You're right." He cupped his hands around his mouth. "Hello? Who's out there?"

He and Megan quieted for a few moments, waiting for some acknowledgement by their visitors, some pause in conversation or break in laughter, but the disembodied voices carried on.

"Okay, that's rude," said Megan. She leaned back, sucking in her breath before bending over and shouting, "Hey! Over here! We're over here!" The only reaction she got, however, was from Ainsley who brought his hands to his ears. "Why are they ignoring us?"

"I don't know. Maybe because you're so loud?"

They both jumped when they heard a child's voice say, "Papa, I don't like it here. When will we be in the elf town?"

"In only a few days, little one," replied a deep voice. The child whimpered, and the man tutted to her. "Now, now. There's nothing in these woods . . . hasn't been for years. You're perfectly safe, and we'll be out by the time the sun is high in the sky tomorrow."

Megan pulled her map from the pile on her blanket and brought it over to Ainsley. They both peered at it by the light of the campfire.

"They're talking about Hylark," she whispered. "But this doesn't make sense." She tapped the map. "Look where the edge of the forest is. There's no way they could make it out by tomorrow morning. It's at least a day and a half from here."

Ainsley grimaced and scratched his head. "Maybe they're not as close to us as we think."

"What do you mean?"

"I think I might have amplified the sound waves so we're able to pick up distant conversation. I wanted some sort of sound to replace your . . . to replace the silence, and this was the result."

"You think we're listening to conversation from miles away?" Megan laughed. "Do you realize how crazy that sounds?"

Ainsley crossed his arms and raised an eyebrow. "I have wings sprouting from my back and just healed your broken wrist in less than a minute. You tell me what sounds crazy."

Megan sat on the blanket. "I guess it's possible."

"How much do you think these critters will fetch in Hylark?" one of the invisible voices asked then. He rattled something and was rewarded with the squawking of several birds. The men began to talk about commerce and poultry and their plans to increase gains for the coming year. While they talked, one of them pulled out a traveler's harp and began plucking the strings.

Megan scooped the contents of her knapsack back into their rightful home and carried the knapsack and her blanket to Ainsley's side of the fire. "Can you tune into someplace more interesting, like Pontsford?"

Ainsley looked at her in disbelief. "I'm not a satellite radio, you know."

"Fine, fine."

The young child must have been just as bored as they, for she demanded that her father tell her a story.

"Of course, Dariel, but after this, it's bedtime." A soothing melody filled the campsite, the dulcet tones of the harp, accompanied by the man's voice that delivered an anecdote about the hylark's origins.

"Much better," said Megan.

Ainsley lay back on his blanket, feeling a bit light-headed from the use of magic. He felt Megan nudge him and opened his eyes to see her peering over his face.

"Want half?" She held up the fruit he'd bitten into earlier, along with a piece of jerky. "I found it in one of my stockings. We'll have a feast."

He looked at her for a moment, and then they both burst into laughter. Their mirth continued long after their paltry meal had been eaten and the raconteur had finished his stories. When the darkest part of night came, they let it claim them, dropping into peaceful slumber.

The Inevitable Return

They woke early the next morning at the insistence of their groaning stomachs and the crowing roosters their invisible friends were transporting. All Megan needed to do was lift her head and give Ainsley a sour look, and their wake-up call was silenced.

"What I wouldn't give to be able to fry up one of those birds," said Megan, shaking out her blanket and rolling it into her knapsack.

"I'll catch something while we walk," said Ainsley, cinching his own pack and holding it out to Megan. "Carry this so I can fly, and watch me so you can see where the path is clearest." He tensed his back muscles and soared aloft, climbing above the gray of the forest and reveling in the return of color as he reached azure sky.

"I'm not a pack mule!" Megan called after him before hoisting his bag onto one shoulder and hers onto the other. She strode north, glancing at the sky occasionally but careful to mind her footsteps through the cushiony ash less she tumble face first. Her stomach protested every few yards, and she started to wonder how the motley hide of her belt might taste.

"Heads up!" Ainsley dove straight toward her and Megan flinched, falling backwards from the weight of the packs. Ainsley caught her with one hand, and thrust a dead bird in her face with the other. "I told you not to worry."

Megan resisted the urge to throw up what little food might be left in her stomach. "*Where* did you get that?" she asked, prodding the fowl with her finger.

"I caught it while I was flying." Ainsley pulled a knife from his backpack and severed the bird's head, letting its blood drain onto the ground. "A whole flock of these suckers was heading south."

Megan turned her back on the nauseating splatter. "I'm not looking at it until it's ready to be cooked."

"Well, you're going to have a hard time plucking it, then."

Megan would have looked back to glare at him if he hadn't been holding a decapitated corpse. "You'd better be joking."

"Luckily for you, I am." Ainsley siphoned magic into his hands, and with the sound of an exploding down pillow, feathers burst off the bird and floated to the ground.

Megan whirled around at the outburst and nodded at the bird, which now resembled something her mother would purchase from the butcher. "Much better. *That* is something I can cook."

"No need." Ainsley wrapped his hands around the body, and smoke curled from beneath his fingers. The tantalizing aroma of roasted fowl made Megan feel lightheaded on such an empty stomach, and she reached for a drumstick.

"Just one more second," said Ainsley, jerking the meal out of reach until the skin had turned crispy. "Okay. Give me something to set this on."

Megan spread one of her shirts on the ground, too hungry to care about diminishing her wardrobe. Ainsley placed the roast bird in the center, and he and Megan tore into it, leaving nothing but the gristliest pieces behind.

"I'm glad you were able to get this so easily," said Megan, licking her fingers, "but I wish you wouldn't use magic to clean and cook it."

"This from the same person who wanted me to tune in Pontsford last night? Trust me. I've already started down a doomed path. At this point, nothing I could do would make it worse."

Megan bit her tongue at the words "doomed path." She was trying her hardest to stay upbeat despite the situation, but Ainsley seemed intent on reminding her of how thin their strand of hope was. Until it actually snapped, however, she was unwilling to give up.

Megan hoisted her pack onto her back and got to her feet. "Still, you don't want to be speeding up the process by drawing on more magic than is absolutely necessary." She reached for Ainsley's pack, but he grabbed it and slid it over his arm.

"Don't worry about me. I'll do what it takes to get you home in one piece." He smiled at her reassuringly, but his wings ached for flight, and it had been all he could do earlier to keep from opening his mouth and scorching the bird with the fiery breath he knew he was now capable of. He couldn't tell Megan that all these little acts of magic he performed were to scratch at a much larger itch. If he didn't satisfy it every so often, he knew it would consume him until he reached a point from which there was no return, which he couldn't allow to happen with Megan in his care.

Instead, he settled for walking beside her and zipping above the treeline every now and again to check their progress.

"We should be out of here by day after tomorrow," he told her around dusk when he had returned from his last survey for the day. "I can see other colors besides gray on the horizon."

"Excellent," said Megan. "Let's make camp in that clearing ahead."

Ainsley disappeared to hunt for the evening's meal after promising not to use magic to clean or cook his prey, and Megan took a turn setting up camp and gathering firewood.

"Ainsley!" She called to the sky when she had finally stacked her collection in a neat pile. "I need a light."

She heard him approaching through the trees and turned away to find a sturdy branch on which to spear his catch for roasting. "It took you long enough. What did you do, go back to Guevan and get a doodah from Parksy's Den or something?"

Ainsley didn't answer her. Megan looked up and saw that he had started the fire but had disappeared from sight again, leaving only a swinging tree branch in his wake.

"If you're going back out for drinks, make mine a cola!" she hollered.

"They're fresh out, I'm afraid," Ainsley spoke from behind her.

Megan yelped and whirled around, swinging her branch at him. Ainsley caught it with one hand, the other carrying a dead rabbit by its ears. "This is the thanks I get?" he asked as Megan sheepishly lowered her makeshift weapon. "I even found us some salad." He pulled a handful of leafy greens from his belt loop.

"Sorry. I didn't think you'd double back so quickly. Where did you get the rabbit and the plants?"

"Double back?" Ainsley stared blankly at her for a moment, then shook his head, deciding the strange comment wasn't worth pursuing. "The forest actually cuts off a lot sooner if you fly west of here, so I found this little guy," he raised the rabbit, "munching on some of these." He raised the handful of vegetation.

"Well, I suppose if they're safe enough for a rabbit to eat . . ." Megan took the plants and reached for a flask of water to clean them.

"Since you did such a good job on that fire, do you want to skin this rabbit, too?" Ainsley asked hopefully.

"Thanks for the credit," Megan smiled as she opened her flask, "but I just put a bunch of sticks in a pile. You were the one that lit them."

Ainsley shook his head, wondering if being away from civilization was beginning to take its toll on Megan. "I just got back when you were talking to yourself about soda. I didn't light the fire."

"You . . . you didn't?" Megan stiffened and turned to look at the branch she had seen swaying earlier. "Someone did."

Ainsley followed her gaze. "Well, they're gone now, and they don't seem to want to do us any harm. Otherwise, they would have acted while you were on your own."

Megan chewed her lip. "I guess you're right." But she still felt at her waist for her dagger, making sure she could pull it free at a moment's notice.

Ainsley yawned. "Do you mind if I lay down for a little bit before starting dinner? All that flying wore me out."

Megan nodded sympathetically. "Don't worry. I'll take care of it."

Ainsley smiled, dropped onto his blanket and closed his eyes. He didn't dare leave them open any longer, afraid Megan might witness the magical madness creeping into them.

He had lied to her. There had been no sudden end to the forest where a plump rabbit just happened to be waiting. He had used magic, forcing the plants to grow from the ashes of the forest floor and drawing the animal into the gray. He knew she would be disappointed in him if she knew the truth, but he also couldn't let her go hungry.

Megan waited until after the sun had set before she decided to prepare the rabbit. In the dark, she mused, the skinning and cleaning wouldn't be as disgusting.

"Okay. I can do this." She held the rabbit at arm's length and turned her head, trying to saw at its neck without looking.

"Need some help?"

Megan screamed and dropped the rabbit. Her grip tightened on the dagger as she spun and jabbed at a shadow behind her.

The figure dodged her strike. "Don't attack, it's me!" said a masculine voice. He stepped into the light of the campfire, and Megan gasped.

She had forgotten just how handsome Garner was.

It had only been a few weeks since their last encounter, but Megan had done her best to force him out of her mind after she'd seen him in Pontsford flirting with a handful of giggly girls. He seemed so different now than when they'd first met in the stables in Raklund, but he was still just as breathtaking.

Ash coated his leather-clad chest, streaking on his muscular arms, which gleamed with sweat. His curly brown hair had been cut since she had last seen him so that his striking green eyes became the focal point of his face.

The scar on his upper lip quivered as he spoke. "Imagine finding a beautiful blossom in such a dead forest."

Ainsley would have gagged at such a line, but Megan started to feel lightheaded, and all she could muster in response was, "Hi." She tried inhaling deeply, but the earthy scent of him filled her nostrils and made her even woozier.

"I wondered what happened to you after you left Pontsford." He glanced around the forest clearing and grinned. "With you being such an adventurer, I should have guessed this was your idea of entertainment."

Megan blushed and slid her dagger back under her belt. "Well, it's not the same as having members of the opposite sex fawn all over you, but—" She pursed her lips the instant the words had left them. She hadn't meant to ever mention that to him.

Garner frowned. "I'm sorry?"

"It's nothing." Megan waved her hand. "There were just all those girls with you in the city and I thought—" She paused, uncertain how to finish that statement. Since Garner had never declared feelings for her, she knew she had no claims over him. "Never mind."

Garner's eyebrows furrowed in concern. "No, you were going to say something." He drew closer until his chest was almost touching Megan's. "What did you think?"

Megan stared at her feet, where her tongue seemed to have fallen. "You . . . well, we . . . I mean . . . I . . . should finish making dinner." She stepped away from him, colliding with a tree. "Stupid thing," she giggled nervously and rubbed the abrasion on her nose. "Who put this here?"

Garner smiled, and Megan felt her legs weaken. Had she not been backed against the tree, she would have surely fallen to the ground. "You seem a little nervous. Is it the forest . . ." he leaned forward conspiratorially, "or is it me?"

"Uh," Megan bit her lip and wished she were biting Garner's. She pinched herself for the thought and swiped the dead rabbit from the ground. "Would you like to stay for dinner?" she asked, using it to shield her face from his.

Garner looked momentarily taken aback, then smiled. "I hope you're planning to clean it and cook it first."

"I'm trying, but I'm not very handy in the wilderness."

"I guessed that when I heard you yelling for help with the fire." Garner took the rabbit from her.

"Were *you* the one who started that? Thanks! I—" Megan narrowed her eyes. "Wait. How long have you been spying on us?"

Garner reached for the dagger at Megan's waist and slid it from her belt. "Long enough to know that Ainsley has the Illness."

The Tagalong

Ainsley awoke at the sound of his name and saw Megan cornered by someone with a knife. Drawing himself into a crouch, he tensed his back and launched himself at the attacker, wings outstretched.

"Stay away from her!"

With a flurry of wings and fists, Ainsley brought the stranger to the ground. His opponent seemed as adept at combat at Ainsley, dodging almost every blow and managing several of his own.

"Ainsley!" Megan yelled. "It's just Garner!"

Ainsley blinked rapidly, the unfamiliar blur of the stranger's face coming into focus. The fact that he hadn't recognized Garner earlier frightened him, but having seen Garner with a knife frightened him more. "He wants to kill us."

Megan yanked on one of Ainsley's wings, but he shook her loose, and she went somersaulting through the ashes.

"Megan!" Garner, blood shining from a gash on his temple and his lip, extracted himself from Ainsley's grasp and ran to where she lay shaking her head.

"Oh, no you don't!" Ainsley tackled him around his midsection and rolled him toward the campfire. He grabbed Garner by the throat and inched him toward the blaze. "I can stand the heat, can you?"

"Please," gurgled Garner, "you don't know what you're doing."

"I'm keeping Megan safe from a knife-wielding psycho," he said, refusing to loosen his grip.

With a grunt, Garner strained his neck and slammed his forehead against Ainsley's. Momentarily dazed, Ainsley felt Garner kick him, and then he was floating above Garner for just a moment before the world around him turned upside down and he found himself crashing into the midst of the campfire. Sparks filled the air, along with several fiery branches, but Ainsley felt nothing but the throbbing jolt to his forehead. Megan screamed and ran toward him, pulling him away from the flames and stamping on his clothes.

Garner, looking unconcerned, knelt beside Ainsley. "I'm not here to hurt either one of you. I borrowed Megan's knife to skin that rabbit you found."

Ainsley turned his head and nodded but continued to lie on his back, embarrassed that he had been bested by a stablehand.

Garner straightened and faced Megan. "Are you okay?"

She reeled back her fist and punched him in the nose, knocking him to the ground beside Ainsley. "What the hell is wrong with you?" She twisted her foot into his chest to pin him down. "You don't toss people into fires! You could have killed him!"

Garner swiveled his head toward Ainsley who shrugged. "I guess you should have been more worried about her kicking your ass than me, huh?"

Garner nudged Megan's foot off his chest. "Well, I'm glad you're so concerned about my well-being." He sat up, pinching his nose and wiping at the blood on his face. "Ainsley's fine, by the way. Those scales he's developed have made him impervious to flame, so there's no way I would have killed him . . . with fire, at least."

"What?" Megan grabbed Ainsley by the scraps of shirt he had left and pulled him to a sitting position.

Now that the pain in his skull was starting to recede, Ainsley realized that Garner was right. He lifted one of his arms, where the sleeve had been burned off, and touched it experimentally. He felt his finger press against the flesh, but no pain accompanied it. "Cool."

"Cool?" Megan shoved him backwards. "Cool? None of this is cool. Between you," she pointed at Garner, "and you," she pointed at Ainsley, "with your constant flip-flop between sanity and insanity, I'm this close to growing hair all over my body and living with the Icyll."

"Well, that's a lovely image," said Ainsley.

"What did I do wrong now?" Garner pulled his hand away from his nose.

"You? You make me feel like . . . like I'm on a roller coaster." Megan stormed off.

Garner leaned over toward Ainsley. "What's a roller coaster?"

Ainsley was thinking of how best to explain when he saw a dead rabbit come hurtling toward him. He caught it, along with the knife aimed for his lap. "Very nice, Megan! You almost cost me future children."

"Good!"

Garner gazed from the rabbit Ainsley was holding to Megan. "Do you want me to stay and—"

"Follow her before she does something stupid." Ainsley waved Garner away. "Just make sure you keep your crotch protected."

He watched Garner dart between the trees and, when he was certain he was alone, willed magic from his hand into the rabbit. Its fur split open near the tail and fell from the body in one neat piece like a peel off a banana. With a satisfied whistle, Ainsley started to gut the rabbit.

"Megan, wait a moment, will you?"

She turned and saw a wingless shadow jogging toward her. "What do you want, Garner?"

He slowed to a walk. "I want to know what I've done to upset you . . . I mean, other than fighting with Ainsley. What is this roller coaster I make you feel like you're on?"

"It's like . . . one of those airpads in Pontsford going up and down really fast."

"Oh. I see." Yet Garner's response was one of confusion, not recognition.

Megan rolled her eyes and felt warmth in her cheeks as if she were leaning into the campfire. "Look. I liked you, but it's clear I wasn't the only one, and it's also clear that you prefer dainty, beautifully made-up women who giggle at everything you do to . . . those like me. But here you are now, acting as if you're interested because there's nobody else around."

Megan didn't have to see Garner's face to know she'd overstepped an invisible line.

"You certainly have the measure of me, don't you? Shallow, shallow, shallow with nothing to lead me through life but a skirt and a pair of breasts." He stepped toward Megan, and a splash of moonlight hit his face, exposing his hurt and anger. "I've already told you they were my boss's daughters, and I would have gotten fired if I hadn't entertained them."

"You 'entertained them' to keep some lowly job working in a barn?" The question escaped before Megan could stop it. She brought her hand to her mouth, hoping to scoop the stinging words back where they belonged.

Garner retreated into the shadows. "Perhaps you should deal with your own petty judgments before condemning someone else."

Megan grabbed for his hand. "Wait, that didn't come out the way I meant it."

Garner shook her loose. "Oh, I think it did." He stormed back to the campfire, and Megan followed.

Ainsley had finished cleaning the rabbit and speared it on a sharp stick, holding it over the fire. "Hey, can someone else take this for awhile?" he asked when he saw Megan and Garner return. "My arm's getting tired."

Neither one spoke. Garner lay on his back on the opposite side of the campfire from Megan, who shot him an exasperated look.

"Okay, then." Ainsley let go of the stick, and it floated in midair.

"Ugh!" Megan stepped forward. "Ainsley, I thought we agreed on this." She grabbed the stick and jerked it from his magical hold. "By the time I bring back the cure, you're going to be too beyond help for it to work."

"I hope you're not talking about curing the Illness," Garner peered around the edge of the campfire. "Because there is no cure."

"Actually," Megan spun the rabbit on its spit, "there is. Arastold knows it. I just have to find her and ask for it."

"What?" Garner sat up. "You can't go looking for Arastold. It's too dangerous." He shook his head at Ainsley. "It's too dangerous," he repeated.

"I know that, but she's dead set on going."

"So, detain her."

"Uh, excuse me." Megan waved her free hand. "I think I should choose how I run my life, and I'm going."

"Then, I'm coming with you," said Garner.

"Not necessary," said Ainsley. "I'll be there."

Garner placed a hand on Ainsley's scaly arm. "I mean no offense, but you are turning into a flesh-eating dragon. Probably not the ideal companion for a young woman."

Ainsley pulled himself out of Garner's grasp. "I would never hurt Megan."

"Not intentionally, no, but as a dragon . . . you'll have no control over your actions. I'm coming with you." He looked at Megan. "At least until I find a dainty woman."

Megan almost dropped the roasting stick into the fire. "That's fine," she said in an even voice. "We would appreciate any assistance you could offer."

Ainsley looked from Garner's clenched jaw to Megan's clenched fist. "I'm missing something, but I don't think I want to know." He sniffed. "That meat's ready, Megan."

She divided the rabbit into equal portions spread onto the outside of her knapsack, along with the washed greens.

"I can probably add something to this." Garner disappeared into the trees and returned with his travel sack.

"Wow," said Ainsley, watching Garner pull out two cloth-wrapped items. "You weren't in these woods by accident, were you? Are you looking for more unicorns to breed with horses?"

Garner shook his head. "I'm not a lowly stablehand anymore."

Megan winced at the verbal jab. "So . . . uh . . . what are you doing out here?"

"The Other Side has chosen me to be a nascifriend, and I have heeded the call. My initiation rite is to restore life to The Folly." He passed out the contents of the cloth: soft cheese and bread.

"Is that possible?" Megan accepted hers without meeting his eye. "I mean, wouldn't someone have already done that if they could?"

"It is a daunting task, to be sure, but I requested a challenge befitting of my people."

"Your people?" Megan couldn't resist looking at him now. When she did, she realized that the swollen lip Ainsley had given him had returned to normal. She studied his mouth for any visible signs of trauma, but nothing save the sole scar on his upper lip remained. "Didn't you have a cut right—" she looked at the side of his head and gasped. "Holy crap." She raised a hand and pointed at him, grinning. "You . . . you're—"

"What?" Garner held his arms out on either side and looked down at his clothes. "What is it?"

"An elf!" Megan burst into laughter.

"*What* are you talking about, Megan?" asked Ainsley, looking around. "There's nobody here but us." Then, he realized her finger wasn't directed behind Garner but at him. "Ohhhh."

When they had last met Garner, he had worn a bandana that had pulled the hair from his eyes and, subsequently, covered his ears. With his locks cut short, the bandana was no longer necessary to restrain them and his pointed ears were now on full display.

"I'll be damned," whispered Ainsley. "You *are* an elf."

"Is that a problem?" Garner squirmed in his seat under Ainsley's fascinated gaze.

"It's kind of cool, actually." Megan crawled up to Garner and bent forward to study his ear, prodding the point. "I've just never known an elf before."

"You know Pocky Nates," corrected Ainsley.

"Well, he's a Ponzipoo, so that's a little different. They're not immortal and they're pranksters. But *you*," Megan grabbed Garner's arm, "you've got all the elven traits. You can heal and you're noble and selfless."

Garner ducked his head and laughed. "I don't know about the last bit, but I can heal."

He touched a fingertip to Megan's nose until golden light shone in her eyes. When he withdrew his hand, she tentatively rubbed her nose where she had scraped it running into the tree.

The abrasion had vanished.

"Thanks. It was starting to sting a little. I guess I'm becoming dainty." She smiled at Garner, and he returned it.

"Well, I usually prefer a heartier girl, but I suppose I could make an exception for you . . . if you don't mind being admired by a skirt-chaser." He bumped her with his shoulder, and Megan couldn't help but giggle. She nudged him back, and he shifted so that she was leaning against him.

"Ugh, come on!" Ainsley stood and carried his dinner to the opposite side of the campfire. "Whatever bizarre flirting you're doing has to stop. I'm trying to eat."

Megan and Garner laughed and returned to their own meals.

"So how did you find us?" Ainsley asked when he was certain the romantic discourse was over. "I mean, it's kind of a big coincidence that we should run into you in the middle of nowhere." He ignored the warning glances, and the rabbit bone, Megan threw at him.

"I sensed a great deal of magical activity from this section of the woods and decided to investigate," said Garner. "I was afraid someone else was trying to influence the forest's growth in a negative way." He frowned. "Strangely enough, I'm not sensing the magic as strongly as I was last night, and I should be since I'm in your midst."

"Last night you say?" asked Megan, giving Ainsley a pointed look.

"Could it have been caused by something like *this*?" Ainsley closed his eyes, and a moment later, the clearing filled with the noise of the invisible travelers.

Garner's eyes widened and he nodded. "A caravan. Incredible."

"We listened last night to keep from going crazy. The father was telling stories," said Megan, listening to the many voices, "but it doesn't sound like he will be tonight."

"But the harp player's going strong," said Ainsley, focusing on the sound.

"That's not a harp," said Garner. "It's a dulcimer."

"Whatever it is, it's good music," said Ainsley, swaying to the melody. "It reminds me of that dance Bornias showed us when we were little, do you remember, Megan?"

Megan nodded. "You kept stepping on my toes."

"Well, I wasn't as graceful at ten as I am now." Ainsley grinned.

"Do you still remember how?" She stood and held a hand out to him.

Ainsley laughed and leaned away. "Forget it. I'm too old for that."

"Actually, The Hylark Blade is a dance for adults," said Garner, grabbing Megan's hand and twirling her to face him.

She curtsied. "Are you my partner, then?"

Garner placed his hands on her waist and stepped forward with his right foot. Megan's hands gripped his shoulders and she stepped backward with her left. His hips swiveled to the right and he stepped to the side, his right foot leading with Megan mirroring the movement. They continued on with Ainsley correcting Megan's missteps from his seat at the campfire.

"Would you like to dance with Garner instead?" she snapped at him.

"The way he's holding you right now? Not on your life." Ainsley leaned back and closed his eyes, listening to the music and imagining himself with a beautiful elf maiden who appreciated a man of magic.

Megan smiled as she watched him drift off to sleep. "I wish he could be so peaceful all the time."

Garner grabbed her arms and wrapped them around his neck so that his face was inches from her own. "*That* is why I admire you."

Megan blushed and leaned her cheek against his chest. "What do you mean?"

"Your compassion for others. It's as if your heart had mixed with gold."

"Well, not gold exactly . . ." Megan smiled, thinking of the Pearl of Truth. "But Ainsley's my best friend, and I promised I would take care of him." She pulled away from Garner with a frown. "I just wish the Illness wasn't so quick to claim him. I know he's putting up a tough front, but I can see its effects. He doesn't smile or joke as much anymore, and he gets angry much quicker than he used to."

She knelt beside Ainsley and tried to smooth down some of his wild hair. "Even though he's with me, I miss him. I miss who he was." She looked up at Garner, her throat constricting. "Does that sound strange?"

"Not at all." Garner grabbed her hand and led her away from Ainsley.

They talked awhile longer before falling sleep, and Ainsley, who had been feigning his own slumber, finally let it claim him, knowing that Megan was safe for another night.

North of Oblivion

For the second morning in a row, the crowing of the roosters woke them. Ainsley put an abrupt stop to the racket while Garner shared more food from his knapsack.

"I don't know how those people can sleep through that," Ainsley growled, refusing the chunk of bread Garner offered him. "There'd be no roosters alive to take to Hylark if I were with them."

"Well, it's not as if the travelers are still sleeping at this hour," said Garner. "Only the ill or elderly remain abed after sunrise."

Ainsley raised his hand. "Uh, I believe I fall into the first category."

"Yes," Garner said with a grin, "but your strength rivals that of any healthy man . . . maybe even two healthy men."

"Easy with the compliments, Garner," said Megan around a mouthful of fruit. "Ainsley's ego's already very inflated. We don't want him floating away."

"Nice." Ainsley made a face at her. "Luckily I've mastered these," he beat his wings rapidly, "so that shouldn't be a problem."

"Are you confident about that?" asked Garner.

"Sure. Why?"

"Because I only have room for one more on my mount, so someone has to walk. If you can fly as well as you intimate, however, we should be able to make excellent time."

"You won't be waiting on me," promised Ainsley.

"You have a mount?" asked Megan. "Is it a zipper by any chance?" She had thoroughly enjoyed her previous ride on the unicorn-horse hybrid that had shot like a rocket across the plains.

"Unfortunately, no. It's a regular horse. I left him close by with the rest of my gear."

"Awww." Megan stood and brushed the crumbs from her lap. "You left the poor thing alone all night? What if something had attacked him?"

"Frankly, I was more worried of him getting attacked if I brought him to your campsite." Garner glanced at Ainsley. "No offense."

Ainsley shrugged. "I'd be offended if it wasn't true, but I can't guarantee I wouldn't have enjoyed a nice horse steak."

"Nasty." Megan wrinkled her nose. "Where is he, Garner? I'll get him while you guys finish."

"Not necessary." Garner brought his fingers to his lips and released an ear-piercing whistle.

Megan raised an eyebrow. "Is he a horse or a dog?"

"Nithan is a highly intelligent animal. Do you remember Sparks, the young zipper I lent you in Pontsford?" Ainsley and Megan nodded. "Nithan is Sparks's father."

A moment later, a handsome, white stallion emerged from the trees and trotted to a stop, his muscular body shivering as Garner patted his neck.

Megan stepped forward and offered Nithan her fruit core. He nosed eagerly at her hand while she stroked his face. "Hello, Nithan. What a beautiful name."

"It means 'strength from within,'" supplied Garner. "He was a premature foal, and my parents didn't think he was going to make it. Look at him now."

As if aware he were the topic of conversation, Nithan tossed his head and butted Garner, almost knocking him down.

Garner laughed. "You're ready to run, aren't you?"

"I can understand that," said Ainsley. He kicked ash onto the campfire and struggled to get his pack over his wings. "I need to get airborne. Are you two ready?"

"Almost." Megan gathered the few items she had used during the night and stuffed them in her knapsack.

"You can probably leave that in your bag," said Garner, gesturing to the knife Megan was sliding under her belt. "You'll be more comfortable and less likely to lose it."

"Actually, I'll feel more comfortable with it out," said Megan. "In case we get attacked."

Garner burst out laughing. "You're quite the jester," he told Megan, grabbing her bag from her and strapping it behind Nithan's saddle. "In case we get attacked."

Megan forced a giggle and slapped Garner on the arm before joining Ainsley. "Was that really funny?" she asked, through her teeth. Ainsley shook his head.

"Are there no dangers between here and the Pass of Light?" he asked Garner.

Garner slid a bit into Nithan's mouth. "Oh, no. I'm sure we'll encounter at least a few bandits along the way and . . . possibly some shirkbeasts." He held a hand out to Megan.

"Then why do you think it's funny that I want to defend myself against them?" she asked. She stepped into the stirrup without help and swung herself onto the squeaky leather of the saddle.

"That knife is an Abbat, used to eradicate spirits, and we won't meet any where we're going." He grabbed the front of the saddle and hoisted himself up behind her without using the stirrups. "No evil ones at least."

"Oh." Megan was distracted, watching the muscles in Garner's upper body flex from his arms to his broad-shouldered back. "How interesting."

"Please," muttered Ainsley as Garner grinned and wrapped his arms around Megan, reaching for the reins.

Although he felt nothing more than a fraternal love for Megan, Ainsley hated to see the horse-loving elf smothering her and pretending to be the ideal guy. The way Garner talked and acted around Megan reminded Ainsley of himself around the opposite sex, and if Garner's motives were the same as Ainsley's, he knew their fight the previous evening wouldn't be the last.

"Ainsley?" Garner nudged Nithan forward. "Are you ready?"

At a leisurely gallop, Nithan covered over ten miles that morning. Ainsley found it easy to match the stallion's speed in the beginning, but the closer it got to noon, he noticed himself lapsing behind Megan and Garner at greater and greater lengths.

At last, Garner reined in Nithan at the remains of a broken camp. Megan slid down first and plucked a feather from between a set of wheel tracks. "This must have been where our invisible visitors stopped two nights ago."

"Too bad they didn't leave any lame birds behind," said Ainsley, clutching his growling stomach. "Looks like we'll have to eat your little mouse friend, Megan."

Bit squeaked from her perch on Megan's shoulder, and Megan cupped a protective hand around her. "Don't you even think about it. If you're so hungry——"

"Shh!" Ainsley and Garner put their fingers to their lips at the same time. Ainsley scanned the woods to their west, and Garner the path they had just taken.

"Megan, take Nithan and start heading north," whispered Garner, unstrapping a bow and quiver of arrows from the side of his saddle.

"What?" she hissed, grabbing Nithan's reins. "What's out there?"

"Highwaymen. I count two," said Garner. He slid the quiver over his shoulder and nocked an arrow without taking his eyes off the trees. "Ainsley?"

Ainsley crouched in a runner's stance as if poised to launch himself into the forest. "I've got three, but they won't be around for long," he said, magic crackling at his fingertips.

"No magic, Ainsley," said Garner. "I can handle them without it."

Ainsley raised his eyebrow and twisted to face Garner. "Well, I could handle *all* of them *with* magic . . . and you wouldn't even have to wrinkle your pretty vest."

Garner scowled. "Some thieves are capable of capturing magic and using it against their attackers. *No magic.*"

"Whatever." Ainsley turned back around.

"We don't have anything they want, anyway, so they'll just leave us alone, right?" Megan slid her dagger out from under her belt.

"Megan," Ainsley spoke through his teeth, "this isn't Robin Hood and his Merry Men. I can smell blood and hatred on these guys."

"You need to leave now, Megan. They're moving closer," said Garner, "and they're forming a circle around us."

Megan pointed Nithan's muzzle north and swatted him on the rear. The horse whinnied and took off at a gallop. Garner glanced back at her and groaned.

"Megan, what—"

"Two each for you guys and one for me, right?" She brandished her dagger before her.

Ainsley rolled his eyes, not even needing to turn around to know what she intended to fight with. "Megan, bring that here and I'll modify it into a sword."

She took a step toward him, but a calloused and bandaged hand grabbed her by the hair and pulled her against a sharp point that grazed her spine.

"You're a pretty one, aren't you?" A hoarse voice growled in her ear, and the pungent scent of alcohol and sweat assaulted her nostrils.

The remaining four thieves made their appearance, clad in leather rags with their hair tied back in greasy ponytails. Garner released an arrow into the nearest highwayman who staggered into one of his fellows. The other two leapt onto Ainsley with knives flashing. Still in his runner's stance, Ainsley transferred his weight to his arms and kicked up with both legs. He succeeded in knocking one of the thieves away, but the other landed upon him and planted his knife deep in Ainsley's shoulder.

"Ainsley!" Megan flipped the dagger in her hand and jabbed the man holding her in the thigh. He screamed and shoved her away. When he did so, Bit leapt from Megan's shoulder and chomped down on his wrist holding the knife. It dropped from his hand, and when it hit the dirt, Megan scooped it up.

With a banshee's scream, she charged toward the man atop Ainsley with her dagger in one hand and the knife in the other. Beside her, Garner twirled his bow, blocking the knife jabs of the thief he hadn't injured.

Having heard her screams, the thief that had stabbed Ainsley yanked his knife from Ainsley's shoulder and turned to face Megan. He slashed his knife in a diagonal motion toward her neck, but Megan blocked it with her own dagger and thrust her borrowed knife toward his stomach.

The man leapt backward, tripping over Ainsley, who grabbed his ankle and wrenched it sideways. There was a snapping of bone, and the thief hit the ground.

"Look out!" Ainsley kicked Megan's feet out from beneath her just as the thief she had stabbed in the thigh appeared behind her clutching a rusty spike. Megan rolled to her back as the thief descended upon her.

Suddenly, his eyes bulged wide and he dropped to his knees, clutching at his chest. Around his fingers, a circle of blood blossomed and Megan could see a hint of steel arrow poking through his scant leather top. As he dropped to the ground dead, she screamed and leapt out of the way, almost tripping over another thief Garner had taken down with his arrow.

"You . . . you killed four of them." Megan kicked one of the men in the foot to make sure he was truly dead.

"They were going to kill us if we didn't get them first," said Garner without a hint of remorse. He brought his fingers to his lips and whistled for Nithan. "We won't be able to rest here. More will come."

Megan helped Ainsley to his feet, and he winced as she prodded his injured shoulder.

Megan turned to Garner. "Could you—"

"I can do it myself," Ainsley interrupted, bringing his hand to his wound. Warmth flowed into his shoulder, and the pain disappeared. He rotated his shoulder experimentally. "There we go."

"You shouldn't use magic to heal that," said Garner, grabbing hold of Nithan's reins as the horse trotted forward.

Ainsley stared at him. "I wouldn't have needed to heal a wound at *all* if I could have used my magic. But I guess *some* people hate feeling inferior because all they know how to use are sticks and strings."

Garner's cheeks reddened but he calmly stroked Nithan's neck. "You did perfectly fine. I'm sorry if you can't feel like a man without magic."

Ainsley smiled at him, but fire danced in his eyes. "I'm hungry. Anyone in the mood for . . . barbecue?" He stomped the ground with his boot and a ring of fire sprang up around him, Garner, and Nithan. Frightened, the horse whinnied and reared, and Garner fought to control him.

"Ainsley, stop this!" Megan reached toward the flames, but before she could burn herself, Ainsley extinguished them.

"You might want to consider finding a different boyfriend," he told her, glaring at Garner. "This one appears to be missing a set of balls."

Garner reached for Ainsley, but Megan stepped between them. "Enough! If more of those highwaymen are coming, then it would probably be a good idea if we weren't here to greet them." She swung into the saddle and gestured to Garner. "Come on."

Ainsley and Megan were never so grateful as when they finally broke through the gray of the forest into the colorful palette of the countryside early that evening. They emerged beside the Riorim River, and when Ainsley saw sunlight reflecting off its mirrored surface, he broke into a sharp nosedive and immersed himself in its cool depths like an oversized duck.

"Why didn't you tell us to slow down a little?" asked Megan when Ainsley finally surfaced and crawled out of the water.

"We were making good time." Ainsley folded his wings behind him and lay on his back in the grass. "Don't worry. I'll get used to this. It was just my first time to fly for such a long stretch."

"Are you going to be able to keep going tomorrow morning or will we need to wait a day?"

"I'll jog beside you if I have to, but I think I'll try those first." He pointed to a bush covered with red berries. "Can you get me some, please? I just found a comfortable position with these wings."

"Ugh." Megan plucked enough to fill her palm and passed them to Ainsley who shoved them into his mouth, wincing.

"Man, these are so much worse when you have heightened senses."

Garner led Nithan to drink downstream from them. "Are the two of you hungry? There are plenty of fish in this river."

"I know," said Ainsley. "I felt them nibbling at my wings."

"Is this river even safe for humans?" asked Megan, peering at the silvery shapes darting through the water. "I thought people dumped magic byproducts in here."

"The elves would never." Garner waded into the river with Nithan and splashed water on the stallion's sweaty front quarters. "They respect nature too much to alter its essence."

"In that case . . ." Megan cupped her hands in the water and downed several mouthfuls. "Man, that's good." She waded in until the water was thigh-high, her skin breaking out in goosebumps as her sodden clothes clung to her. "Crap." The fish that had been plentiful moments before had all but disappeared. "I scared them away."

"Stand where you are until they get used to your presence," said Garner, heeding his own advice. "They'll come back."

"I could levitate them onto the shore if you . . ." Ainsley trailed off at a glance from Garner. "Or you could bat them out of the water like bears, I guess."

"Shhh." Feeling something brush against her knee, Megan bent at the waist and waited with her hands under water. Her rear end jutted in the air, making a tempting target, and it was all Ainsley could do to keep from booting it with his foot.

And then suddenly Megan toppled forward with a squeal, falling face-first into the river with a splash that scared the fish into Garner's waiting hands. He deftly snatched one up and tossed it ashore then waded over to Megan and helped her to stand upright.

"Wow," said Ainsley, trying hard to keep a straight face. "You really get into your fishing, don't you?"

"Oh, shut up!" She reached into her pocket and found Bit, soaked and shivering. "Are you okay?" She stroked the narshorn's head and it relaxed. She placed Bit gently on the grass and then whirled on Ainsley, her soggy mop of hair spraying him with water. "You did that on purpose!"

Ainsley couldn't hold back his mirth any longer and burst into laughter. "I . . . I . . . swear," he gasped between giggles, "I didn't . . . oh no!" He doubled over in hysterics, pointing to Megan's head.

One section of Megan's hair had started to jump and twitch as if coming to life. With a scream, she swiped at her head furiously until a minnow freed itself from her curls and plopped back into the water. Ainsley roared with laughter until his eyes watered and he started to cough. To Megan's embarrassment, Garner was stifling a chuckle of his own while he helped her wick away the excess water.

"Ooooh, shut up!" She bent and shook her head to make sure she wasn't harboring any more bait, then flounced off to sit by herself and dry her clothes.

After half an hour had passed, and Megan's temperature had cooled, Garner had a fire crackling and a row of plump pink filets cooking on a forked branch. Ainsley wolfed his and headed back into the water to catch the next day's breakfast. Megan seated herself as close to the flames as she could, and it wasn't until she had downed several bites of the warm, flaky fish that she inched away from the fire.

"Feeling better?" Garner lowered himself beside her, handing her the hardened end of a crusty bread loaf.

She nodded and twisted off a corner that seemed palatable. "I'm sorry you had to see me like that. I'm not normally so dramatic."

Garner's cheek dimpled. "I thought it was rather endearing, actually. Most of the ladies I have known wouldn't have dared to get their feet wet."

Megan pulled a piece of dough from the center of her slice of bread and rolled it between her fingers. "You always speak about all the ladies you know. How well do you know them?"

She didn't have to look at Garner to tell he was blushing, so long was the silence that followed her question.

"Pretty well, then, huh?" she tried to make it a joke but couldn't bring herself to follow it with a laugh. "I'm sorry. That was too personal of a question."

Garner shook his head. "No, it's well timed. I know you still have notions of me being some lust-driven lecher, and I need to dispel them." He brushed crumbs off his lap. "In my lifetime, I have . . . entertained two ladies—"

Megan squished the bread between her hands. "Two, huh?"

Garner held up a finger for silence. "But I have known none."

"Oh!" Megan relaxed her grip, and the dough slowly expanded to its original size. "Well, that's not bad at all!" She groaned inwardly at how cheery she had sounded, but Garner didn't seem to notice.

"Any respectable elf will find his or her soul mate, and they will love only each other. It was that way with my ancestors, and it is that way with me."

"So . . . the girls you entertained . . ." Megan did her best to appear nonchalant.

Garner sighed. "I can't deny that elves have the same urges as man, but with my past relationships . . . we knew they would only go so far before it had to end."

"Mmm . . . great." Megan tossed her meal scraps in the fire, not enjoying the uncomfortable turn the conversation was taking. "So, tell me more about being a nascifriend."

Garner blinked. "Erm . . . sure."

The conversation flowed smoothly between them, but even as Megan responded to his questions about her journeys over the past weeks, she couldn't stop thinking of his words, "it had to end." She knew it was the typical route of many relationships, but the way Garner spoke, it seemed as if the ending was predicted even from the beginning.

"Come now, you can't dodge the question you asked me." Garner prodded her shoulder, and Megan realized she hadn't even heard what he'd asked.

"Sorry. What?"

"How many men . . . or elves . . . or any other race for that matter . . . have you known or entertained?" Garner raised an eyebrow.

"Oh! Um . . ." Megan blushed, "kissed one, and that's it."

"Really?" Garner's voice conveyed the same enthusiastic relief Megan had felt at his answer, and she decided to downplay the situation even more.

"It wasn't even a big deal. It was, like, three years ago, and Ainsley and I—" Megan's eyes grew wide. "Um . . . I mean, the guy and I—"

Garner snorted. "I should have known, the way he acts around you."

Megan crossed her arms. "What do you mean by that?"

"He still cares for you, and he thinks his magic will make you swoon for him."

"Ugh, gross, no, he doesn't!" Megan grabbed Garner's arm as he tried to storm off. "If you would have let me finish," she yanked him down to a sitting position, "you would have heard me say that Ainsley and I felt sick to our stomachs afterwards, and we've pretty much been disgusted by each other since."

Garner opened his mouth to reply, then paused. "Really?"

Megan nodded. "It was like kissing my brother . . . if I had one."

Garner squeezed Megan's hand, and Ainsley chose that moment to toss an armful of wriggling fish in their laps.

"Am I the master, or what?"

"How did you get all these?" Megan jumped up and kicked Ainsley's haul away from the fire.

Ainsley shrugged. "I just waded into the water, and the current moved them straight to me."

Megan narrowed her eyes. "You mean you moved them straight to you with magic! I swear, Ainsley," she said, "if you don't stop it, I will kill you and then stab you with the spirit-banishing knife."

"The Abbat," corrected Garner.

"Whatever. Either way," she shook her finger in his face, "you'll be dead."

"I'm telling you, I didn't do anything." Ainsley crossed his heart. "I mean, I thought about it, but I didn't move a muscle."

Garner studied Ainsley for a moment. "Your powers are advancing more rapidly. If you thought of an action, you probably performed it."

Ainsley and Megan looked at one another.

"What do you mean?" asked Ainsley. "I can just will stuff to happen with my mind now, and I don't have to lift a finger?" He grinned. "Cool."

"Yes, just what you need." Garner poked at the fire with a flaming branch. "Another disturbing power you can use to control the world around you."

Ainsley clenched his jaw, and suddenly, Garner was battling to keep the flaming branch from poking at him.

"Ainsley, knock it off!" Megan grabbed the stick and hurled it at the fire.

"Sorry, sorry!" said Ainsley, but he cackled and rubbed his hands together, his red eyes glowing bright as hot coals. "Oh, man, this is gonna be fun."

Megan exchanged a nervous glance with Garner. "Are we . . . losing you here, Ainsley?"

Garner leaned toward Megan. "I told you. He thinks magic is the answer to everything."

Ainsley jerked his head toward Garner, anger sparking in his eyes. "It can certainly answer the question of how to kill annoying elves." Ainsley gasped and slapped a hand over his mouth while Megan and Garner stared at him. "I'm sorry," he said through his fingers. "I'm sorry. I didn't mean that."

Garner said nothing. Instead, he crawled over to his bag and pulled it into his lap.

"Garner?" Megan reached out a tentative hand. "Are you okay?"

He looked up at Megan and smiled, placing a hand over hers. "This has gone on long enough. Forgive me."

"Forgive you?" Megan squeezed his arm. "Forgive you for what?"

Garner held his free hand in front of her face, palm up, and blew on a soft powder that tickled her nose. The muscles in her hand relaxed their grip on Garner, and she slumped over in his arms. The world around her blurred, and she reached out for Ainsley, whispering, "Help me," before a curtain of darkness fell across her eyes.

Ainsley took a few steps toward her, but his legs crumbled beneath him and he pitched headfirst into the fire where he could see nothing but orange and then nothing but black.

The Living City

"Megan? Wake up now."

Someone nudged her shoulder, and she shifted under cotton-soft blankets. Her eyelids felt as if they were weighed down with bags of sand, and she struggled to lift them. "What . . ."

She brought a hand to her forehead and massaged it, trying to assuage the jackhammer that seemed to be drilling its way through her skull from the inside out. She found herself staring up at a wispy canopy of soft blue gauze. She swiveled her head to the side and saw that Garner had drawn a chair beside the bed where she lay. "What did you do?"

"I did what I had to protect you." Garner placed a hand on her temple where the pain surged the greatest, and it faded at once. "This journey was getting too dangerous for you and Ainsley."

"Ainsley? Where is he?" Megan jerked away from him and sat up, scooting to the furthest corner of the bed. "Where am I?"

Garner settled back in his chair with a hurt look. "You and I are at my relative's home in Hylark, and Ainsley is with our high priestess."

"Priestess?" Megan was starting to become more aware of her surroundings, chief among them that she was draped in nothing but a strategically wrapped length of olive fabric secured with gold cords.

"Where are my clothes?" She wrapped her arms around herself and shot Garner a horrified look. "Did you take them off?" She covered her lower half as much as she could.

"I can hear that our guest is awake." A tinkling of chimes accompanied the voice of a raven-haired woman standing in the archway. Her green eyes matched Garner's in hue, though hers held amusement and were fixed on Megan while Garner's looked glum and held fascination with the floor. She stepped into the room and reached above the entrance to draw down a thick, floor-length curtain that had been wound about a marble hook. "I am relieved to see that you are well, Megan."

"This is my aunt," said Garner, rising so she could take his chair. "She's the one who . . . undressed you, not me."

He blushed for the first time Megan could recall and stood with his hands clasped in front of him.

Garner's aunt took his seat at the side of Megan's bed and beckoned her forward. "I am Tatia of the House of Ph'linx." She pressed the middle finger of her right hand to her forehead, then to her lips, before pressing it in the center of Megan's forehead. "That which is mine is also yours."

Megan stared at her for a moment, then started to lift her own hand while glancing askance at Garner. He shook his head. "Only if she were a guest in your house."

"Given the circumstances under which you arrived, it is the very least I can offer. I can assure you the House of Ph'linx does not condone his actions . . . even if they were performed with the best intentions," she glanced at her nephew, who shifted uncomfortably.

"What actions?" Megan narrowed her eyes. "Garner, *what* did you do?"

"It was nothing really," he said, but he had started to back away. "I just . . . I put you and Ainsley to sleep so I could bring you here with no complications."

"What?" Megan leapt from the bed and advanced upon him. "You . . . you used that poison powder and kidnapped us?"

"Not poison," Garner raised his hands defensively. "I would never poison you."

"Oooh!" Megan's hands reached toward his neck, but she resisted the urge to wring it. "That's not helping!"

Tatia placed a hand on one of Megan's shoulders and motioned with her head toward the curtain. "You are dismissed, Garner."

After giving Megan one last hopeful smile, he left the room.

Megan turned to Tatia. "I need to see Ainsley."

Tatia smiled at her. "You need to eat something. Ainsley can wait."

"I ate earlier when . . ." Megan paused, glancing out the window, which was also draped in the blue gauze, "how long have I been here?"

"Garner arrived with the two of you last night. He thought it best to sneak Ainsley in under cover of darkness until he can be given the priestess' protection."

"This priestess he's with . . . is she going to kill him?" Megan allowed Tatia to lead her by the elbow to a wooden table that held a porcelain bowl and pitcher.

"Ainsley has sanctuary in the Temple of Embrace," Tatia emptied the pitcher of cold water into the bowl. "No harm will befall him."

Megan dipped her hands into the water and splashed it on her cheeks. She considered using it on her upper body but realized that she didn't feel the familiar stickiness of travel and perspiration. "Have I been bathed?"

"By my daughter, not my nephew," said Tatia in an amused voice, handing Megan a towel. "Would you like a meal with my family now?"

"I don't want to be around Garner," she said, dabbing at her face. "When will Ainsley and I be allowed to leave?"

Tatia spread her arms. "Whenever you wish. You were brought here without your consent, and you have harmed none. We have no right, legally or ethically, to hold you."

"Then I'll take something with me to eat now and go meet Ainsley."

Tatia nodded and held the curtain back for Megan. "All your clothes have been washed, and your pet has been fed and tended to."

"Bit!" Megan patted the folds of her dress, expecting to hear a muffled squeak. "Where is she?"

"The last time I saw the narshorn, she was burrowing into your travel bag, which awaits you at the front door."

Megan looked Tatia in the eye. "You knew I wouldn't stay long, didn't you?"

Tatia smiled. "I wouldn't have." She led Megan down a hallway of white marble walls accented with gold leaf designs stamped onto their polished faces. Sunlight poured through the diamond pane ceiling, reflecting off the golden ink to create even more light.

"Is this real marble?" Megan ran her fingers along the cool surface of one of the walls. "How can the Hylark stand the weight of structures like these?"

"It is a hearty, resilient flower that could endure a city twice this size," said Tatia with pride, "almost self-sustaining."

"What do you do to care for it then?" asked Megan, remembering what Bornias had told her and Ainsley about the hylark's symbiotic relationship with its residents.

"We keep any pests away that wish to nibble its leaves and roots, and our joy and love act as additional nourishment."

The hallway ended in a triangular living room with two other archways disrupting its remaining faces. A door occupied one of the archways, and Megan guessed it opened into the outside world.

Tatia rested a hand on Megan's arm. "Please wait a moment so I can arrange a travel package for you," she said, disappearing through the other open archway.

Megan wandered the room, admiring a mantle that seemed to run the length of the living space and was arranged with covered urns of various sizes and designs. Each seemed to be a tableau, depicting a different significant moment in Sunil's history. One of the most beautiful ones was iridescent with gold etching of a horse and man locked in battle, the man clutching what appeared to be a gold cone in one hand while the other gripped a chain wrapped about the horse's neck.

Glancing guiltily at the open archways, Megan pulled the vase from its shelf and turned it over in her hands.

"Be careful with that," Garner spoke in Megan's ear, startling her.

"Gah!" The urn slipped in her fingers and she hugged it close to her body, catching the lid on her foot. Breathing a sigh of relief, she turned to scowl at Garner. She considered berating him but realized how guilty she must look holding something valuable that belonged to his family.

"Sorry," she said, easing the urn to the floor. "I was just wondering why these were so special." She retrieved the urn's lid and clamped it firmly in place.

"My aunt collects them." Garner picked up the urn and placed it back on the shelf. "They're from different parts of the world at different times in history." He steered Megan toward a rectangular one. "Does this remind you of anyone?" A horrific black dragon crushed several figures underfoot and belched flames on a thatched-roof house.

Megan's face darkened. "Ainsley isn't like that."

Garner crossed his arms and chuckled sympathetically. "Not yet, but he will be soon."

Megan resisted the urge to slap the mirth from his face. "No, he won't. I'm going to get the cure. Arastold—"

Garner threw his arms up in exasperation. "Arastold has been dead for years, Megan, killed by Lodir Novator! There is nothing left for you to do."

"That's not true. I saw her with my own eyes." Megan turned away, her lower lip trembling.

Garner brushed his fingers against Megan's arm, and she stiffened. "Why can't you see me bringing you here as a blessing? You've seen Ainsley. You can't save him."

Clenching her jaw, Megan threw an elbow back into Garner's ribcage. He gasped and backed away.

"Don't ever tell me what I can and can't do," she hissed.

Drawing a deep breath, Garner shook off the pain and pulled himself to his full height. "You can't leave."

"There will be no disrespect of visitors in the House of Ph'linx."

Megan and Garner turned from their quarrel to see Tatia standing by the front door holding a woven bag bulging with foodstuffs. "Megan is free to travel as she pleases. You do not own her, son of Ph'linx."

Spots of pink mottled Garner's perfect complexion. "I care for her."

Tatia walked toward them. "As a nascifriend in training, you must learn when a creature needs your aid and when it doesn't." She grabbed Megan's arm and pulled her away, offering the bag to her. "This should be enough food to last you and Ainsley several days. By then, you'll have reached the Pass of Light."

Megan emptied the bag's contents into her own weightless pack. "I hope my friends are still there." She handed the netting back to Tatia. "You wouldn't happen to have a summoning pool, would you?"

"There is one in the Temple of Embrace." Tatia opened the door for her. "Follow the street to the left. It will end at the outer cloisters of the temple."

Megan nodded. "Thank you for your hospitality." She turned to Garner who had crossed his arms again. "Thank you for your concern."

Though she was angry with him, she had expected Garner to at least be a little sad at her departure. Instead, he nodded curtly but said nothing.

Shaking her head, Megan left the House of Ph'linx. The door clicked shut behind her, and she took a deep breath, inhaling the floral aroma that hung thick in the air. Standing in the center of a two-mile long flower, she would have expected no less. The pollen beneath her feet was a deep cucumber green and cushioned her movements. After one last glance at the closed door behind her, she started down the elf-made avenue.

As she gazed about her, Megan wondered what role the Ph'linxes played in the community, for the few dwellings at the same intersection as the House of Ph'linx shared none of its regality. The walls of the other homes were made of finely polished wood that looked slippery to the touch, and their roofs, while angled, were covered with smooth screens that reminded Megan of aingan.

She turned left as Tatia had instructed and saw the bell tower of the Temple of Embrace off in the distance. She judged, by the structures lining the avenue, that she had entered Hylark's commercial district. Bursts of laughter brought Megan's attention to a store where a gaggle of pointy-eared children had gathered.

From their level of excitement, she assumed it had to be a toy store, but walking past, she noticed nothing but wooden wind chimes dangling from the eaves of the storefront. Curious, she approached just as a slight breeze swept past the building. The wind chimes plunked against one another, and the children became ecstatic. The few adults among them smiled as well.

"Could I interest you in a set of wind chimes for a younger sibling, miss?" asked the craftswoman.

Megan shook her head. "I'm an only child. I'm just surprised how much these children seem to be enjoying them. Where I'm from, wind chimes aren't exactly popular toys."

The craftswoman smiled. "These aren't toys. They allow the young ones to listen to the wind. When they get older, they'll be able to do so without the chimes."

"They can't hear the wind right now?" asked Megan.

The craftswoman smiled again. "There is a difference between hearing and listening. The wind chimes help them understand what the wind tells them, I should say. Those who listen to the wind usually grow up to become nascifriends."

"Ohh." Megan watched the children more closely, and sure enough, they stood in silence, staring at the chimes until the slightest wind rustled them. Then, they clapped and chattered to one another.

Megan turned to the craftswoman. "Can a lot of humans hear . . . I mean, listen to the wind?"

"That one seems to be able to," the craftswoman nodded toward a young girl with violet eyes. She stood apart from the others but remained as transfixed as they.

"Dariel!"

The human girl reluctantly turned away from the chimes and ran toward the man who had called her. He stood in front of a gypsy wagon, raising one of the side panels to act as a roof for his customers. Megan strolled toward the wagon, watching the man wedge pieces of wood into the panel hinges so it would remain propped open. When he saw Megan, he removed a tattered cap and bowed before her.

"My lady, I'm just opening for the day, but if you would like to browse my wares while I set up, I'd be most honored." He indicated two crates on the ground that were filled with a hodgepodge of items, from elegant folded fans to leather riding whips. Despite her desire to reach the temple, Megan couldn't help but sift through the top items in each box.

"Where did you get all these things?" she lifted a necklace of teeth and grimaced.

"Part of the glamour of the gypsy life," chuckled the man. "I travel Sunil buying a little of this and selling a little of that. What is commonplace to someone here is worth good money to someone in a foreign land. Those for instance," he indicated the necklace Megan was preparing to drop back into the crate, "are authentic dragon's teeth. They can help you find treasure."

Megan gave the man a doubtful look. "And how much does something like this cost?"

The man grinned. "How much money do you have? Maybe we can reach an agreement."

Megan was about to tell him she had no money when she remembered the two gold coins Bornias had given her at Kaelin's cottage. She found them easily in her bag and held one out to the man.

He clicked his tongue and shook his head. "That's not enough for the necklace, I'm afraid. But I may have something more in your price range." He dug into the box from which Megan had pulled the necklace and produced a strip of leather with a fang attached.

"It's still a dragon's tooth," he said, "but this one will only find you a dragon, not its treasure, and it doesn't work over long distances."

Megan regarded the bracelet for a moment before handing over her coin and allowing the gypsy to tie the leather about her wrist. She had doubts about its authenticity but it made her feel a bit closer to Ainsley's plight. Thanking the man, she continued toward the temple, feeling slightly guilty about seeing Hylark without Ainsley.

It took quite a bit of self-control to stay on course as she passed a fletcher who was offering free archery lessons and an apothecary selling liquid strength, but when Megan reached a corner bakery just across the street from the temple's outer cloister, she had to pause.

A bumblebee the size of a sheep was darting about the store, wearing a banner over its thorax that declared "A Sweet Contest to Find the Best Honey in Hylark." The patrons inside didn't appear to be concerned about the massive insect or its stinger that could pierce them through and through. They sidestepped it in their shopping, and one woman even reached out to straighten its banner.

"Whoever wins will have an all-expenses paid booth at Carnival," a voice spoke behind Megan.

Megan didn't have to turn to know who it was. "Did you come to whisper discouraging words in my ear, Garner?"

She felt him brush against the back of her tunic, his hands upon her arms, and her heart rate accelerated to match the beating of the giant bumblebee's wings.

"No, I came with an apology," he said, bowing his head so that it rested against hers. "I'm fond of you, Megan, and I acted out of jealousy. I shouldn't have dissuaded you from helping your friend."

Megan leaned against him. "You know that . . . that I like you, too, and Ainsley is nothing more than a friend. What happened—"

"Was in the past, as you said," Garner cut her off. "And if you can forget about mine, I should be able to forget about yours."

Megan smiled and turned, wrapping her arms around Garner's neck. Out of the corner of her eye, she could see the Temple of Embrace. "Can we talk more when I get back?"

She felt Garner's head shift up and down. "I still haven't shown you Carnival."

Megan pulled back, letting her hands travel down his arms until their fingers intertwined. "Wish me luck."

Serenity

The stench of brimstone filled Ainsley's nostrils, and screams of agony cursed his ears. He gasped, his lungs filling with the intense heat of fire, and his eyelids flew open. He was laying on his back between the dragon's legs, looking straight up at its scaly belly.

Turning onto his stomach, he could see Penitent facedown in the rubble several yards away.

But so could the dragon.

"Penitent!" Ainsley called to him, but his companion didn't stir.

Ainsley felt the ground shudder beneath him and watched as the dragon's trunklike legs inched it toward Penitent.

"Leave him alone!" Ainsley leapt to his feet and willed the magic to stir within him. He transformed his hands into lethal blades and punched them upwards, but the dragon's magic had magnified so that its stomach was now swathed in the same sturdy armor as the rest of its body. Ainsley found himself being dragged forward, his hands still buried deep within the dragon's hide.

"What do I do? What do I do?" He withdrew his hands and dropped to his knees. Tensing his back muscles, his wings moved with a hummingbird's speed, hurtling him toward Penitent's unconscious figure. Grabbing Penitent under his arms, Ainsley lifted him up and away just as the dragon lowered its head to enjoy the man morsel. As they always did, the canyon walls stretched before Ainsley, always out of his reach, though this time that fact worked in his favor.

With a roar of outrage, the dragon charged after Ainsley on foot, its thunderous footfalls rattling even the air through which Ainsley flew.

"Come on, wings, don't fail me now!" Ainsley began to sweat, uncertain of how much longer he could bear his weight and that of another.

With its massive stride, the dragon was quickly closing the gap, and Ainsley's arms were beginning to weary of carrying Penitent. Crying out in pain and fear, Ainsley shot straight upwards, hoping to find a roosting spot beyond the dragon's reach. In his hands, he felt Penitent stir.

"Ainsley?" Penitent looked up at him with fear-filled eyes. "I'm slipping."

"Hang on!" Ainsley's hands scrabbled with cloth, and then they scrabbled at air as Penitent plunged, flailing, toward the open mouth of the dragon. "Penitent! No!"

Tears spilled down Ainsley's cheeks and he sobbed until his breathing was reduced to hiccups. Eyes clamped shut, he prayed for solace, for an end to his personal hell.

And it came.

A gentle hand clutched Ainsley by the shoulders, shaking away the darkness. "Wake up, now! Wake up!" Softness enveloped him, the sweet perfume of wildflower and honey replaced the brimstone, and the air he breathed became cool and crisp.

He drew open his eyes and gazed upon the kindest face he had ever seen. A woman, no older than his mother, smiled down at him from the edge of the pallet where he lay. Soft blonde locks framed her heart-shaped face and flowed into the folds of her gown, a wisp of white material that could have been plucked from a passing cloud. Her eyes were pools of blue in which Ainsley could see not his reflection but unfathomable depth.

"Fear not, innocent. You're safe in the Temple of Embrace."

Ainsley wiped at his eyes, wet with tears carried beyond his nightmarish world. "Where am I?"

The woman offered Ainsley a wet cloth, and he gratefully ran it over his face. "You are in Hylark. I am High Priestess Sciara. Garner, son of Ph'linx, brought you to us."

"That son of a bitch," murmured Ainsley, squeezing the cloth in one hand so that the water dripped down his arm. "What did he do to Megan?"

"He took her to his relative's home for care." Sciara frowned. "Your tone conveys disapproval, which I do not understand. Your friend has done you a kindness."

"Can't you see what's wrong with me?" Ainsley held his arms open wide. "He's no friend. He brought me here to die."

She smiled again and took back the cloth, placing it into a ceramic bowl on a tray before her. "Of course I realize you have the Illness. But you are also cognizant of who you are."

"So?" Ainsley watched her select a stick of incense from several lining the tray and hold it in front of his nose.

"Those with such advanced cases of the Illness are already lost to it. Light this, please."

Ainsley shrugged. "If you want me to get even more sick . . ." He puckered his lips and blew on the textured end until a spark appeared and the incense smoke tickled his nostrils.

Sciara stood over him and traced a circle of smoke around his head. "Using your magic isn't increasing your Illness. Your degradation lies in how you view magic."

Ainsley watched as the ring drifted down about him. "I don't understand what you mean."

"Do you ever take your magic for granted?"

"No . . . I don't . . . maybe." Ainsley tried to think while the heady fragrance of jasmine teased his senses. "I guess sometimes I just expect it to do what I want."

Sciara nodded. "Currently, you take what you can to get what you want, and magic does the same. Your relationship with magic should be one of equality. You should devote yourself to understanding and appreciating its intricacies, and it, in turn, will aid you."

Ainsley sighed and studied his scaly arms. "Well, it's a little too late for that now."

Sciara placed a hand on his head and knelt beside him. "I would not waste my breath with this advice if you were beyond salvation, son of Minks."

Ainsley's head jerked up to meet the high priestess' gaze. "You . . . you know who I am?"

Sciara's eyes crinkled as she smiled. "Your father used to visit us when he was governor of the Protectors. I see him in you."

"Yeah, but he was way better than me." Ainsley pulled his legs to his chest and buried his chin between his knees. "Somehow, I don't think I'll be appointed governor after this."

Sciara laughed, and the innocent delight it held made Ainsley crack a smile. "I expect you may be right about the governorship, but comparing yourself to your father is like comparing the moon and its stars. You are different people, and you have different qualities that make you extraordinary."

Ainsley cleared his throat and tried to look uninterested. "Like what?"

"Your father was devoted to learning as much as he could to better himself, and you seem just as devoted to those you care about." She got to her feet. "Which is why, I assume, you keep staring at the temple doors."

Ainsley smiled apologetically. "I really need to find Megan."

"Leave the Temple of Embrace and join your friend. Your destination is still several days coming." The high priestess extended her hand to Ainsley, but he hesitated in taking it.

"Uh . . . I'm not going to exactly blend in with the crowd," said Ainsley. "Isn't everyone going to panic when they see someone with the Illness?"

She shook her head. "Elves do not fear the Illness. Ours is a symbiotic relationship with magic. It will not turn on us."

"Oh." Ainsley got to his feet and allowed himself to be led toward the main entrance. "What about the humans in the city?"

Sciara pulled him before a window so that Ainsley could see his reflection. "You have been marked with my blessing," she indicated a hazy white outline circling his head like an ill-placed halo, "and none may harm you in the city lest you do harm first."

She nodded to one of the men attending the doors, and he drew the left one wide, its hinges creaking with the effort. Dust motes flitted about in the noonday sunlight that peeked through the widening gap between the doors, and a northern breeze carried the scent of a busy city to Ainsley. He blinked against the brightness and stepped into the daylight splashing across the temple steps. From where he stood, the rest of Hylark spread before him, its ground carpeted in green pollen, a reminder of the colossal flower it was named after and built upon. In the distance, he could see one of the hylark's massive white petals to the east. It rested innocuously upon the grass ready, along with its four counterparts, to fold up at a moment's notice and protect the city within.

"The House of Ph'Linx lies south along the main road, two houses past the bee farm."

Ainsley nodded. "Okay. Um . . . where is your best blacksmith?"

The high priestess looked taken aback. "Shettel is the best, I suppose. His smithy is as close to that petal as you can get." She pointed where Ainsley had been looking earlier. "He needs a great deal of water from the river to cool his metalworks. Do you wish for a weapon?"

"For Megan, not for me. All she has is some soul-killing knife, and I have a feeling she'd probably like something better."

Sciara placed a hand on Ainsley's back and nudged him toward the steps. "Why don't you ask her?"

Ainsley followed Sciara's gaze. Megan waved at him, her face split in two with a massive grin, and broke into a run, her green gown fluttering about her dainty frame. Ainsley glided down the dozen steps to meet her, and Megan knocked all sense of grace out of him, tackling him in a bear hug.

"Are you okay?" they both asked at the same time.

"I'm fine," said Megan, still grinning.

"Me, too." Ainsley held her at arm's length and surveyed her outfit. "What happened to your clothes? Garner didn't . . ." he leaned close, "try anything, did he?"

Megan blushed fiercely. "Of course not. He's a gentleman . . . more or less." She turned to the high priestess and curtsied. "Good afternoon."

"I am High Priestess Sciara." The priestess repeated the welcoming gesture Tatia had done in her home. "I am relieved to see you in a better state."

"I'm relieved to see Ainsley in the *same* state." Megan impulsively reached for Sciara's hand. "Thank you for giving him sanctuary."

She clasped her hand over Megan's. "If I cannot protect the innocent, I am nothing. Is there anything more I can do to assist either of you?"

Ainsley shook his head, but Megan nodded. "Actually, I was hoping we could look into your summoning pool to find some friends of ours."

"Of course." Sciara led them around the side of the building and through an iron gate to what appeared to be a stone well with a shingled roof.

Megan frowned. "Um . . . we don't need water. We—"
She stopped when she realized there was no hoist, no
bucket, and no mouth to the well. Instead, a piece of mirror had been inserted flush with the inner lip of the well
so that its surface was smooth.

"Who are you looking for?" Sciara closed her eyes and
dragged her index finger across the mirror, though it left
no streak or imprint.

"Frieden Tybor and Cordelia Maudred," supplied Ainsley.

After a few whispered words of Elvish, the high
priestess opened her eyes and stepped back from the mirror so Ainsley and Megan could see.

Frieden and Lady Maudred were still together, and
they were standing inside a building made of woven reeds
speaking with a man who seemed to be pushing some
product on them. A green powder coated their shoes and
the hems of their clothing.

"They're in Hylark!" said Megan, yanking on Ainsley's arm.

"At the shop of one of our more persistent knack merchants, from what it appears." Sciara sighed and shook her
head.

"Where is it?" Megan's hand grabbed for Ainsley's.
"Let's go meet them!"

Sciara shook her head. "Your efforts would prove fu-
tile. That merchant is on the opposite side of town. By the
time you reached him, your friends would be gone."

She turned her face skyward, whistling to the bell tower of the temple. A white dove fluttered down onto her shoulder, and she cooed to it. It responded in kind and took to the sky once more, soaring over the tops of the buildings.

Sciara turned to Ainsley and Megan. "She will find your friends and speak to them."

"But Frieden's not a nascifriend anymore," said Ainsley. "He won't know what she's saying."

"He will know she comes from the temple, and that will be enough." She placed a hand on each of their shoulders. "Come fill your stomachs while we await their arrival."

Ainsley ate ravenously, foregoing any manners and diving into the dishes before him with one fist after the other. From what he had tasted, the elven diet consisted mainly of fish, herbed vegetables, and honey bread.

"I should have fed you when you first awoke," said Sciara, watching Ainsley in fascination as she gestured for one of her acolytes to bring more food. "It appears you haven't eaten recently."

"Oh, I've eaten." Food dribbled out of Ainsley's mouth. "I just haven't eaten well." Speaking with Sciara had raised his spirits considerably, giving him new hope and a new appetite. He tapped Megan on the arm, diverting her attention from the windows that overlooked the temple entrance. "Are you gonna eat that roll?"

"Take whatever you want." Megan pushed her plate toward him. "I'm not hungry."

"Your friends are coming," Sciara assured her. "My messenger has already returned."

"I know." Megan smiled at her. "I'll just feel better when I actually see them." She turned back toward the window and jumped to her feet almost instantly. Boots clomping against the stone floor of the temple, she yanked open one of the entrance doors.

Lady Maudred and Frieden blinked in surprise, Frieden still with his hand wrapped about the silk cord to ring the door chimes.

"It took you long enough to find us!" said Megan. She laughed through her tears as she found herself snuggled in Frieden's arms. He squeezed her tight until she wasn't sure if she were making her own tears or being drained of them.

Frieden stepped back and held her at arm's length. "I was so terrified that I had lost you . . . both of you," his voice even deeper than usual.

"Come now, Frieden, do share the girl," said Lady Maudred with a shaky voice, holding out even shakier arms to Megan who willingly stepped into them.

"It's good to see you, too, Lady Maudred," said Megan.

"And you!" Lady Maudred released Megan and bustled toward her grandson who had joined them. "What were you playing at, wandering off into the Folly?"

"I'm half-dragon. What did you expect?" Ainsley swallowed against the lump of emotion that rose in his throat.

Lady Maudred smacked Ainsley on the side of the head, and then pulled him to her. "You little fool! Don't ever do that again." Her voice was muffled both by her tears and the fabric of Ainsley's shirt.

Ainsley felt another, more masculine hand squeeze his shoulder and looked up at Frieden, who winked at him through watery eyes. "It's very good to see you in one piece."

Megan attached herself to the hugging mass, which soon turned into a laughing mass when Lady Maudred exclaimed, "My bosom is too large for me to reach around to all of you!"

The group finally disentangled themselves from one another when the high priestess padded forward, a blissful smile on her face. "So much love have I seen surrounding these two in a single day's span," she indicated Ainsley and Megan, placing a hand on each of their foreheads. "You give me hope in mankind, and you challenge the darkness I have seen of late. I bless you both." A glow emanated from beneath her hands and it swirled around Ainsley and Megan. "In the darkest hour, hope finds a way."

The Pass of Light

"So, you didn't find Arastold?" asked Megan.

She and Ainsley walked behind Frieden and Lady Maudred along a road west of the Temple of Embrace.

"As soon as we realized you two hadn't made it with us, we started devising a way to find you. Our first notion was to come to Hylark." Frieden climbed the steps of a structure named "The Sea-faring Fay" that seemed to be built of bamboo strapped together with marsh grass.

Ainsley placed his hand on one of the walls and pushed with his body weight but felt no give. "These are some strong sticks."

"They should be," said Frieden. "These . . . sticks are the same ones merchants out of the Port of Scribnitch use to build their boats." He held open the door, and it became clear to Ainsley and Megan why the owner had named the building so.

Nautical paraphernalia seemed to have exploded across the entire interior. Canvas sails had been fashioned into curtains for the windows, which were actually portholes. An inverted capstan hung from the ceiling, its arms each holding a snow light so that it acted as a chandelier. Even the railing of a staircase seemed to be a refurbished piece of gunwale.

"Wait here while I gather our things." Frieden indicated a group of barrels that had been cut in half and flipped closed, end up.

"So you've been here for the past week?" Megan asked Lady Maudred. "Did it take you that long to search the city?"

"Well, no," said Lady Maudred. "That took only a few days, and I asked Frieden why we weren't using a summoning pool to find you, too." She leaned closer to Ainsley and Megan even though there was nobody else in the room. "He explained that because you weren't born in this world, we wouldn't be able to track you, so we both started thinking of other people to whom you might have gone."

"Why didn't you just track Bit?" asked Megan.

The narshorn popped her head out of Megan's knapsack at the sound of her name, and Lady Maudred yelped at the surprise visitor.

"Unfortunately," said Lady Maudred, clutching her chest and swallowing, "summoning pools can only track intelligent beings . . . not that your pet isn't intelligent," she amended.

Ainsley frowned. "Well, then, how are we supposed to know exactly where to find Arastold?"

"I've got that taken care of!" With a triumphant smile, Megan jangled her wrist in Ainsley's face, indicating a jagged piece of flint on a leather thong.

"And I thought I was the one going crazy," said Ainsley, examining the object. "What is this?"

"It's a dragon's tooth. I stopped at a peddler's wagon on the way to the temple, and he was selling them."

"You bought something off a peddler's wagon?" asked Lady Maudred at the same time Ainsley asked, "You paid *money* for this?" He raised Megan's arm over her head and waved it back and forth. "I don't see Arastold."

Megan jerked out of his grasp. "That's not how you use it. When you're close to a dragon, the tooth will point in that direction, like a divining rod."

"Ah," said Ainsley, "and it's not pointing to me because . . ."

Megan regarded the bracelet, wondering the same thing. Aloud she said, "Because you're not a full dragon yet. Duh."

Ainsley turned to his grandmother who was shaking her head. "How much money did that peddler take her for?"

"Oh, it's a real dragon's tooth," said Lady Maudred. "I'm just unsettled by how the peddler must have gotten it."

"Everyone ready?" Frieden appeared with a bag slung over each shoulder. "Our Roc will be at the pick up site behind the temple."

"Why are we stopping to pick up a rock?" asked Megan.

"It's picking *us* up, actually." Frieden ushered her out the door. "And it's R-o-c, not r-o-c-k."

From somewhere behind him, Ainsley heard a high-pitched cry, as of a hawk. He turned and looked to the sky. "I'm guessing it's a huge bird of some sort?"

"Very good," said Frieden with a grin. "Has Bornias told you about them before?"

"Just a lucky guess." Ainsley pointed where he was looking, and they all glanced up.

A snowy white bird with the size and wingspan of a dragon soared toward them, making a beeline for the Temple of Embrace. Around its massive neck, it wore a yellow band.

Frieden glanced at a slip of parchment in his hand. "That's our Roc. Let's get moving."

Behind the Temple of Embrace, a wooden platform and tower had been erected. A square basket the size of a car rested on the platform, its handle wrapped in the same yellow fabric as the Roc's collar. A pulley system between the platform and tower indicated how the basket had been hoisted from a multicolored collection on the ground below.

Frieden took the steps up to the basket two at a time. "Everyone inside." He climbed in himself and then helped Lady Maudred up the basket's grooved steps.

Megan followed next, wincing as she kicked a leg over the side of the basket and heard the rip of fabric. Ainsley beat his wings once and was standing in the center of the party.

From within the tower, a man emerged and shouted to the Roc in a foreign tongue. The Roc emitted a piercing shriek in reply and wrapped its talons around the basket's handle, carrying the foursome off the platform and into the afternoon sky.

For the first fifteen minutes or so of flight, they all stood near an edge of the basket, looking at the terrain below them. Then, Frieden yawned, followed by Lady Maudred.

"Tired already?" asked Megan.

"We haven't," Frieden yawned again, "slept well since we've been without the two of you. I suppose it's catching up to us."

"If the three of you don't mind, I'm going to catch a quick nap before we land," said Lady Maudred, slumping in the basket and tucking her pack behind her head.

"That sounds like an excellent idea," said Frieden, sitting down opposite her and pulling the hood of his cloak over his eyes.

Ainsley and Megan watched the adults until they had fallen asleep, as their parents had often watched them, and smiled at one another.

"We haven't had a chance to talk alone in a while," said Megan, joining Ainsley on his side of the basket. "How are you?"

Ainsley frowned. When he and Megan had been at the Sea-faring Fay, he had planned to tell her how good he was feeling, that things were finally starting to seem more hopeful with their party reunited.

But things didn't feel right anymore. In the time that had passed since they'd gotten into the basket, something had changed.

"I don't know." Ainsley shook his head. "I feel strange."

"Well, you have the Illness," said Megan. "Of course you feel strange."

Ainsley didn't answer her. Instead, he turned to the mountains. For a reason he couldn't explain, he seemed drawn to them. The longer he watched, in fact, the more insistent the pull became. It began to overwhelm him, and he found himself fighting to resist the urge to leap from the basket and fly toward it.

He knew what was calling him, and his stomach turned as he realized that Arastold was the only thing he now cared about. He knew what was happening, what had changed, and there was no way to stop it.

"Megan," he whispered, "I'm losing myself."

"What?" With a distracted smile, Megan turned away from a breathtaking aerial view of the hylark, but her happiness faded when she saw Ainsley's horrified expression. "Oh, shit, no. Frieden? Lady Maudred?" she called without taking her eyes off Ainsley. "Something's wrong with Ainsley!"

A single tear fell from Ainsley's eye, and he knew that by the time it reached his chin, it would be meaningless. "It's too late now."

Megan's eyes grew wide. "Frieden, Lady Maudred!" She kicked them both until they stirred. "Help me!" She turned back to Ainsley and placed her hands on either side of his face. She tried to push the emotion from her voice, but instead, it pooled in her eyes. "Don't go, okay?"

Ainsley could see fear and great sorrow on Megan's face, but he felt nothing in return. It was as if an invisible switch controlling his emotions had been flipped off in his brain. He looked to Lady Maudred and Frieden and felt neither animosity nor affection for them. A distant force called to his soul, and he longed to answer it.

"Ainsley?" Megan tightened her grip on his arm. Beside her, Frieden clambered to his feet and grabbed Ainsley by the shoulders.

"Stay with us, Ainsley. You can fight it."

Ainsley knew he could, but he didn't care to be in charge anymore. He wanted someone else to think for him, to control him, and somewhere in the Icyllian Mountains resided that puppet master.

"Goodbye," he said almost casually to the others as he tensed his wings and jetted out of the basket.

"No!" cried Megan. The basket began its descent with Ainsley still soaring high above. "Follow him!" she hollered up at the Roc. She tried to reach up and grab the Roc's claw, but Lady Maudred pulled her to the floor of the basket.

"The Roc only follows its handler's bidding," she said, rummaging through her bag. Her movements were less fluid than usual, almost jerky and aggravated. "You can shout until you expire and it won't make a difference. Here, put this on." She forced a black woven facemask into Megan's hands. "We'll have to follow Ainsley once we get to land."

Megan just stared at the mask for a moment, then to Lady Maudred whose lips were pressed in a thin line.

"How can you be so callous about this?" fumed Megan. "He's your own grandson!"

Megan knew her words were harsh, and for a moment, she was afraid of what the old sorceress might do. Lady Maudred took hold of Megan's hands but did nothing more than look her in the eye.

"I have experienced a great deal of hardship in my life-time: the loss of my husband, the disappearance of my son, along with many other things you couldn't begin to imagine. Each horrific event has made me stronger and taught me what is in my power and what is beyond my control." She squeezed Megan's hands. "But you and Ainsley have taught me to hope, and as long as I have that, I refuse to add this experience to my list of hardships. This is a challenge I can still win."

Lady Maudred said these words with such conviction that Megan's heart leapt, and she threw her arms around the older woman. "I think we can still win, too."

Lady Maudred squeezed Megan and patted her on the back. "Then, let's get ready for some chilly weather."

Megan nodded and slipped the mask over her head. Instead of cutout eyeholes, tinted lenses allowed her sight. "Hey! Why is everything so dark?"

"Your eyes will adjust," promised Lady Maudred. "The snow in the Icyllian Mountains absorbs so much light that you'll go blind if you look at it directly. You should also change into warmer clothes."

Lady Maudred blocked Megan from Frieden's line of sight, though as an extra precaution he kept his back to them, watching Ainsley's flight path. After Megan had changed into her tunic and breeches, she joined him. The Roc's speed was far faster than Ainsley's, and he was becoming a speck behind them.

"What are we going to do about Ainsley?" she asked while Lady Maudred and Frieden donned their masks.

"If my understanding of the Illness is correct," said Frieden, "he's gone to find Arastold. With his mind now fully infected by the Illness, he no longer sees himself as the master of magic but vice versa. Since the curse originated with Arastold, he seeks to do her bidding."

Megan slipped her cloak around her shoulders with a shiver. The temperature had fallen noticeably the farther north they flew, and now that they were almost at the Pass of Light, it was all she could do to not set the basket around her on fire for extra heat.

"Don't we have any warmer clothes in the bags? We'll freeze before we reach Ainsley."

Frieden removed his own cloak and wrapped it about her, rubbing her arms. "Our basket will land at an Icyllian outpost where we can purchase supplies. I wish we could have gotten them in Hylark with the masks, but I didn't want to risk being weighed down."

Megan nodded and curled into a ball on the bottom of the basket to conserve body heat. A moment later, Lady Maudred and Frieden were sitting beside her.

"The Roc will be dropping our basket on the platform any moment now."

"It's going to *drop* us?" Megan tried to remember all the safety tips she had ever heard a flight attendant spout, but none of them seemed applicable to riding in an oversized picnic basket carried by an oversized bird. While she contemplated placing her head between her knees, the basket shook beneath her and then stopped moving altogether. She glanced up to see the Roc circling around with another basket headed back to Hylark.

"Welcome to the Pass of Light," Megan heard someone outside the basket say.

Getting warily to her feet, she found herself staring at a man whose body and face were covered with a sleek coat of white hair. His facial features were human, but the hand he extended to her had a thumb and three fingers arranged symmetrically opposite it, like a bird's claw.

Doing her best not to appear repulsed, Megan smiled and took the proffered hand with its long, spikelike fingernails.

"Ow! Careful now." The hirsute man chuckled as Megan stepped on the platform, and she realized she had trodden on his foot, which was as flat and round as a manhole cover.

"Sorry." She backed away, her boots crunching in the snow that covered the platform, which, from what Megan could see, was isolated amidst mountainous drifts.

"Megan, this is Orex," said Lady Maudred, smoothing her dress after her unceremonious removal from the basket. "Orex, this is Megan, Frieden's niece."

Orex nodded. "So, I'm guessing you found who you were looking for, eh, Frieden?" The Icyll helped him out of the basket.

"One of them, yes," said Frieden. "The young man flew out of the basket and toward the mountains."

Megan had to give credit to Orex for his nonchalant acceptance of this news. "Not to worry. Rocs fly much faster than any other winged creature, and I expect that includes humans."

"But, he'll go blind . . . or freeze to death," said Megan, her own teeth chattering against the cold.

"You have to remember that he's not entirely human any more," said Frieden. "Dragons are cold-blooded creatures, so the temperature won't affect him, and the pigmentation in his eyes will block out any excessive light."

"Oh. G-good t-t-to know," stammered Megan.

Orex gestured her to him. "Come, come. I often forget how cold this weather can be for those wearing naught but skin. We'll get you some warmer gear and send you after your friend."

Orex stepped off the platform into the snow and indicated a hole that had been burrowed in the ground directly beneath the wooden structure. He sat on his rear with his feet dangling inside and, with an enthusiastic cry, pushed off from the ground, disappearing inside the hole. Lady Maudred tucked her skirts around her legs and followed suit, foregoing the gleeful caterwaul.

Megan walked to the rim of the hole and saw that it slanted slightly to form an icy slide ending roughly twenty feet below the surface. She could see Lady Maudred rearranging her skirts but standing fully upright before she disappeared from view.

Megan turned to look at Frieden. "Where does this . . . um . . . go?"

"The Icyll *do* live under the snow," he told her, "but their walls and ceilings are made of solid ice and are very secure. I promise you'll be safe."

Megan swallowed hard and sat on the edge of the tunnel but couldn't bring herself to push off.

Frieden stooped beside her. "If you stay out here, you'll freeze to death, and this is the only way we can save Ainsley."

Megan nodded and closed her eyes. "Just push me."

She felt his hands on her back, and then she was skidding down the icy tunnel with her stomach in her throat. The ground evened out beneath her and she collided with a mound of snow. Lady Maudred helped her to her feet, and Frieden slid in behind them.

"Everyone here?" asked Orex. "Let's shove off, then."

Megan glanced about as they walked, relieved that the tunnel wasn't as snug as she had feared. She stood on tiptoe and rapped her knuckles on the ceiling, which felt like an ice block. She nudged the wall beside her and didn't hear so much as a faint crackle.

"Are you satisfied now?" Frieden whispered in hear ear.

Megan nodded. "But I'd still like to get out of here as soon as possible."

"Mind the railing!" Orex called over his shoulder. "If you fall over the side, it's a long way down." He chuckled to himself, and for a moment, Megan glanced around in confusion. Then, he and Lady Maudred moved out of her line of sight, and Megan stepped into the top level of a multitiered rotunda, sanctioned off from its hollow center by a low steel wall.

Though the ice underfoot was covered with a rough layer of snow, Megan still exercised caution as she crept to the wall and peered down. Icyllian people bustled about each level, along with a few random elves and humans bundled in thick coats, and far, far below, Megan could see the bottom floor.

"We keep snow clothing on this level," said Orex, "since our visitors can't make it much farther down without it." He chuckled again and padded along the floor, stopping outside a circular hole in the wall of ice with Icyllian writing carved above it.

"Our furrier." Orex motioned for them to enter the shop, where an Icyll woman sat behind a counter stitching two pieces of hide together. She reminded Megan of a hairier version of Sari.

Upon hearing them, the furrier looked up and smiled. "Good day to you all. It appears you have reached me just in time." She placed her piecework on the counter and directed their attention to a collection of wooden shelves fitted into grooves in the ice. The shelves bulged with white fur, as if a sleeping animal lay on each with its back turned.

"Full-length coats for each of you, then?" The furrier went from shelf to shelf and pulled out three fur garments of varying sizes.

"We'll need a fourth one to take with us," said Frieden. "In a young man's size."

Megan sniffled, heartened by the fact that Frieden saw Ainsley's rescue as a certainty and not just a possibility.

The furrier heard Megan and forced her arms through the coat's sleeves. "Here, my dear. I couldn't live with myself if you caught your death."

Hugging the fur to her, Megan felt warm enough to melt into a puddle on the shop floor. "Thank you," she said, feeling even more encouraged.

Frieden paid for the outerwear, and the furrier wrapped Ainsley's coat in a waxy paper, assuring them it was water-resistant.

"What do you need now?" asked Orex. "Food? A heat source?" He chuckled to himself. "Water?"

"Just a team and a sleigh," said Frieden. "Ainsley may have caught up with us by now."

"Of course, of course." Orex led them around the rotunda to the opposite side where two holes had been cut into the ceiling. Beneath one of the holes, a series of metal pikes had been hammered into the ice. Beneath the other, the wall was riddled with holes but no climbing apparatus.

"For our foreign visitors," Orex indicated the metal pikes, "and for the Icyll," he said, stabbing his long fingernails into the existing divots and climbing out of sight.

Orex helped Megan and the others into a tunnel that stank of wet animal fur and drool. They ascended at an angle until they broke the surface beside a kennel of the smelliest animals Megan had encountered.

"Ugh. What *are* these?" she asked as Orex entered the kennel.

"Burgles," said Frieden, dragging a sleigh to the kennel entrance. "They're similar to wolves but with a more outgoing disposition."

Megan backed away from the door when she heard howling and yipping, and a moment later, five burgles lunged from their home and into the snow, dragging Orex behind them.

They *were* similar to wolves, with their facial structure and thick fur, but their legs were equine, long and muscular so that on all four paws, they stood roughly the height of Megan's shoulders.

"These things are *huge*!" she said as one nearly knocked her to the ground in an attempt to lick her facemask.

"That makes it easier for them to traverse snow that would swallow most other creatures." Frieden offered a hand to Lady Maudred and Megan who climbed into the back seat of the sleigh and accepted the bags Frieden handed up to them.

With difficulty, he and Orex fastened the wriggling burgles into the harness. Climbing into the front seat of the sleigh, Frieden took the reins from Orex and tossed him a bag that clinked when he caught it.

"In case I can't bring your animals back in one piece."

Orex tossed the money back to him. "You will." He nodded to Lady Maudred and Megan, and they waved as the burgles trounced off through the snow, pulling the sleigh behind them.

"How are we going to find Ainsley?" asked Megan.

"I already have." Frieden pointed up and to their right at an ill-shaped object dotting the sky. "All we have to do is follow him, and he should lead us directly to Arastold."

The sleigh glided smoothly over the snow, the burgles kicking up flurries of white as they trotted a steady gait. Frieden kept his eyes turned skyward, steering the sleigh beneath Ainsley's flight path and managing to keep him in sight. In his intense concentration, he missed a break in the snow where a pond had frozen over.

"Look out!" cried Lady Maudred. She grabbed Frieden's coat to get his attention but wound up pulling him off the sleigh and into the snow before he could correct their course.

The lead burgle skidded across the ice, yelping, and it became quickly apparent that burgles, while superior in deep snow, were as graceful as donkeys on ice. Still lashed together, the remainder of the team had no choice but to follow, and the sleigh jackknifed behind them onto the pond before colliding with the opposite bank. Megan and Lady Maudred added their screams to the burgles' howls as they were sent tumbling into the drifts.

"Are both of you all right?" Frieden maneuvered around the pond to where Megan was helping Lady Maudred stave off slobbering, whining burgles. Megan could feel Bit shifting about in her coat sleeve, and she fought to keep her hidden from the excited animals.

"We're fine," she said, turning her face up to the sky, "but I don't see Ainsley anymore."

Frieden grabbed the lead's harness and straightened out the team, pulling them, and the sleigh, onto steadier ground. "He must be flying low so he can land soon. We'll just have to keep following the path he was taking until we find him." Frieden kicked their satchels back into place with a little more force than necessary, and Bit popped her head out of Megan's pack, looking ill-treated.

"Bit! How did you get in there?" Megan could still feel something beneath her coat sleeve and she squealed, pulling it back. The dragon's tooth she had tied about her wrist was levitating, its pointed end facing to the southeast. "Um . . . Frieden, this may not be picking up on Ainsley, but it's picking up on *some* dragon."

Frieden considered this for a moment, and then motioned for Megan and Lady Maudred to join him on the sleigh. "It's better than riding blindly." He jerked the reins to the right, and the burgles lumbered forward.

Megan rode beside Frieden with her arm outstretched. The dragon's tooth continued to defy gravity, swaying slightly to and fro as Frieden dodged obstacles, but it always pointed them back to the southeast.

"There he is!" Megan pointed to a dark shape that crested a hill and disappeared from sight. She leapt from the sleigh when they reached the hilltop, her boots sinking to meet the ground. "I think he found Arastold."

In the midst of a valley blanketed by snow, a rocky structure the size of a football stadium stood naked, its russet-colored surface exposed. A crevice split the rock at ground level, and it was through this Ainsley slipped.

"Come on!" Megan beckoned to Frieden and Lady Maudred and half-ran, half-slid down the hill to the base of the bald mountain.

"Wait a moment." Frieden caught up with her. Sword drawn, he prowled the opening in the rock, sniffing at the air. He motioned to Megan and Lady Maudred, and the three stepped inside.

Megan felt as if she was facing a blast furnace, and it became obvious to her why the cave had no snow covering its outside. She peeled off her mask and gloves while Frieden and Lady Maudred looked into the opening of several branching tunnels. Spying gold dust trailing into one of the tunnels, Megan followed it with hand on dagger.

The tunnel widened into a shadowy cavern, and in its center lay Ainsley's knapsack. "Ainsley?"

A burst of sound from above hit Megan's ears, and several chunks of rock smashed against the ground to her left. She jumped, scanning the darkened ceiling of the cavern.

"What have you found here?" asked Frieden, entering with a torch held aloft. The light was just enough for Megan to see the source of the falling stalactites. She screamed as a dragon, black as the shadows, roared and spread its massive wings, swooping down. Frieden forced Megan to the ground, and she lay flat on her stomach, waiting for teeth or claws to tear into her flesh. The dragon, however, pulled up from its dive at the last minute and landed like a swan upon water. It regarded Frieden and Lady Maudred, then looked down at Megan. "Your willingness to sacrifice yourself for your friend is rather noble. But then, those who wear the Pearl of Truth usually are."

Megan lowered her arms from above her head and pulled herself to a kneeling position, gaping at the dragon. "You . . . you can talk?"

The dragon snorted twin puffs of steam. "I'm not sure whether to find your disbelief offensive or the result of an outworlder's innocence."

Megan stood and exchanged a nervous glance with Lady Maudred and Frieden. "Outworlder? What do you mean?"

The dragon lowered its massive head to meet Megan's eye, and she could feel the heat resonating from its snout. Megan stood her ground, though fear quaked her body. "Please don't play games with me. I know your mind."

"Okay," said Megan in a small voice.

Frieden stepped in front of Megan. "Are you the dragon Arastold?"

The dragon bared its teeth in what must have been an amused fashion, and Megan was relieved to see no scraps of Ainsley's clothing between them. "You know I am."

"Wh . . . where's Ainsley?" Megan locked eyes with Arastold, but the dragon was far too intimidating to stare down, and Megan found herself bowing her head.

Arastold rested on her haunches and brought her front claws together on the ground. With a flash of light, Ainsley appeared between them, crouched with head bent and wings folded about him. He raised and swiveled his head to take in all three human faces with no recognition, no emotion behind his eyes.

"Awake, young mind," said Arastold. "I release you."

Life Swap

Ainsley blinked several times, his cognizance increasing with every open and close of his eyelids. His first blink awoke him from a slumber he hadn't realized he'd been taking. His second blink brought him to the realization that he was no longer in a basket flying over Arylon, and his third blink brought him recognition of the people standing before him. With the fourth shuttering of his eyes, he noticed that his mind was no longer bound by the Illness.

After that, he couldn't stop blinking to fight back the tears. He no longer felt afraid to live and enjoy life, as if it might suddenly be taken from him. All worries that he might hurt his loved ones had vanished, and the dread and despair coating his insides had melted away. He felt as he did when he first arrived in Arylon.

He felt free.

Ainsley whooped, pounding his chest like Tarzan. "I'm . . . I'm me again!" He noticed the black scales on his arms and felt the weight of his wings. "More or less."

"I knew we could do it!" Megan launched herself at him, smothering him with hugs and kisses on every square inch of his face. He returned the hugs and, though he would forever deny it, enjoyed the kisses.

Megan grinned up at Arastold. "Thank you so much!"

Arastold remained impassive, as if she had done nothing remarkable. "I do not think it fair that a youth unfamiliar with magic should share the burden of the greedy of this world."

"I couldn't have said it better," said Lady Maudred, approaching her grandson with arms open wide. Megan stepped away, lest she be included in the enfolding.

Ainsley extracted himself from his grandmother and turned to the dragon with a look of humility. "So . . . can you change me back the rest of the way?"

Arastold dropped to her stomach and crossed her front claws before her. "Actually, I was hoping we could exchange one favor for another."

"What do you have in mind?" Frieden stepped between the teenagers and the dragon.

"Frieden Tybor." Arastold bared her teeth again. "Ever the diplomat, eh?"

Frieden smiled back politely. "Ainsley and Megan aren't in a position to negotiate for the future of this country. I am."

Arastold jerked her head to one side, and several loose boulders rolled toward her, stopping when they were even with her front claws. "Please, all of you, sit."

Frieden settled on the stone closest to Arastold while Lady Maudred, looking more official and less grandmotherly, sat beside him. Ainsley and Megan shared a boulder furthest away.

"You've learned from the stories," Arastold began, "that Lodir Novator defeated me, and I in turn, cursed his magical greed. Most people also assume he killed me. As you can see, I live and breathe, but I am banished to this cavern."

"You're trapped here?" Megan twirled the dragon's tooth on its string. Realizing who she was sitting across from, she quickly placed her hands in her lap.

Arastold nodded. "I survive on whatever creatures I can lure into my lair and have performed any and every magical spell in an effort to free myself."

"He used a scroll of banishment, didn't he?" asked Frieden.

Arastold nodded again. "So you see my dilemma."

"Indeed." Frieden stroked his goatee.

"Um," Megan peered over Frieden's shoulder. "I don't."

He swiveled on his boulder to face her. "If a living creature is banished by scroll, the only way to reverse it is to destroy that scroll."

"Which Lodir took with him when he left," added Arastold.

"And he wandered off somewhere in these mountains to die." Megan sighed. "So, we're screwed. Uh . . . we don't have a chance," she amended at the confused looks from Frieden and Lady Maudred.

Frieden nodded. "Unless you can think of a quick way to search 64,000 acres of snow."

"This difficulty is precisely why I am willing to make the following offer." Arastold paused until she had their full attention. "If you could find the scroll and destroy it for me, I would be willing to destroy the curse I instilled on Lodir and his kin all those years ago."

"Completely?" asked Lady Maudred. "The Illness—"

"Would become a thing of legend."

"But you would be free to wreak havoc on our people again," said Frieden.

Arastold laughed a hissing breath that smelled of brimstone. "After being imprisoned for so long, I assure you, the last thing I'm interested in is burning villages in search of treasure to bring back . . . here." She sneered at the stone walls around her, as if they had committed her a personal affront. "With my newly found freedom, I'd much rather see the world, see other worlds. In fifty or so years, if I'm not dead, I'll return and you can worry about me at that time."

Frieden looked to Lady Maudred, who nodded, then got to his feet and traced a half-circle on the ground with the toe of his boot. "Your word?"

"My bond." Arastold extended a talon and drew an arc to complete the shape.

The circle glowed with light, and suddenly, Frieden staggered forward, grabbing at his shoulder and screaming. Megan and Ainsley clambered off their boulder to help him, but Lady Maudred thrust her arms out to stop them.

"Let it be." She nodded at Frieden, who had dropped to all fours but was panting now, no longer in pain. Then, Arastold roared and reared up onto her hind legs, thrashing about and knocking rock from the walls with her wings. As Frieden had done, she relaxed and dropped back down, but a luminous white circle now shown on her right shoulder.

"They are now physically bound together by their words," Lady Maudred said in a low voice. "If either breaks the bond, that individual will perish."

"Okay." Ainsley clapped his hands together. "So, let's start looking. I'll take the first 16,000 acres."

Frieden wiped at his forehead with his sleeve and pressed his fingertips into his shoulder. "I'll need to contact Bornias. Finding a dead body buried in all this snow is going to take a legion of men." He swung his arm experimentally.

Megan raised a finger. "Actually, it'll only take *one* man."

Ainsley groaned. "You can't seriously be thinking of Losen. Not after he nearly got us killed again in the dungeons!"

To his chagrin, however, Frieden and Lady Maudred seemed to agree with Megan. "I'll have Bornias and Rayne speak with him tonight," said Frieden, "and if things go well, we'll set off in search of Lodir tomorrow morning."

"For now," said Lady Maudred, "we should have something to eat and get some sleep."

It didn't take them long to devour what Lady Maudred had left in her pack, and after Arastold's assurance that no harm would come to them in the night, Frieden wandered into a side passage to contact Bornias and Lady Maudred resumed her interrupted rest from earlier that day.

Megan, too, lay down with her blanket bundled under her head, the cavern being too warm for covers, but Ainsley leaned against the wall with one of the books from The Traveler's Tales.

"You're not sleepy?" asked Megan.

"Oh, I'm exhausted," said Ainsley, flipping through the pages, "but every time I fall asleep I have these nightmares of Arastold."

Megan rolled onto her stomach to face him. "It's probably because you've been thinking she was evil all along and it's been influencing your sleep. Now that you know she's not, she won't bother you in your dreams anymore."

"I don't think so." Ainsley shook his head. "The Arastold in my nightmares never talks. She just seems angry and out for blood." He paused. "There's something else." He explained to Megan about Penitent, and she frowned.

"Recurring dreams are weird, but dreams that pick up where you last left off?"

"And they seem so real," said Ainsley. "In one of them, I dreamt a rock clobbered me on the head, and when I woke up, I could feel a tiny lump under my hair. Another time I woke up with dirt in my boots."

Megan shuddered. "I don't blame you for wanting to stay awake, but if you do fall asleep and have one of your nightmares," Megan lowered her voice, "imagine I'm with you, and we'll kick Arastold's butt."

"Megan, if you're in my dreams, it's already a nightmare." He smiled at her, and she laughed, thankful to have her old Ainsley back.

Disturbing the Dead

"You have *got* to be joking." Muffled laughter, followed by a puff of warm breath, permeated the man's facemask. He was bundled in warm furs, but his hands were made plain to see, the magic binders circling his wrists. "Is this how your people solve their problems? They send prisoners out into the snow to die?"

"That's a good idea," said Ainsley, turning to Frieden. "Can we do that with him?"

His grandmother grabbed him by the crook of the elbow and steered him away. "You aren't really helping to encourage communication, you know."

"We should be using a different necromancer," grumbled Ainsley.

"Do you know anyone other than Losen?" challenged Megan. "Because you should have suggested it earlier before we called Bornias."

Losen laughed again. "Your king tells me you're looking for Lodir Novator's body. Don't tell me it's to cure him?" He nodded toward Ainsley.

"Yes," said Lady Maudred.

"I'd rather freeze to death," said Losen with a derisive sniff.

"That can be arranged," said Ainsley, reaching for Losen's jacket. "I imagine you're still pretty pale. A good dose of sunlight—"

"Now, wait a moment, Losen." Frieden forced himself between the enemies. "I've spoken with King Bornias and he tells me you agreed to a fair offer."

Losen shook his head. "He's agreed to free my mother, but not me. So I've changed my mind about helping you . . . unless you agree to change our bargaining terms."

Frieden and Lady Maudred exchanged a look.

"I'll have Bornias send someone to take him back to prison," said Lady Maudred, turning toward Arastold's cavern.

"You're bluffing." Hidden behind the mask, Losen's facial expressions were indiscernible, but one of his hands picked at the cuticles of the other, and he seemed to be swaying in place.

"Would you like to wait inside?" Frieden gestured after Lady Maudred. "It might get a little cold out here."

"So, you . . . you don't need me anymore?" asked Losen. He lifted the bottom of his facemask and began chewing on his nails. "You're going to find the body and raise it out of the snow . . . possibly even ice . . . by yourself?"

Frieden shrugged. "We ask very little of you, but you seem to want much more. I don't see how these are fair terms. Do you?" He turned to Ainsley and Megan who both shook their heads.

Losen made a whining sound and gnawed even more vigorously on his fingernails until a dot of blood splashed the snow. "I hear things when I'm down there, things about the future of Raklund, even Arylon itself. Troubled times lie ahead for you. If I divulge what I have and help you retrieve the scroll, will you pardon both my mother and me?"

Frieden fixed Losen with a steady gaze. "Is he lying about what he knows, Megan?"

"No."

She and Ainsley looked from Frieden to Lady Maudred, who had stopped and turned, her hand on the cavern's opening.

Frieden crossed his arms. "If you do all you say, we will free you and your mother with *no* pardon. You will be marked as criminals and distrusted by civilization the rest of your days."

After a moment, Losen extended his bound hands to Frieden. "Done."

Frieden passed one of his own hands over the bindings, and they dropped away.

The first thing Losen did as a free man was shrug off his coat. "I can't work when I'm being smothered," he said, though his teeth had started to chatter. Crouching, he placed his palms on the snow until steam rose beneath them.

"It's this way." He pointed north. "About 10 miles."

"Are you sure?" asked Megan as Losen brushed the snow off his hands. "Could it be someone . . . or something else?"

Losen shrugged back into his coat. "Based on the level of decomposition and size of the corpse, no. I'm sure it's him."

Ainsley helped Frieden ready the team of burgles and then took to the air while Frieden, Lady Maudred, Losen, and Megan rode on the sleigh. An hour later, Frieden reined in the team and Losen removed his coat once more.

"Ah, yes . . . I can feel the bones." Losen's voice seemed almost blissful as he dug his hands into the snow. "*Rexium miter gudar*!" Losen raised his hands above his head, their flesh pink from the chill of ice.

As if sensing the presence of something supernatual, the burgles began to whine and yelp, inching the sleigh forward. Ainsley went to calm them while the others waited in a circle around the spot Losen had crouched. Beneath their boots, they could feel a slight tremor in the snow.

"You may want to step back." Losen told them, heeding his own advice. "It's about to get much more unstable."

They would have been fools not to. With a crumbling and crackling like the start of an avalanche, the snow belched upward where Losen had touched it with his hands. Then a lump of ice the size of a coffin lifted from the ground and settled into the churned-up snow.

Losen cleared the residual snow off the top, and they all peered at the frozen remains of Lodir Novator.

"At least it's mainly bones and clothes," said Megan. "I was afraid the snow had preserved his whole body . . . like a corpsesicle."

"It would have," said Frieden, getting his pack from the sleigh, "if the wild animals hadn't gotten to him first." He pulled out a firepine pod and broke it in half, turning it with the inside facedown and rubbing it on top of the ice.

The ice sizzled and popped, rapidly reducing to water under the intense heat of the firepine pod. When he could finally get to Lodir, he separated the clothes from the bones and searched them.

"We have a problem," he said with a grim set of his jaw, shaking out a brown robe.

"Don't tell us it's not there," said Lady Maudred. She picked up a bag that had been cast aside and dumped it upside down.

Frieden threw the robe onto the bones and cursed. "He doesn't have it with him."

"Maybe . . . maybe it's at his home in Raklund," suggested Megan.

Lady Maudred shook her head. "No, dear. Every item in his house was either auctioned off or put in the library. They would have noticed a scroll of banishment."

"Which means he hid it someplace before he died," Frieden kicked at a piece of tattered gold ribbon and began pacing, "which could be anywhere . . . and now we'll never find it."

Losen clucked his tongue. "What a shame. You ended up getting nothing out of this arrangement but a few pieces of Lodir memorabilia."

Megan prepared herself to keep Ainsley from attacking the necromancer, but he just stared at the scraps of fabric. The hairs on the back of his neck stood on end, but it wasn't a result of the cold Icyllian air.

"Ainsley?" Megan grabbed his arm. "What's wrong?"

"These are Penitent's clothes."

Megan eyed the frozen remains, which Losen was now starting to pick up and analyze. "What? That guy from your dreams? He's Lodir Novator?"

Ainsley nodded. "I think so."

"What is this about?" asked Lady Maudred, stepping closer.

"I keep having these dreams," explained Ainsley, "where this man named Penitent and I are fighting Arastold, trying to make it back to you guys."

"Vivid dreams," added Megan.

Frieden paced closer to them. "How vivid?"

In response, Ainsley rolled back a sleeve and pointed to a scar on his arm.

Lady Maudred and Frieden looked at one another, and Lady Maudred placed a hand on her grandson's shoulder. "You weren't dreaming, dear. You were walking the void between this life and the Other Side."

Losen dropped the femur he was holding and it struck the other bones, striking a hollow note like a macabre xylophone. He scampered to his feet and drew level with Ainsley. "How many times did you do it?" he asked in an awed voice.

"What? Walk the void?" Ainsley shuffled back a few paces to distance himself from the overzealous necromancer. "Five or six I guess."

With an excited squeal, Losen lifted the bottom of his facemask and began gnawing his cuticles anew.

Ainsley looked at Frieden and Lady Maudred. "What I did wasn't normal, was it?"

They both shook their heads.

"Not by any stretch of the imagination," said Frieden.

"The most times anyone has walked the void is two," said Losen around a mouthful of finger. "You are an anomaly!"

"Wait, wait, wait." Megan waved her hands over her head. "What are you saying? That Ainsley actually *saw* Lodir? The *real* Lodir?"

"Yes," said Frieden, Losen and Lady Maudred in unison.

Megan leaned close to Ainsley. "Okay, that's spooky when they all agree on something."

Ainsley smiled, but he was lost in thought about all the instances he'd been in the void. He realized that every time he'd entered, Lodir was always there, even when he should have been flambéed by Arastold.

"I can do it again," he said. "I can walk the void and ask Lodir where the scroll is." Against his better judgement, he turned to Losen. "Can you send me there?"

Losen's eyes lit up. "Of course, but I can't guarantee you'll come back."

"Ainsley, don't do it." Megan grabbed his arm. "There have to be other ways we can find the scroll. Besides, you already have your mental health back."

"For how long?" Ainsley peeled her hand from his sleeve. "This isn't the life I want, always waiting in fear that I might attack someone or that I might lose myself again." He swallowed a thick lump in his throat. "I can save other people from this nightmare." He nodded at Losen. "Are you ready?"

"Stop! Stop him!" Megan turned to Lady Maudred and Frieden for help, but Lady Maudred kissed her grandson on his forehead. Ainsley extended his hand to Frieden who took it in both of his.

"Good luck, son of Minks."

Ainsley cleared the packs off the backseat of the sleigh and lay upon it. "Let's get this over with."

"Ainsley," Megan whispered, clambering onto the floor-board, "please don't. We just got you back."

He gazed down at her and smiled, his blood-colored eyes shining with the same energy and excitement as the blue-eyed boy Megan had saved the world with. "Don't cry or you'll fog up your face mask," he said, reaching out and squeezing her hand.

Megan held it to her chest while Losen stood above them and started to chant. As the last words passed Losen's lips, Megan felt Ainsley's hand go slack in her own, his pulse beating the rhythm of a pallbearer's march.

"And now," said Losen, "we wait."

Walking the Void

Ainsley opened his eyes. The familiar orange glow of Arastold's cavern had materialized around him, and he could feel warmth on his face.

"Get down!"

Ainsley's legs were kicked out from beneath him and he hit the ground.

"What the—"

A pair of hands grabbed him from behind and dragged him into a low-ceilinged side tunnel. Ainsley rolled to his stomach and faced his assailant, the light from the main cavern illuminating the smiling face of Penitent.

"Thank the Other Side you made it," he said. "It's wonderful to see you alive."

Ainsley grinned back at him and squeezed his shoulder. "It's far better to see *you* alive, Lodir."

The other man stiffened and pulled away. "You . . . you know who I am?"

Ainsley nodded. "And I need your help."

A guttural roar and the approach of thunderous footsteps delayed his request. Placing a finger to his lips, Lodir shrank farther into the tunnel.

Ainsley grabbed his arm. "No, it's okay. I've talked with Arastold, and we've struck a deal. I don't think she'll hurt us anymore." He started to back out of the tunnel to greet the dragon, but Lodir yanked Ainsley toward him. Their red eyes locked upon each other.

"You still don't seem to understand the perils of the void," whispered Lodir. "This is not the real world. Here, your worst fears exist for the sole purpose of tormenting you. If you fear your friends will turn on you, they arrive to stab you in the back. If you fear being buried alive, the weight of stone lays heavy on your chest. And if you are inflicted with the Illness and you fear that which you will become . . . Arastold is your tormentor."

"Huh." Ainsley swallowed hard. "Well, I'm glad I didn't actually test Megan's theory."

They waited in the darkened dampness as a scaly black trunk of a leg shifted past, followed by a second and then a seemingly endless tail, plowing the rubble around it.

When the tip of Arastold's tail slithered past, Ainsley poked his head into the cavern and glanced after the dragon who didn't seem to have noticed her quarry. He backed in to sit beside Lodir again.

"Okay, she's gone for now."

"She'll find me. She always does." Lodir wiped at the sweat on his brow.

"I don't understand why you never told me who you really were."

"Because I did so many terrible things." Lodir leaned against the wall. "Banishing Arastold doesn't even begin to encompass my iniquities."

"Well, you can help me set things right," said Ainsley. "If we can destroy the scroll you used to banish the *real* Arastold, she's agreed to revoke her curse forever."

"Truly?" Lodir regarded him with wide eyes. "Perhaps if I could do that, it might be enough to take me to the Other Side."

It was then that Ainsley understood why Lodir had always managed to reappear unscathed in all the times he'd been in mortal peril. "You're trapped here, aren't you?"

Lodir nodded. "Forced to live out the consequences of my most heinous deeds. But now, I may not have to." He reached into his robes and plucked a piece of parchment from the pocket, handing it to Ainsley.

"Is this a map to the scroll?" Ainsley turned the parchment 180 degrees but couldn't discern top from bottom.

"It's better than a map," Lodir flicked it with his fingers, "it's the scroll itself."

"Really? Well, let's end this now." Ainsley grabbed the paper in both hands and attempted to rip it in half. He might just as well have been trying to tear a sheet of metal. The palms of his hands burned from the efforts of twisting and tugging at the parchment.

"That won't work," said Lodir. "Scrolls of banishment can only be destroyed by reversing the process that forged them. It requires materials I don't have here."

"Then, I'll just take it back to the world of the living with me." Ainsley rolled the parchment back up and tucked it into his pants with a nod of finality. "Now, how do I get out of here?"

Lodir blinked at him. "You don't know?"

Ainsley's stomach twisted like the scroll of banishment. "Uh . . . no. I've always just woken up, I guess. Okay, wait . . ." He jammed his eyes shut and concentrated on Arylon. After a minute had passed, however, he could still smell the dusty clothes of his companion and feel the warm, damp air of the tunnel. "Maybe I need to be more relaxed." Ainsley moved to lie on his back on the floor, but Lodir stopped him.

"You could always try the exit."

"The exit?"

Lodir inched toward the tunnel entrance and motioned for Ainsley to follow him. "Do you see those two tall stalagmites that look like pillars?" He pointed to the far end of the cavern. "The world of the living is through there. That's where I've been trying to lead you."

"And all I have to do to reach it is get past the flesh-eating dragon," Ainsley muttered under his breath.

"I could help you by distracting her," said Lodir.

"Why don't I just freeze her in place?" Ainsley demonstrated with his hands.

Lodir raised an eyebrow. "Have you noticed what effect your magic has on her? All you'll succeed in doing is drawing attention to yourself and becoming her new interest. If she defeats me and I journey to the Other Side this time, so much the better."

Ainsley considered this. "You're right. Can you draw her past so I can sneak out behind her?"

In answer, Lodir scrambled out of the tunnel and placed his fingers to his mouth, emitting a shrill whistle. "Come and get me, you vile beast!"

Ainsley scuttled backwards in the tunnel until he could see just the hem of Lodir's robes. A bellow of triumph assured that Lodir's call had been answered, and Ainsley heard footsteps shuffling back and forth outside the tunnel as Lodir taunted the dragon. Then, the shuffling quickened, and he saw the brown robes dart to the right.

Rubble fell like snow into Ainsley's hair as two pairs of clawed feet galloped past, followed by a massive tail. Ainsley took a deep breath and crept out of the tunnel, watching the dragon's hind end grow smaller.

Saying a silent prayer, Ainsley took to the air, beating his wings as hard and fast as he could. To his horror, the twin stalagmites didn't seem to be getting any closer, and he wondered if they were as infinite as the cavern walls. Glancing back over his shoulder, he could hear Lodir shouting insults at Arastold while rock smashed to the ground.

When he turned to face forward again, his heart leapt at how close the stone pillars now were. He dove to the ground and started running, the noise of his stamping feet no longer a care.

"Ainsley, wait!"

Ainsley skidded to a halt on the rubble-strewn floor, fluttering his wings to keep balance, and whirled around. Lodir was charging toward him, singed robes smoking, with Arastold several lengths behind.

"You need this!" Lodir waved his hand above his head, the thumb and index finger pinched together. Ainsley strained his eyes and saw that Lodir was gripping a clump of hair. He flew to meet him halfway, and Lodir forced the hair into Ainsley's palm, curling it shut. "You'll need a willing piece of me to reverse the spell."

Ainsley nodded and redirected the contents of his hand to his pants pocket. Lodir smiled and clapped him on the shoulder.

"Go now, and good luck." Without waiting for Ainsley to answer, Lodir turned back and ran toward Arastold, whooping and zigzagging to get her attention. He glanced over his shoulder and pulled faces at the dragon as she took the bait, following him to the other end of the cavern.

Ainsley watched, smiling, until he noticed that Lodir was still looking back at Arastold and not at the boulder he was rapidly approaching.

"Look out!" Ainsley cried too late. Lodir flipped over the fallen rock and landed on his back with Arastold standing directly above him. With a triumphant roar, she lowered her head and clamped her jaws around his midsection.

"Noooo!" Ainsley dropped to the ground and placed his hands upon the stone. As he willed it to obey his command, he remembered the words of the high priestess and withdrew his hands. With a deep breath, he lowered them back down and asked the land to split beneath the dragon.

The magic surged through him, but this time, it felt different. He felt comforted and reassured instead of the usual anxious rush of adrenaline. It was as if the magic was a companion, not a foe to be bested, and it answered his request willingly.

At the first crackle and groan of the cavern floor, however, Arastold simply stepped closer to Ainsley and away from her peril. Ainsley groaned. She may not have been self-aware, he realized, but she was no stupid monster either.

"Ainsley . . . get . . . out," croaked Lodir. He screamed in agony as Arastold's teeth sank deeper into his flesh. Ainsley heard the splintering of several bones and gagged as rivulets of blood dripped from Arastold's maw.

Though he knew Lodir would regenerate and be made whole, Ainsley couldn't walk away from this man who had sacrificed himself many times over to keep Ainsley alive.

With Lodir's next cry of pain, Ainsley screamed in rage and launched himself into the air at Arastold's snout, pummeling it with several sharp jabs and kicks. The dragon opened her mouth to bite at Ainsley, and Lodir rolled out. While he dodged and ducked her, Ainsley asked the wind to cushion the injured man's fall.

"Ainsley." Lodir wheezed and coughed, clutching his rib cage. "You should have left me."

"I couldn't do that," said Ainsley, looking down at him. "I couldn't just let you suffer." Arastold caught him off guard, and with a puff of air, she knocked him from the sky and to the ground beside Lodir.

"It doesn't . . . look like . . . you'll make it," said Lodir, trying in vain to inch his mangled body away from Arastold.

"I will. We both will." Ainsley grabbed him under the arms and pulled him toward the twin pillars. "In the darkest hour, hope finds a way."

Unsettling News

"How long does it take to get a scroll from a dead guy?"

It had only been a few minutes since Ainsley had slipped into unconsciousness, but already Megan had begun pacing in the makeshift shelter Lady Maudred had conjured. It did nothing to remove the chill from the air, but they were at least able to stop the wind and block the blinding snow.

"Megan, do stay still," said Lady Maudred, bringing her hand to her eyes. "You're making me dizzy walking in circles."

Megan climbed onto the sleigh beside Ainsley and lifted one of his eyelids, but the pupil was still rolled back into his head. "How are we supposed to know if something's gone wrong?"

"With all the magic he possesses, I'm sure he'll find a way to let us know," Frieden assured her as he slid a coat over Ainsley's limp form.

"But what if it's too late?" Megan wrung her hands. "What if Arastold ate him? What if—"

"Be still." Frieden pulled Megan from the sleigh and placed a hand over her mouth.

In the silence that followed, she could hear footsteps crunching through the snow outside their shelter. Drawing his sword, Frieden looked to Lady Maudred who nodded. They both pulled their facemasks on and stepped outside the shelter.

"Well, what a surprise!" said a man's jovial voice, his smooth, easy manner familiar to Megan. "How wonderful to see two of Raklund's finest out here."

"Greetings to you, Evren," said Frieden. "And to you, Master Mage."

The hair on the back of Megan's neck stood on end. She had forgotten that Evren Sandor, the suave former lieutenant of the Silvan Sentry had planned his own expedition into the mountains with Nick Oh, Master Mage of the Community of Amdor. She wondered, however, why in all the miles that spanned the Icyllian Mountains, they had chosen to come here.

Megan wished she could see outside, for there was an awkward pause after which Nick responded, "Greetings, governor and your ladyship."

"I always find the travels of others fascinating," said Lady Maudred in her most flattering voice. "What brings the two of you here?"

"We're looking for soulfire for Nick's knack shop," said Evren.

Lady Maudred let out a light-hearted laugh. "My dear, Sir Sandor, you are looking in the wrong place. Soulfire thrives around the frozen lakes and streams, not amidst the mountains!"

"I did *not* know that." Evren pooled his hearty laughter with hers. "Perhaps that's why it's taking us so long to find it."

Megan clutched at her chest and winced, waving Losen away when he crept toward her.

"Are you all right?" he whispered beneath the outside conversation.

Megan shook her head. "Evren knew exactly where to find soulfire. He's hiding something."

"Well, we really must be on our way if we're to find that soulfire before nightfall," said Evren. "Perhaps we'll see each other again at Carnival."

"At Carnival," agreed Frieden.

Two pairs of footsteps crunched away through the snow, and a moment later, Lady Maudred and Frieden reappeared.

"He's lying to you," Megan said as they pulled off their facemasks. "He knows where to find soulfire."

"I suspected as much," said Frieden. "They're here for something besides soulfire, but that doesn't concern me as much as the master mage's behavior. He didn't seem as animated as usual."

"And neither one of them even asked us what *we* were doing there," added Lady Maudred.

Losen coughed. "Aren't you glad you made your little deal with me?"

Everyone turned to look upon his smiling face.

"Does this," Frieden waved outside of the shelter, "have something to do with what you heard in the dungeons?"

Losen regarded him with a solemn expression. "You should be wary of Evren Sandor. He plans to overthrow your kingdom, and then the country."

Megan snapped her fingers. "Sir Inish told me he *thought* something like this was happening, but he couldn't prove it!"

"Well, we have to warn the master mage then." Lady Maudred reached for her mask, but Frieden grabbed her arm.

"We have no tangible proof of what Evren is plotting . . . merely the hearsay of a convicted man and a teenager." He looked from Losen to Megan. "No offense intended."

"I suppose you're right," said Lady Maudred with a sigh. "It certainly wouldn't be wise for someone in either of our positions to defame him . . . yet."

"Once this ordeal is over, we will speak with Bornias and formulate a plan."

The group quieted once more, and Megan took up her pacing anew, being careful to do it out of Lady Maudred's field of vision. "We need to wake Ainsley. This is taking too long!"

"You won't be able to . . . to draw him back," stammered a voice from outside the shelter. "He'll only r-return when he's ready."

Megan paused and exchanged a surprised look with the others. "Garner?"

The elf stepped into the shelter and removed his face-mask. His cheeks had been pinched by the cold, but he smiled warmly at Megan. "P-please don't hate m-me."

"What are you doing here?" Megan had meant to sound angry, but she was more shocked than anything.

"I-I had to make sure you were all r-right." Garner took her hands, and she could feel his frosty flesh.

"Garner, you're freezing!" Megan rubbed his hands. "And you aren't wearing a very thick coat." She opened her own and pulled Garner to her so they were both wrapped inside.

"I d-didn't have a . . . lot of t-time if I wanted to keep up with you." He spoke through chattering teeth. "I saw him," he pointed to Frieden, "buying a Roc pass and decided to follow."

"You idiot!" Megan lay her head against his chest. "You could have frozen to death."

Frieden pulled another firepine pod from his bag and cracked it open, balancing it on its curved side so the heat radiated upward. "Come sit."

With a grateful smile, Garner shrugged off his hunting bow, quiver, and travel pack and fairly rested *atop* the open pod. While Frieden removed his own coat and draped it around Garner, Lady Maudred poured water from her insulated flask into a mug. She placed the mug over the other pod half until it boiled and steamed, then offered it to Garner whose cupped hands were slowly regaining their flesh color.

"I am in your debt," he said, taking a sip of hot water.

Megan wandered back over to Ainsley and sat on the sleigh beside him. "So, you're saying we can't wake him? We've done it before."

"But this time, he is on a mission, is he not?" asked Garner. "He won't return until he's ready, and the fact that he still breathes proves he hasn't passed on."

Megan studied Ainsley for a moment, listening to his soft breathing. "I suppose you're right." As she adjusted his coat, however, she noticed that his chest seemed to be rising and falling much quicker. "Ainsley——" She looked up at his face and saw him grimacing, sweat beading on his forehead.

She dug through the packs and reached into her own for something she could use as a cold compress. "I think he's only going to get worse." A sudden gust of wind blew through the shelter then, ruffling the fur on her coat and chilling her skin. As it subsided, Megan heard a voice speak softly in her ear.

In the darkest hour, hope finds a way.

She whirled around to face the others and looked at Garner who was drying his facemask over the firepine pod. "What did you say?"

"Me?" He stared up at her blankly. "Nothing. Why?"

"I thought you . . ." She turned to Losen. "Did *you* say something?"

He shook his head. "But the wind in the Pass can make anyone hear voices."

"No." Megan lowered herself to the ground. "This wasn't just a bunch of random voices. It was *one* voice, and it said something the high priestess in Hylark told me and . . ." Megan's skin crawled with gooseflesh despite her heavy coat. "Shit."

Losen stared up at her, uncomprehending. "Who's that?"

Megan ignored him and crawled onto the sleigh, shaking Ainsley by the shoulder. "Wake up!"

"What are you doing?" Lady Maudred tried to pull Megan away from her grandson, but Megan squirmed out of grasp.

"Ainsley's in trouble. We have to wake him!" She saw his brow furrow promisingly and patted him on the cheek. "Come on, now!"

"Megan, I already told you that won't work," said Garner, wrapping an arm around her midsection and hauling her away. "You can't bring him back."

"If he can't come to us, then I'll go to him. He needs help." Megan threw off her coat and lay with it under her head like a pillow. "Losen, send me to the void."

"Of course." Losen rubbed his hands together and advanced on her, but Garner shoved him away.

"Megan, don't be a fool! If you enter the void, you have no hope of coming back."

Megan gripped Garner's bow in one hand and the quiver of arrows in the other. She smiled at him and whispered, "In the darkest hour, hope finds a way."

The images of Garner, Frieden, Lady Maudred, and Losen started to blur into shades of gray. Their voices called to her, their hands shook her body almost violently, but she did nothing in response. Her eyes rolled back into her head, and all the sounds and smells and touches poured into one pot of darkness.

Never Alone

"Lodir, can you walk at all?" Ainsley crouched with his wings outstretched over the man just as Arastold unleashed a torrent of fire.

"If you give me a few hours," said Lodir with a weak laugh. "Then, the wounds will have healed."

Arastold lowered her head to snatch both men between her teeth, but Ainsley shot a handful of ice into her open throat, and she screeched, backing away and jerking her head from side to side.

"We don't have a few hours," said Ainsley. "And I can't keep doing this. Magic isn't enough against her. I need something different." Ainsley glanced around the cavern floor, barren except for the fallen boulders. "Man, I'd trade all these rocks for just one sharp pointy stick."

"Look out!" cried Lodir as the dragon's tail swung toward them like a battering ram.

Ainsley ducked, but his outstretched wings still jutted upward, and Arastold's tail collided with them, sending Ainsley flying several yards through the air to hit the ground on his back. Flipping to his feet, he turned just as Arastold lowered her gaping maw once more on his injured companion.

"Lodir!"

And then suddenly the dragon reared back and roared again. It turned its head from Lodir and spouted fire on the floor directly to his right. When the flames cleared, there stood Megan, bow drawn and arrow notched against the bowstring.

"You missed me," she told the dragon.

She relaxed her fingers, and the bowstring thrummed forward, propelling the arrow into Arastold's snout. Her hand reached into the quiver for another arrow while Arastold rubbed against the cavern wall, trying to loosen the projectile.

"Ainsley, are you okay?" called Megan, notching her next arrow.

"I'm fine," Ainsley took to flight and joined her. "And I have the scroll of banishment. The way out is through those two pillars."

"Well then," Megan let fly another arrow, which completely missed Arastold, "let's get out of here."

"That was a horrible shot," said Ainsley, pushing Megan to the ground beside Lodir and covering them both with his wings as Arastold spewed flames at them.

"Give me a break. I only took two weeks of archery at summer camp. I'm just lucky her head is roughly the size of a house." Megan reached into her quiver, but it was empty. "Okay, I'm out of arrows. *Now* would be an excellent time to leave."

Arastold's jaws opened directly behind Ainsley, and Megan screamed, grabbing the bow by one end and jamming the other into the roof of Arastold's mouth. The dragon snorted and backed away, opening and closing its maw in an effort to dislodge the bow.

"I can't leave Lodir here like this," said Ainsley. "We have to get him some place safe until I can figure out a way to release his spirit."

"Are you serious?" Megan looked down at Lodir. "Hi, by the way. Nice to meet you."

"Greetings," said Lodir with a feeble wave. "I'm sorry to make your acquaintance under such uncomfortable circumstances."

All conversation stopped as Arastold let loose another blast of fire. Ainsley forced his companions to the ground, and Megan yelped as she landed wrong on the handle of her knife. Rubbing her side, she regarded the Abbat with awe.

"Wait a minute, you're a spirit?" She sat upright and stared at Lodir as Ainsley launched himself into the air.

Lodir nodded.

Megan's fingers closed around the handle of the dagger, and she slid it from her belt, the blade flashing the Silverskin insignia.

"You have an Abbat?" Lodir turned hopeful eyes upon her.

"It looks like you're free to go," said Megan with a grin, holding the spirit-eradicating dagger out to him, handle first.

Lodir shook his head, and pushed her hand away. "I can't do it myself. You have to."

"No, no, no." Megan forced the Abbat back. "I can't kill you . . . I mean, I know you're dead, but I . . . I can't re-kill you. I'm not that kind of person."

"Please, you mustn't be afraid." Lodir wrapped a hand over Megan's. "Show me mercy. It's the right thing to do."

His words reminded Megan of Rella's, and she knew that in the same situation, Rella wouldn't have hesitated if it meant protecting a loved one.

"Okay." Megan drew a deep breath and tightened her grasp around the Abbat. Lodir lay back and closed his eyes.

"Please forgive me," said Megan, raising the dagger. She bit her lip until her teeth pierced the delicate skin and she could taste blood. Then, she stabbed downward, plunging the Abbat into Lodir's heart.

From his vantage point in the sky, Ainsley could see everything, and he screamed as he dove downwards, knocking Megan aside. "What the hell are you doing?" He grabbed the Abbat's handle and tried to pull the dagger free, but it seemed almost melded with Lodir's body. A circle of white light outlined the dagger's entry point as blood would a mortal wound. "Lodir?"

The injured man nodded at Ainsley reassuringly and smiled at Megan. "Thank you," he said.

The white light in his chest began to swirl and rise like motes of dust in sunlight, drifting through the cavern and past a stunned Arastold.

"He *is* going to the Other Side now," said Ainsley as the last particles slipped from Lodir's body into the air.

Something clinked on the ground beside them, and when Ainsley and Megan looked down, there was nothing left but the Abbat. The two teenagers looked at one another.

"I'm glad you came," said Ainsley.

Megan grinned. "Me, too."

From the mouth of a tunnel behind them, Arastold roared. They turned and watched as she finally succeeded in snapping the bow into two splintered pieces with her massive jaws. The bow ends clattered to the ground, held together by only their string.

"Let's get out of here," said Ainsley.

"She'll kill us before we reach the pillars," said Megan, snatching up the Abbat and sliding it back into her belt. "They're too far."

Ainsley glanced at the dragon and the shattered pieces of bow beneath her. He noticed how her body brushed up against the tunnel walls, and he smiled. "Then, I'll just have to buy us some time. Don't run until I tell you to."

Before Megan could protest, he flapped his wings and shot above Arastold's head. As always, the ceiling retracted where he flew.

"Come and get me," he taunted the dragon.

She spouted more fire at him, but when she saw he was impervious to flame, she leapt upward, snapping at him with her jaws. Ainsley darted out of the way at the last second, and her snout crashed into the tunnel roof with a thunderous boom, knocking loose several large rocks that struck her massive head.

"Over here." Ainsley fluttered beside her right eye and she whipped her head about at an angle. Ainsley escaped by a hair's breadth, and Arastold bit into a section of the wall. He darted to her other side and Arastold turned her head to clamp down on a mouthful of nothing more than rock again. Twice more he taunted her, and twice more she collided with the tunnel's walls.

Where she had smashed into the tunnel's ceiling, the stone had started to crack and sever. With each successive attack upon its sides, the roof seemed to tremble even more.

"One more for the road," said Ainsley, darting between the dragon's legs and landing on her back. "Maybe we can ride you home, huh?"

With a deafening screech, Arastold tried to physically turn in the narrow tunnel to bite at the pest on her back. Her front flank slammed into one wall and her hindquarters collided with the other. Jarred by the motion, Ainsley toppled from her back before he could even flex his wings.

And then, in a shower of boulders, the walls quivered and the entire tunnel collapsed upon Ainsley and Arastold.

"Ainsley!" Megan clawed at her face with her fingernails as the dust settled and neither dragon nor dragonboy emerged. She ran toward the pile of rubble and started to dig, her knuckles bleeding from the rough stone she hauled. A section of rock shifted, and she gasped, uncertain which victim was trying to escape. Then, she saw a human hand feeling its way out between two slate-sized stones, and she squealed with joy. "You made it!"

Megan worked to help him out from the pile, and when he was free, Ainsley broke into a coughing fit, collapsing in her arms.

He looked up at her and smiled. "It's . . . okay to run now," he wheezed.

Reversal of Fortune

Ainsley gasped and sat up, the coat that had been thrown over him sliding into his lap.

"You're alive!" Lady Maudred clapped her hands together and hugged Ainsley to her. "Losen, run and get Frieden."

"How's . . . Megan?" he spluttered as his grandmother squeezed him like a boa constrictor.

Garner, who had been sitting beside Megan, nudged her shoulder gently. "Megan?"

She, too, gasped for air but rolled into Garner's arms, coughing and shivering.

"Is she all right?" Garner asked the others with a worried glance.

"She just got back from her first trip to hell," said Ainsley with a grin. "Give her a break."

Megan smiled as Garner helped her into her coat, though her lips trembled from the chill that leaving the void had given her. "I'll be fine."

"Is it true?" Frieden burst into the shelter, arms full of flowers, with Losen behind him. He ground to a halt at seeing Ainsley and Megan and dropped his bundle. "It is! You survived the void."

"*And*, I have the scroll of banishment," said Ainsley, pulling the rolled parchment out of his waistband and handing it to Frieden.

"Excellent, excellent!" Frieden hugged him. "I've never been more proud of either of you." He unfurled the scroll and beamed. "This is it, and with these," he pointed to the pile of flowers with his toe, "we have all the ingredients we need except . . ."

"Oh!" Ainsley reached into his pocket and removed the handful of hairs Lodir had given him.

"Perfect!" Frieden placed them and the scroll into Garner's empty water mug. "Now, let's end this."

They packed the sled and readied themselves for the journey to Arastold's cavern. Garner tossed his bow onto the pile of Lodir's remains.

"Sorry about what happened there," said Ainsley, noticing the broken string, snapped-off tip and teeth marks in the wood, "but it came in handy."

"That's all right," said Garner. "I'm just glad you both escaped in one piece. When I noticed my bow disintegrating before my eyes, I was prepared to enter the void and bring you back."

Megan grabbed him by his shirtfront and gave a mock growl. "You doubted me? I told you I was going to save Ainsley, didn't I?"

"I'm glad you did." Garner lifted the bottom of Megan's mask and touched his lips to hers. Startled, she tried to pull away, but Garner wrapped his hands over Megan's. "I'm proud of you," he said, kissing her again. This time, Megan didn't fight him.

"Ugh. They're using tongue!" Ainsley made a sour face and turned away. "We should go before there are little human-elf hybrids crawling all over the sleigh."

Lady Maudred smacked him on the back of the head. "Don't be disgusting." After a minute had passed, however, with the kissing couple still locked together, she called, "Megan, a lady always leaves her suitors wanting more."

"Now, *that's* disgusting," said Ainsley, rubbing his scalp.

Megan blushed beneath her mask, but she was laughing as she settled herself on the sleigh beside Lady Maudred.

"Losen?" Frieden gestured to an open portal where two Silvan Sentry stood waiting. "We'll converse when I return to Raklund."

Losen hesitated. "And my mother?"

"I've informed the king to grant her, *and* you, freedom after we speak."

Only then did Losen join the guards and allow them to shackle his wrists.

"Would it be possible for me to return with him to Raklund?" Garner asked Frieden. "I feel as if I should visit my parents and let them know I'm still alive."

Frieden nodded, patting Garner on the shoulder. "Thank you for caring for my . . . niece and nephew."

Megan stood up in the sleigh. "Wait . . . you're leaving?"

Garner grabbed her hands and kissed them. "Only for a little while. Come tomorrow afternoon, we'll be strolling the halls of Raklund together."

Megan smiled as he walked away. "I'll hold you to that."

Garner stopped before Ainsley, extending his hand. "I apologize for my earlier actions. I only wanted what was best for Megan . . . and you."

Ainsley locked eyes with Garner, trying to gauge the sincerity of his words.

"Oh, for crap's sake, Ainsley," cried Megan, leaning over the back of the sleigh, "shake his hand so they can leave already!"

Garner smiled, but Ainsley held an impassive expression. "I can forgive you once, but I won't forget." Their hands connected and Ainsley pulled Garner toward him. "If you *ever* do anything less than kind to Megan again," he whispered in the elf's ear, "I'll make you wish you were walking the void."

Ainsley drew back, satisfied at how Garner stumbled a step away. With a covert glance at Megan, Garner nodded.

"Of course." Then, he plastered on his usual good-natured smile and waved to the others. "Until we meet again. May your adventures lead you safely home." He joined Losen and the guards, and the four men disappeared in a flash of light.

"Now to Arastold," said Frieden, taking the leads in his hands. "Ainsley? Will you be riding or flying?"

Ainsley flexed the muscles of the back so that his wings lifted him from the ground. "I think I'll fly," he said, glancing lovingly over his shoulders at the wings, which had saved him on more than one occasion. "I won't have them much longer."

Though the return trip to the cavern took the same amount of time, to Ainsley it seemed to rush by, and it was with some reluctance that he lessened the beating of his wings and settled to the ground as the sleigh bearing the others slowed to a stop.

"Leave the packs here," said Frieden, though he picked up his own. "With any luck, we should be leaving in an hour's time."

When they entered the cavern, Arastold was waiting for them, and she looked pleased.

"I could sense your triumph from a mile away. First, let me keep *my* end of the bargain."

"Wait!" Ainsley hurried forward before she could begin the counter-curse. "I know this is going to sound strange, but . . . could I keep my wings for the rest of the time that I'm here?" He fluttered them almost bashfully. "I . . . I'm pretty fond of them now."

Arastold bared her teeth in a smile. "You once thought them a disfigurement but now see how beautiful they can be. They shall remain with you as long as you remain in Sunil."

"Thank you." Ainsley bowed and backed away.

Arastold closed her eyes and began an incantation, half dragon hisses and half words. When she had finished, rays of golden light, like dozens of shooting stars, fell down upon her and soaked into her hide. The white circle that had scarred her shoulder shimmered and faded away.

"It is done," she said, opening her eyes. "All the Illness that is and ever will be has been returned to me."

They turned to look at Ainsley who was studying his tan, scale-free arms. He raised his head and grinned at them, and his eyes sparkled their beautiful sapphire blue.

"Is it me?" he asked Megan.

"It's you." She grinned. "Plus wings."

Frieden bowed to Arastold. "Our country thanks you. And now, we shall uphold *our* end of the agreement if you can provide a spare scale."

———

"It really is quite clever how you managed to defeat me . . . or rather, the evil version of me . . . in the end." Arastold took her first steps outside her cavernous prison and followed Ainsley and Megan to the sleigh where Frieden and Lady Maudred were waiting. The burgles whined and cowered in the harnesses at the sight of the dragon, but she paid them no mind. "I must congratulate you."

"I couldn't have done it without Megan," said Ainsley, grinning at her.

Arastold lowered her head toward the teenagers. "You'll remember that, won't you? Both of you? In the days to come, you must rely on more than magic to see you through."

Megan looked at Frieden and Lady Maudred, who were preoccupied, then took a step toward Arastold. "Things are going to get worse, aren't they?" she whispered.

"Fear not." The great black dragon breathed a puff of steam that encircled Ainsley and Megan in its warmth. "Difficult times lie ahead, but if you allow the truth to guide you, good will prevail."

"Ainsley, Megan, let's go!" Frieden called from the sleigh.

"And now I must take my leave." Arastold spread her massive wings. "There is so much I have yet to see, but I wish good luck to you both."

She flapped her great wings and sent Ainsley and Megan sprawling onto their backs, and when they got to their feet, she was gone.

"I was starting to get nervous," said Frieden as Ainsley climbed onto the seat behind him and Megan joined Lady Maudred.

"Arastold was just giving us some good advice," said Megan. Under her breath, she added, "I think."

"Well," Frieden clicked the reins, "let's return this sleigh and head to Pontsford."

"Pontsford?" Ainsley and Megan said together.

Frieden and Lady Maudred laughed.

"We thought the two of you deserved to have a little fun after what you've endured these past weeks, and we'll be there just in time for the best week of Carnival."

"Awesome!" said Ainsley.

"What about our parents?" asked Megan. "And Garner?"

"We'll have Bornias tell them. Your parents won't mind being without you for another day or so, I'm sure."

"Will they have anything good to eat there?" asked Ainsley. "Any Mariner's Mash?"

"Are you kidding, my boy?" asked Lady Maudred. "You will experience dining that almost *rivals* the Port of Scribnitch. Chocolates and fruits and pastries from other lands—"

"Don't forget the entertainment," added Frieden. "And the exotic auctions."

Megan smiled and settled back in the sleigh, listening to Ainsley rattle questions to Lady Maudred and Frieden, occasionally interjecting ones of her own. She even laughed with Ainsley as Lady Maudred and Frieden recounted *their* first trips to Carnival.

But in the back of her mind, she couldn't forget Arastold's warning.

This ends the second book in
The Silverskin Legacy trilogy

Acknowledgments

Always, always, always for my husband, family, friends, and fans.

For my maker, who fills my brain with stories to tell.

For Cynthia Leitich Smith who so selflessly promotes other authors and makes them feel like stars.

For the fabulous people at Llewellyn but especially: Andrew Karre, my editor and personal cheerleader; Rhiannon Ross, my copyeditor, who has unfathomable patience with me; Kelly Hailstone, my ingenious publicist, who exceeds my expectations; Gavin Duffy, the creative designer who makes the Silverskin legacy real to me with his artwork; Drew Siqveland, editor-in-chief of New Worlds magazine, who always grants me an outlet for my voice; and Jennifer Spees whose kind words make me feel like a real author.

For Anne Stokes, a charming woman and the fabulous artist of Arastold.

For anyone who's ever been stricken with an illness that shatters their world.

And for Terry Brooks, the man who made me realize that even ordinary people can do extraordinary things.